A Thousand Yesteryears

A Point Pleasant Novel

Mae Clair

LYRICAL PRESS
Kensington Publishing Corp.
www.kensingtonbooks.com

First Electronic Edition: April 2016
eISBN-13: 978-1-60183-777-6
eISBN-10: 1-60183-777-1

First Print Edition: April 2016
ISBN-13: 978-1-60183-780-6
ISBN-10: 1-60183-780-1

Printed in the United States of America

Behind a legend lies the truth...

As a child, Eve Parrish lost her father and her best friend, Maggie Flynn, in a tragic bridge collapse. Fifteen years later, she returns to Point Pleasant to settle her deceased aunt's estate. Though much has changed about the once thriving river community, the ghost of tragedy still weighs heavily on the town, as do rumors and sightings of the Mothman, a local legend. When Eve uncovers startling information about her aunt's death, that legend is in danger of becoming all too real . . .

Caden Flynn is one of the few lucky survivors of the bridge collapse but blames himself for coercing his younger sister out that night. He's carried that guilt for fifteen years, unaware of darker currents haunting the town. It isn't long before Eve's arrival unravels an old secret—one that places her and Caden in the crosshairs of a deadly killer . . .

A THOUSAND YESTERYEARS
A Point Pleasant Novel

Books by Mae Clair

Weathering Rock
Twelfth Sun
Myth and Magic

Point Pleasant Series
A Thousand Yesteryears

Published by Kensington Publishing Corporation

This book is dedicated to the memory of those who lost their lives in the Silver Bridge collapse of December 15, 1967. To their families and loved ones, and to the few who survived that terrible day. It is also dedicated to the people of Point Pleasant, whose town has endured much over the decades, yet remains resilient despite adversity and change.

Acknowledgements

Thank you to my two wonderful critique partners, Laura Lee Nutt and Mary E. Merrell, who were with me from the beginning to the end of this story. I appreciate all of your input and the suggestions that went into polishing this story.

Thank you also to my wonderful editor, Corinne DeMaagd, who made working through edits and galleys a pleasure. I can't say enough about your impeccable eye for detail. Thank you for working so hard to make my story shine.

Finally, to my wonderful husband, the love of my life, who indulged me with two trips to Point Pleasant so I could complete research for this novel and those which follow in the series. Friend, soulmate, and life partner, God blessed my life the day we met.

Author's Foreword

As someone who has long held an interest in folklore, urban legends, and the mythology that shapes different cultures, I was first drawn to the legend of the Mothman in 2013. What I knew about the creature at that time was minimal, but the story intrigued me enough to engage in further research. As a result, I unearthed the history of the Silver Bridge and the elements that contributed to its tragic collapse on December 15, 1967. In my mind, none of these were supernatural in nature, but it seems that the Mothman and the bridge are forever linked in folklore.

I've taken a different approach for my story. The shadow of the Silver Bridge tragedy hangs heavily over my characters, but as a ghost of the past. In addition, I've employed my own interpretation of the Mothman. It should be noted that none of the characters in this book are meant to resemble persons living or dead in any fashion. The Parrish Hotel and many of the other businesses I've created are fictional, but certain locations such as the TNT and Tu-Endie-Wei State Park are places you can visit.

Having been to Point Pleasant and the TNT twice since beginning this series, I can vouch it is an area rich in history—not just in relation to the Silver Bridge and the Mothman, but to an era when riverboats ruled the waterways, and even farther back, to the days preceding the American Revolution. A lot has changed since then and the glory has faded, but the town's heritage remains strong.

That said, I hope you enjoy A Thousand Yesteryears and the novels to follow in this series. There is plenty of myth, mystery, and romance to come.

Mae Clair
July 2015

Prologue

December 15, 1967
Point Pleasant, West Virginia

"Do you think Caden Flynn will go?" Eve Parrish kept pace with her friend, Sarah, as a brisk December wind pushed them down Main Street toward the Crowne Theatre. Eager for a glimpse of the movie poster that had everyone in the tiny river town of Point Pleasant, West Virginia talking, she barely felt the sting on her cheeks. Her mother would box her ears if she knew what Eve was up to, but all the boys at school said the poster hung in the window, plain as day for anyone to see. That had to mean she could sneak a peek. She was twelve now, practically a teenager.

Her parents had called *The Graduate* racy, and Mrs. Quiggly, who sold brown eggs and fresh milk from her farm outside town, said the poster was shameless. She wanted to bring a petition against the theater and make them take the "vile thing" down.

"Silly, busybody," Aunt Rosie had chided behind her back. Never one to get hung up on proper behavior, Aunt Rosie did artsy things like taking photographs and hosting moonlight picnics for friends. She even had a darkroom in her home and occasionally sold shots to the local paper who proudly displayed them with the byline *Photo courtesy of Rosalind Parrish.*

"I heard Caden tell Wyatt Fisher they should take their girlfriends to see it," Sarah said, interrupting her thoughts.

Eve gasped. It was bad enough the boys might see a movie as shocking as *The Graduate,* but more appalling that girls would go, too.

"Maybe they'll chicken out." She had a hopeless crush on Caden, an awkward situation given he was eighteen and the brother of her friend, Maggie. Although careful not to make a fool of herself whenever Caden was around, she usually ended up tongue-tied.

Sarah shrugged and tugged the collar of her coat higher against the wind. Several cars drove by in the pre-holiday rush, the glow of headlights holding the night at bay. Sunset was still a half hour away, plenty of time for Eve and Sarah to reach the theater and ogle the poster. The movie didn't open until next week, but the buzz it generated had already swept through their school.

"I wish Maggie was with us," Eve said with a touch of melancholy.

Sarah rubbed her reddening nose. "Me, too."

The walk to the Crowne was only a few blocks from the Parrish Hotel, owned by Eve's parents and Aunt Rosie. Despite the short distance, it was cold enough to make her wish she'd brought a scarf. At least she'd have something titillating to share with Maggie once she saw the poster. Maybe her gushing about how improper the advertisement looked would make her friend smile.

"Do you think she really saw the Mothman?" Sarah's voice was barely audible. Nervously, she glanced over her shoulder as if fearing the giant birdlike humanoid would sweep from the sky. "Was she near the TNT?"

Eve shook her head.

A remote area of dense woods and small ponds, the TNT had once been used to store ammunition during World War II. Eve's father had taken her there on a few occasions, allowing her to explore the abandoned weapons "igloos." But ever since the Mothman was first spied in the region, she hadn't been back. Her father said bad things happened there, and Mrs. Quiggly insisted the place was a haven for UFOs.

"She was visiting Nana and followed Mischief into the Witch Wood."

A fat orange tabby, Mischief belonged to Maggie's grandmother, an elderly woman who everyone called Nana. She lived in a sprawling house snuggled up to a thicket of woods at the farthest end of town. Eve and Maggie had dubbed the thicket the "Witch Wood" after discovering a sycamore tree that resembled an old woman with legs.

"But it's too cold to go into the Witch Wood now," Sarah protested.

Eve nodded. She, Maggie, and Sara occasionally played there, but usually in the spring and summer when the trees were green with leaves, making it easy to catch caterpillars and grasshoppers.

"Maggie was afraid Mischief would get lost."

Sarah made a *pffing* sound. "As if! He's always getting into trouble and always finds his way home. I wish she hadn't followed him."

"Me, too." Eve bit her bottom lip, worrying it between her teeth. She'd visited her friend for a brief time yesterday, finding Maggie huddled beneath the blankets in her bedroom. She hadn't been to school for three days. "She's afraid to go outside."

They had almost reached the theater. Farther down the street, traffic was lined up at the red light that led to the Silver Bridge. Her father would be home soon, returning from Gallipolis, a neighboring city nestled on the Ohio side of the river. He'd headed there earlier in the afternoon to meet a friend, and like everyone else, would need to cross the Silver Bridge.

"I heard the Mothman's eyes are red," Sarah said.

"Maggie thought so. She told me when she couldn't find Mischief, she got an odd feeling, like something bad had happened. Her skin broke out in goose bumps."

Sarah's eyes widened. She rubbed her nose again. "My mom says people get a weird sensation when they see the Mothman. I've heard her talking about it to my dad when she thinks I'm not around."

"My parents do the same thing." How strange to be focused on something scary when everything around them reflected the festive mood of the coming Christmas holiday. The streetlights on Main were decorated with cheerful ribbons, wreaths, and pinecones, and a lighted Christmas tree brightened the display window of G. C. Murphy, the local five-and-dime. At the store entrance, a man in a Santa Claus suit called out holiday greetings and beckoned shoppers inside. A sense of excitement and seasonal cheer hung in the air.

"Maggie was scared." Eve wet her lips, remembering what her friend had told her. "She thought she heard a noise. Like scraping, or someone digging."

"What did she do?"

"She crept closer, but stayed hidden behind the trees. At least, she thought she was."

There was no mistaking Sarah's nervousness as she squeezed her mittened hands together. "But she wasn't?"

Eve shook her head, only then realizing how frightened she was for her friend. A lot of people thought the Mothman was trying to warn the town about something terrible, like a looming disaster, and that's why it kept reappearing. But Maggie said the creature was awful. A hideous monster with hateful eyes that bored into her soul. Those who'd seen it said its eyes were so ghastly, they couldn't recall any other feature of its face. Rumored to be at least seven feet tall, it had large wings that allowed it to fly vertically like a helicopter. Most said it was gray in color, and the Mothman's terrifying eyes glowed scarlet even in the daylight.

"She got close and peered through the trees," Eve explained. They stopped in front of the theater, but the poster they'd come to see no longer felt important. Someone blew a horn as the light for the Silver Bridge turned green, but traffic remained at a standstill. "That's when she saw it, crouched on the ground."

"What was it doing?" Sarah's eyes filled with fear.

"Maggie didn't know. It was hunkered down with its wings draped around it like a cape. Then it turned and saw her, and she screamed."

Sarah looked like she wanted to do the same.

A chorus of horns blared from the stalled traffic, causing Eve to knit her brows. "Why do you think all the cars are backed up like that?"

Sarah appeared too focused on the story to pay attention to the vehicles bottled up at the entrance to the Silver Bridge. "Did she run? Did it chase her?"

"Of course she ran. Wouldn't you?"

"I would have screamed my head off."

"Me, too." Her heart kicked into a prickly rhythm. Was it because of her fear for Maggie, or the cold sensation that crept over her as she stared at the unmoving traffic two blocks away? Instinctively, she headed for the backup, Sarah keeping pace beside her. "Maggie heard it chasing her, but she managed to get away and run to Nana's home. She didn't tell anyone about it until two days later. She pretended to be sick so she wouldn't have to go to school."

"But Dr. Pullman couldn't find anything wrong with her." Sarah's observation was half question, half statement.

"Nope. And that's when she had to tell the truth."

"How awful." Sarah soaked in the story as they continued walking, seemingly unconcerned they hadn't stopped to gawk at the poster for *The Graduate* as planned. The sidewalk was busy with Christmas shoppers heading in and out of G. C. Murphy and the local bank.

Any other time, Eve would have delighted in the festive mood, but something didn't feel right. Was she the only one who sensed the ominous undercurrent in the air? And why were there so many birds flitting around overhead, as if they couldn't find a place to rest?

"What happened to Mischief?" Sarah asked.

"He came back later. I heard he was fine."

"He's such a bad cat." Sarah shook her head. "I feel just awful for Maggie. Do you think anyone believes she saw the Mothman?"

"Her parents didn't. They tried to convince her she saw a large bird or something."

"What about Ryan and Caden?"

Ryan was Maggie's other brother. Only a year older than the three of them, they often hung out with him and his friends. Fun and kind of goofy, he was unlike Caden, who Eve thought as dreamy and mysterious as an ancient knight.

"She said Ryan believes her, but Caden thinks she's overreacting."

"Well, he is eighteen." Sarah shrugged. "He's one of them. An adult."

How could she have a crush on an adult? "My mom was talking to Mrs. Flynn earlier, and she said Caden was going to try to get Maggie to go Christmas shopping tonight. You know how she's wanted to visit that new department store in Gallipolis? He thought that might get her out of the house."

"I hope it worked."

"Me, too." Eve's stomach did a queasy flip-flop. Did she really hope so? It would mean Caden and Maggie would be on the Silver Bridge. "It's getting near dinner time. If it worked, they're probably headed back right now." *Like my dad.* "Do you notice all the birds?"

Sarah eyed the sky. "Yeah. Weird, isn't it?"

More horns from the stalled traffic.

"Something's wrong." She started walking faster, bypassing the Santa who waved shoppers into the five-and-dime with a hearty "ho-ho-ho." As the doors opened and closed, the cheerful notes of "Jingle Bells" carried onto the street, spurring her into a jog.

"Eve, wait." Sarah hurried to catch up. "What's wrong with you?"

"The traffic." Goose bumps broke out on the back of her neck. "Look." She'd never seen it stacked up like this before. Friday nights were always busy, especially around rush hour, but even with the addition of Christmas shoppers, there were far too many cars.

The pungent tang of exhaust snarled with the rumble of idling motors as they neared the entrance for the bridge. From her vantage point on the sidewalk, she spied the tall rocker towers erected against the sky. The sun had yet to set, the fiery ball ebbing toward the horizon, painting the silver framework with splashes of tangerine and copper.

"The light's green," Sarah said at her side. "Why aren't they moving?"

Eve glanced at the traffic signal just as it cycled to yellow, then red. Not a single car had inched forward. "The light must be out on the Ohio side. Everything's backed up."

"So people are going to be stuck on the bridge."

Like her father. Like Maggie and Caden.

It shouldn't have bothered her, but an unsettled feeling gnawed at the pit of her stomach. The Silver Bridge defined Point Pleasant, much like the Parrish Hotel. Eve had been on the bridge once when the rocker towers swayed slightly, but her dad had told her they were designed to be flexible, and she shouldn't be afraid. The towers moved with suspension chains to help reduce strain on the bridge piers. She didn't understand the construction, but knew the people of Point Pleasant were inordinately proud of their beloved Silver Bridge.

Sarah shook her head, apparently deciding they'd seen all there was of interest. "Hey, we missed the poster for *The Graduate.* Let's go back."

Eve nodded, trying to mask her uneasiness. "Okay. If my dad's on the bridge, he's going to be stuck in traffic anyway."

She started to turn from the sight when a deafening boom split the air like thunder. A woman's shrill scream knifed deeply into her bones. Within seconds, the terrified shriek was echoed by a dozen more voices raised in horror. Those stalled in traffic poured from their vehicles. On the ramp for the Silver Bridge, reverse lights flashed as cars tried to back away from the traffic signal amid a mad chorus of blaring horns.

"Oh!" Sarah shrieked. "Oh, no. No, no, no!"

Her friend lurched forward, rushing toward the bridge, and Eve jerked in her wake as if pulled by an invisible string. A sob built in her chest. It wasn't happening, couldn't be happening! But even before her gaze fell on the rocker towers looming above the Silver Bridge, she understood the horrified screams, the frenzied bleat of car horns, the chaotic cries of starlings wheeling overhead.

As if trapped in a slow motion bubble, the solid framework twisted sickeningly above a bridge crippled with stalled traffic. Christmas shoppers, truckers, workers returning at the end of the day, even visitors crossing from state to state. How many lives were clustered in that frozen string of cars? Her father. Her friend. Caden.

"Daddy." The name was a pitiful squeak, pushed past the lump in her throat. She lurched another step, vaguely conscious of people swarming past her. They came from cars and stores, from traffic that had stopped haphazardly on Main Street. Screams and voices that made no sense. Birds shrieked above her. Somewhere in the background "Jingle Bells" still played through the open doors of the five-and-dime. Even the suited Santa raced past, waving and hollering for people to get off the entrance ramp.

A scream built in her lungs. Someone yelled for police, someone else for an ambulance. Three steps ahead of her, a woman huddled on the street, hugging a small child to her chest. From the look of the open car door behind her, she had been on the ramp but managed to scramble free, abandoning a brown station wagon. Both the woman and the child were sobbing.

No more than thirty seconds had passed, Eve was sure. Why couldn't she scream? Why couldn't she look away from the twisting rocker towers? In the span of a single heartbeat, they collapsed, the entire bridge folding like a mammoth deck of cards. A heap of metal, steel, and headlights plummeted into the Ohio River.

Eve stumbled to her knees, the scream in her chest ripped lose in a mournful wail.

In little more than sixty seconds, the Silver Bridge was gone, claiming the lives of those she loved.

Chapter 1

June, 1982
Point Pleasant, West Virginia

Eve Parrish stared through the windshield of her Toyota Corolla at the two-story house her aunt had bequeathed to her in her will. A house she remembered fondly from childhood, it had been in her family for four generations, just like the old hotel in downtown Point Pleasant.

Tightening her grip on the steering wheel of the parked car, she vowed to worry about the hotel later. *One problem at a time.*

At twenty-seven, it was staggering to find herself the sole owner of her family's homestead *and* the Parrish Hotel. She'd inherited the latter after her father died, and Eve's mother had signed her ownership of the property over to Aunt Rosie. Not long afterward, her mother had uprooted them, determined to put the tragedy of the Silver Bridge in the past. It had always been Aunt Rosie who came to visit Eve and her mom in Pennsylvania.

But Aunt Rosie was gone.

Why couldn't she have told them about the cancer? Eve would have done something, anything to help. Insisted she get treatment.

"She didn't want treatment," Adam Barnett, Rosie's lawyer had explained as he'd passed her the keys for the hotel and the house earlier that day. "She went quickly, which is how she wanted it."

Eve swiped a tear from her cheek. Aunt Rosie had planned to marry in the summer of '68, but the Silver Bridge altered those plans. Shaken by the tragedy, Eve's aunt had called off her engagement to Roger Layton and never married. Was that why she'd allowed herself to go so quickly once diagnosed with breast cancer? Did she think no one loved her?

A spasm of guilt twisted Eve's stomach. Her small apartment was only six hours away in Harrisburg, but her mom had drilled a steady dislike of Point Pleasant into her head from the time they moved away. It was the place where her father had met his end in the icy waters of the Ohio River only weeks before Christmas and a hotspot for bizarre Mothman and UFO sightings. Was it any wonder her mother had insisted on burying the town in their past?

Right or wrong, Eve hadn't returned in fifteen years. She barely recognized the sparse streets now, so changed from the thriving river community she remembered. She'd been glad to see the Crowne Theater still in operation, but saddened to know G. C. Murphy's had closed its doors. How she, Maggie, and Sarah had loved their soda fountain.

Taking a deep breath, she popped the door on the Corolla and stepped onto the street. Aunt Rosie's house—the same house in which her father and his sister had grown up—was located several miles from downtown Point Pleasant. Every bit as imposing as she remembered, the large two story was offset by a covered porch and a towering chestnut tree in the front yard. Her father had once hung a tire from the lowest branch at Aunt Rosie's behest so Eve and her friends would have a swing when they visited.

Reluctantly, Eve glanced to the house next door. Not quite as large, the cheerful colonial looked in far better condition than the imposing structure Eve had inherited. The paint appeared fresh, the shrubs neatly trimmed. Colorful blooms had already sprouted in the flowerbeds, and a pot of pansies welcomed guests to the front porch.

She'd spent countless afternoons playing in Maggie's home. Countless Friday night sleepovers when they'd stayed up late eating Mrs. Flynn's peanut butter cookies and giggling about boys. She'd never told her friend about the crush she'd had on Caden, but Maggie had known. Best friends always did. Unlike his sister, Caden had survived that fatal night on the Silver Bridge.

With an inhale of determination, Eve hooked her purse onto her shoulder. She would leave her overnight bag and suitcase in the car for the time being. She'd packed light, hoping to finalize plans for the house and hotel within two weeks. Hopefully, Adam Barnett could recommend a real estate company capable of handling residential and commercial sales.

He'd warned her about the break-in. "Nothing taken, it appears. Just vandalism. It happens sometimes when a house sits empty. Probably teenagers looking for a thrill. I had all of the damaged items removed and disposed of as you requested."

The key turned easily in the lock. According to Mr. Barnett, the vandals had gained entrance through the screened porch in the rear, and then busted the kitchen door. Both doors would require reinforcing. With any luck, the rest of the damage would be minimal.

As she stepped inside, a swarm of memories assaulted her. The house smelled stale, closed up for too long, but a trace of Aunt Rosie's signature scent lingered beneath the mustiness. A light bouquet that whispered of spring flowers and clover. On the heels of having visited her aunt's grave at the cemetery, the fragrance brought tears to Eve's eyes. Hugging her arms close to her chest, she blinked them away.

Mr. Barnett had made sure all of the utilities were working, but it was stuffy in the house. She'd have to set the ceiling fans to circulate the air. At least no one had covered Aunt Rosie's pretty furniture with those dreadful white sheets people used when closing an estate.

Her aunt had kept most of the furniture Eve remembered from childhood. The gold and crystal lamps on the end tables were new, but the heavy-footed couch and easy chairs upholstered in crimson brocade were as she remembered, if faded from time. Black walnut tables and thick butternut drapes covered with climbing grapevines accentuated the décor. Surprisingly, there was little damage to the room.

Tracing her fingers along a chair rail, she headed for the dining room. Whoever bought the old monstrosity would have to crave a home with character. It certainly had that. From its wide windowsills to arched openings and massive moldings, it echoed the detailing of a different time.

In the kitchen, she found the door leading to the screened porch reinforced with plywood to prevent further break-ins. The upstairs fared worse. The room her talented aunt had employed as a dark room had been completely ransacked. Mr. Barnett had been hesitant to volunteer the information but said there were chemical spills, and many of her aunt's beloved photos had been found torn and littered on the floor. Looking at the damage, Eve felt a slow burn of anger that someone would destroy her aunt's work. They had no right! As if in mockery of the act, the vandals had used black spray paint to leave a large squiggle on the wall like a brand. Stupid, stupid kids.

Two of the bedrooms had barely been touched, but the last—her aunt's room—had suffered nearly as badly as the dark room. The contents had been dumped from the dresser and closet. At least Mr. Barnett had seen to it that her aunt's lovely clothing had been piled on the bed for her to sort through and replace. Someone had obviously overturned the bureau—the mirror was shattered— and the bedspread had been ripped off and thrown on the floor. This time when the tears welled, she couldn't stop them. It wasn't fair. Her aunt had been taken prematurely at forty-nine by an ugly disease, and this is how her memory was honored? Lifting a soft terry robe from the bed, she inhaled her aunt's scent and pressed the fabric to her cheek.

"I'm sorry, Aunt Rosie. I'm sorry I wasn't there for you when you needed me."

Eve jerked reflexively when a sharp pounding interrupted her thoughts. Given the vandalism she'd witnessed, her heart lurched frightfully, sending a flutter through her stomach. It took a few seconds before she placed the sound as someone banging on the front door. Mr. Barnett had indicated somcone from the sheriff's office would likely stop by to talk to her about the damage. She hadn't expected them so soon, but was eager to learn the details of the report. Tucking a stray strand of hair behind her ears, she hurried down the steps, then yanked open the door.

"Why hello there." The petite woman standing on her front porch offered a friendly smile.

"I…" Eve mentally stumbled, her mind doing cartwheels. Something about the woman was familiar. The appearance was off—there was gray in the woman's hair that hadn't been there before, and her eyes looked watery, not bright like Eve remembered—but the inflection of her voice was the same. She swallowed hard. "Mrs. Flynn?"

"I saw your car. Maggie said you were coming."

"Excuse me?"

Her dead friend's mother smiled indulgently and patted her hand. "It's all right. I realize things are different now." Turning, she roamed to the edge of the covered porch and rested her hands lightly on the railing as she gazed over the front yard. "Maggie has waited a long time for you, Eve."

Flummoxed by her unexpected arrival and the strange comments, Eve trailed after her. "Mrs. Flynn? I…don't understand what you mean." Surely, her best friend's mother wasn't discussing Maggie as if she were still alive. Perhaps the woman was ill. Her odd behavior made the whole scenario seem like a dream.

A car passed in front of the house, sending a flutter of leaves into the yard on a puff of air. The breeze smelled of honeysuckle and exhaust, and a clingy kiss of sunlight warmed Eve's face. She couldn't be dreaming.

"Did you know they didn't find her body until June of '68?"

Eve bit her lip, uncertain how to respond. When her mother had uprooted them the spring after the bridge collapse, the bodies of three victims were still missing. She'd later learned that Maggie's remains had been located during the summer, but there was no talk of returning for the funeral. Her mother wouldn't hear of it.

"I'm so sorry." At least her father's body had been discovered in the debris pile on the Ohio side of the river, allowing him the dignity of a proper burial. Not Maggie. For nearly six months, her remains had been battered and misshapen by the cold currents of the river. If the knowledge ripped at Eve's heart, how much more the heart of her friend's mother?

"Would you...would you like to come inside?"

"No thank you, dear." Mrs. Flynn turned to face her. "I just wanted to welcome you back. Maggie asked me to."

Oh, God. The woman was certifiably crazy.

She might have contemplated the thought further but for the arrival of a police car in front of Aunt Rosie's house. Mrs. Flynn shook her head at the sight, then quietly left the porch without so much as a goodbye. She was halfway across the yard when the man in the car stepped onto the street.

"Mom," he called.

Mom?

Eve felt her eyebrows launch into her bangs as she watched the man dart around the rear of his car to greet Mrs. Flynn on the grass. They exchanged a few soft words before the woman continued her path back to her home and the man jogged toward the porch. As he hustled up the steps, Eve got the shock of her life.

"Ryan?"

"Hey, you remembered." Maggie's brother grinned and extended his hand.

When she slid her fingers into his, he yanked her close, hugging her tightly. In no time, she found herself laughing breathlessly.

"It's so good to see you, Ryan." She hugged him back, delighted by the warmth his unexpected presence brought. "Mr. Barnett never said you worked for the sheriff's department."

"Yep. A sergeant." He tapped the badge pinned to his neatly pressed uniform, then held her at arm's length, his smile igniting a sparkle in his blue eyes.

It was hard to believe the skinny thirteen-year-old she remembered had matured into such a tall, broad-shouldered man. His black hair, no longer curly but wavy, lay tousled over his brow, his grin as infectious as always.

"God, it's good to see you after all these years." Ryan seemed reluctant to release her. "I ran into Adam Barnett at the bank, and he told me he'd given you the keys. I can't believe you're really here."

"I can't either." She hugged him again, then laughed. "You got so tall."

"And you got so..." He paused and wiggled his eyebrows, molding his hands in the shape of an hourglass. "Curvy."

She swatted his arm. "You always were a trouble-maker. Do you want to come in for a while? The house is a wreck, but—"

"Actually, that's why I'm here. I wanted to go over the vandalism report with you." He sobered abruptly and stepped away. "And I'm sorry about my mother. I hope she didn't say anything to upset you."

"No, I..." How did she explain the odd conversation? She'd only been in Point Pleasant a short while. The last thing she wanted to do was offend a childhood friend by pointing out that his mother was off her rocker.

Ryan shook his head, clearly conscious of what may have been said. "Sometimes she gets confused and gets caught up in the past."

Eve let the remark slide without comment. "I was just going to get my bags out of my car." She steered the conversation elsewhere. "Maybe you could give me a hand?"

"Sure."

Together, they trudged to her Corolla. Ryan grabbed her suitcase and overnight bag while Eve snatched a jacket from the backseat along with a few boxed goods she'd brought for the trip. Later, she'd hit the grocery store and stock up on perishable items. At least the refrigerator was in working order.

In the house, Ryan carried her luggage upstairs while she detoured to the kitchen with her small parcel of crackers, instant rice, and peanut butter. She wished she had something to offer him, but the best she could manage was peanut butter and crackers. Mentally, she bumped the grocery store higher on her to-do list.

"I put everything in the spare bedroom for you," Ryan announced, entering the kitchen. "I guess you saw Rosie's room is a mess."

Eve added her box of instant rice to the nearest cupboard, nudging aside several cans of Campbell's soup left behind by Aunt Rosie. A vivid memory flashed through her mind as she recalled her aunt feeding her tomato soup and a grilled cheese for lunch on a brisk autumn day.

"Her dark room, too." Eve shut the cupboard and turned, bracing her back against the counter. "The vandals hit the upstairs hard. Do you have any idea who would have done such a thing?"

"Afraid not." Ryan motioned her toward the dining room. "Let's sit down."

At the dining room table, he withdrew a folded sheaf of papers from his breast pocket. "I thought you should have a copy of the vandalism report."

Eve eyed the papers he handed her. It was standard stuff—date, time, damage done. "Who reported it?"

"No one. I still live next door with my mom. It's um…complicated." He cleared his throat awkwardly. "After Rosie died, I kept an eye on the place. Several days after her death, I was walking around the house when I noticed the door on the screened porch had been busted. I guess the vandals chose it because it was hidden from the street. Easy entry."

"Did they take anything?"

"Not that I could tell, but Rosie isn't here to answer that question. I should have said it before, Eve, but you have my sympathies." He covered her hand with his where it rested on the table.

She managed a wan smile and nodded a thank you. It was good to see him again, a familiar face that made the shock of returning to her childhood home less traumatic. Even if he was grown, no longer the thirteen-year-old boy she remembered, he was still the brother of her one-time best friend.

"So you think it was just kids out for some fun?" She winced, unable to comprehend how anyone could view destroying the home of the recently deceased as entertaining.

He hesitated. "It looks that way."

"Is there something you're not telling me?"

"Nothing of importance." He patted her hand again and stood, then paced a short distance away. "What are you going to do with the place?"

The million-dollar question. "Sell it, of course." It hurt to say, as if she was turning her back on Aunt Rosie and all her aunt held dear. "Vandalism aside, the home needs work to make it desirable. I'm no expert, but it looks like it could use a new roof and several of the rooms should be repainted. If I want to put it on the market, I'm going to have to fix it up first." It was a sobering thought. "I don't suppose you could recommend someone?"

He surprised her with a quick answer. "Do you remember Caden?"

"Your brother?" Her heart lurched again. How could she forget her childhood crush?

"He has a contracting business. Home remodeling, repairs. That sort of thing."

"It sounds ideal." For some reason she hadn't considered encountering him when she'd returned to Point Pleasant. "Do you have a phone number for him? I'd like to talk to him about taking on the repairs."

"How about if I have him stop by tomorrow? Will that work?"

"Perfect." She was planning on addressing the hotel tomorrow, something that would probably take most of the day. "Do you think he can stop early? Around nine? I was planning on visiting the hotel later."

"It shouldn't be a problem." He shot her a sideways glance as if measuring her reaction. "The hotel is still the center of town."

"I thought as much." Eve glanced at her hands, thinking back to the years when her parents and Aunt Rosie had made the hotel the focus of their lives. It had been her family's defining legacy long before she was born. Her great grandfather Clarence had paid for its construction in 1922, then quickly turned the establishment into a thriving operation, bolstered in part by Point Pleasant's blossoming river trade. It hadn't taken her more than a few hours in town to realize those days were nothing more than a memory. "I noticed things are different."

A shadow crossed Ryan's face. "A lot's changed since you left."

"The Silver Bridge affected everything."

He nodded, shoulders slumping as he stuffed his hands in his pockets. "It wasn't just the catastrophe. Bruce Mechanical closed up shop shortly afterward. That dried up half the employment in town. Point Pleasant isn't the thriving river community it used to be."

How sad. Eve had fond memories of watching riverboats and tugs traverse the waters of the Ohio and Kanawha Rivers, ushering barges loaded with coal from Ohio to West Virginia and vice-versa. When Bruce Mechanical launched a new boat, the event was guaranteed to draw a crowd. She, Maggie, and Sarah had eagerly raced to the docks as the newly built ships slid sideways into the water, tilting so far she feared they would capsize before righting themselves.

Ryan returned to his seat at the table, then reclined comfortably, crossing an ankle over his knee. "Main Street is pretty much a ghost town these days. I'm sure you noticed."

She nodded. "They moved the Silver Bridge."

"We call it the Silver Memorial Bridge now, but you're right." A frown flitted across his mouth. "The new bridge diverts the flow of traffic out of town, bypassing Main. As much as we appreciate the Silver Memorial Bridge, it's partially responsible for sapping Point Pleasant's lifeblood."

"What about the hotel?" She had to know.

"It holds its own." Ryan gave a one-shouldered shrug. "It may not pull the traffic it did in its heyday, but according to Rosie, it was solvent. I'm sure you've seen the books."

"Enough of them." The hotel was a juggernaut she needed to tackle.

"So you really want to sell it?" Ryan asked.

She glanced at her hands. The Parrish Hotel was as much a part of Point Pleasant as the historic Silver Bridge. Her family had invested decades in its growth. The idea of fluffing it off for financial gain was nothing short of sacrilege.

"I'm still undecided." It wasn't an entire lie. Part of her resisted the idea of unloading an institution that had been her family's legacy. "Right now I'm using two weeks of my vacation time from Labor and Industry. I do clerical work, not the most exciting thing, but it's a Commonwealth job, and the benefits are good. I don't know the first thing about overseeing a hotel."

"That's what a manager is for."

"I'm not sure I want to go that route." The thought of entrusting so much to someone she didn't know left her uneasy.

"You've got a lot on you," Ryan conceded. "Half of the businesses on Main Street were forced to close."

"But the hotel survived."

"Along with the Crowne Theater. At least for now. Your aunt saw to the hotel's prosperity. The Parrish name still has enough clout to draw visitors from neighboring states."

She nodded and laced her hands on her lap. "I'll look into it tomorrow." Wrapping her head around the house was enough for the day. Suddenly, she didn't want to think about the past or the pressing matters looming over her head. She simply wanted to bask in the warmth of seeing an old friend. "Thanks for bringing the vandalism report. I never would have pegged you as a cop. You always got into so much trouble as a kid."

He laughed. "Odd how things turn out. What about you? Did you marry?"

"No."

"I didn't either. No luck yet, or just not ready to settle down. I can't figure out which."

"That doesn't surprise me." He'd always been a free spirit, much like Rosie, playful and prone to trouble. "What about Caden?" She hoped the query appeared as nothing more than the innocent probing of an old friend trying to catch up on the present. Her heart gave a little flutter when she thought of him. Amazing her long-buried attraction was still there.

"Caden's single, too." Ryan shook his head. "He'll probably end up an old man living alone unless he moves past his guilt."

"What do you mean?"

Ryan waved a hand as if brushing away the thought. "He hasn't forgiven himself for taking Maggie shopping that night. Most of us have moved on. Caden hasn't."

She thought of herself, her mother. Their world had come to a crashing halt that cold December night when her father's car fell into the Ohio River. And yet somehow they'd rummaged up the strength to continue. It had taken uprooting, leaving the shadow of the disaster behind in Point Pleasant, but somehow her mother had managed to put the pieces together for herself and her twelve-year-old daughter. Eventually, her mother had remarried, and Eve found herself with a stepfather. As much as she loved the man, part of her understood Caden's refusal to relinquish the past.

"What about your parents?" She couldn't help venturing the question given the odd discussion she'd had with Mrs. Flynn. Should she tell Ryan what his mother had said about Maggie…talking about her as if she were still alive?

He shrugged, and she sensed his reluctance. "My father passed away a few years ago."

"I'm so sorry." She had fond memories of Mr. Flynn.

"It was his lungs. All those years spent working in a coal mine finally caught up with him."

"What about your mother?"

"She's accepted his death, but Maggie's…" Again a shrug that said far more than words. "A part of her died when that bridge went down."

Eve bit her lip. She could understand Mrs. Flynn's pain.

"Most of the time she's okay," Ryan continued. "But other times, she retreats into the past and insists Maggie is still alive. She talks about her as if they share discussions. It's the reason I still live at home…to take care of her. She can be a handful when she's in the past."

Eve wasn't sure what to say. So much tragedy had happened when the Silver Bridge collapsed. The town had suffered, but more than that, the populace had crumpled under the blow of individual losses. Fifteen years later, splinters of that residual pain reached far and wide.

"I'm sorry." There were no words for the loss or the choking reach of its tentacles.

"We do the best we can." As if deciding he'd had enough gloom, Ryan stood. "It's good to have you back, Eve, even if only for a short while. I'll tell Caden to drop by tomorrow morning."

She walked him to the door, thankful to have encountered a familiar face. It had been a stroke of luck to learn Caden was a contractor. It would save her the trouble of looking for someone to do the repairs and speed the sale of the house that much more quickly.

"What about Sarah?" she asked as he stepped onto the front porch. Eve stayed inside on the threshold, a breeze scuttling past her like an uninvited guest. "Does she still live in town?"

He nodded. "She works in the records division at the courthouse. We had a bad situation there several years back. I'm not sure if Rosie told you about the bomb blast."

She had. A suicidal ex-convict had forced his way inside with a shotgun and a homemade explosive device. Despite attempts at negotiation, the bomber had leveled the entire first floor, killing three and injuring six others. After hearing about it, Eve had called her aunt to make sure she was safe.

"Another tragedy in a town plagued by them," Aunt Rosie had said. "Fools around here are saying it's the curse of Cornstalk come to blight us again."

"I saw it on the news when it happened," Eve told Ryan. At the time, she'd wondered if it was in some way connected to the Mothman. She didn't believe in the curse of Cornstalk, an Indian chief who'd been murdered in the days preceding the American Revolution. Local legend said he'd cursed the town with his dying breath. You couldn't grow up in Point Pleasant without having the shadow of that legend leech into every event that took place.

"Sarah wasn't hurt, was she?" Cold fear gripped her stomach as she thought of her childhood friend.

"No, she wasn't working then, but we lost a lot of good people. Strange how things keep happening in this town." He raised a hand in farewell. "Stay in touch, Eve. Don't leave without saying goodbye."

She stayed at the door, closing it only after he'd driven off in his police cruiser. The emptiness of the house settled over her with a marked hush, and she wondered how Aunt Rosie had managed living there on her own for so many years. Then again, like the hotel, the house was part of Parrish history.

* * * *

A loud bang woke her from a sound sleep.

Eve sat bolt upright in bed, panic spiking through her chest. The unfamiliar surroundings made her inhale sharply until she remembered where she was. Wind rattled the rafters, sending creaks and groans through the old house. After a trip to the grocery store and a phone call to her mother, she'd spent the remainder of the day sorting through the mess the vandals had left. She'd concentrated on Aunt Rosie's bedroom, wanting to clean up the violation as if the destruction had been a personal affront to her aunt. Dinner had been a can of soup heated on the stove, after which she'd taken a shower and collapsed into bed. Whether it was the emotional toll of returning home after fifteen years or the long hours she'd spent cleaning and disinfecting to erase every last trace of the vandals, she'd fallen asleep easily.

A glance at the bedside clock told her it was after two in the morning. Another bang reverberated through the upstairs hallway.

Easing from bed, she slipped on her robe and padded to the bedroom door. Hesitating, she wrapped her fingers around the doorknob, straining to hear. Her heart pumped a frenzied beat as she debated switching on a light. Part of her wanted to call the police. She feared the vandals may have returned, but knew she'd looked foolish if the noise turned out to be something trivial. Maybe a stray animal had found its way inside through the broken kitchen door.

Bang. Bang. Bang.

The noise came again, steady and in sync, like someone pounding on a wall.

Not an animal.

Whatever the cause, it originated in Aunt Rosie's room. Deciding she had no choice but to investigate, Eve eased open the door and crept down the darkened hall to her aunt's bedroom. As she neared, the sound stopped, then started again. The frantic flutter of her heart had her gulping down fear as she peered into the room. By then, her eyesight had grown accustomed to the dark, allowing her to pick out shapes easily. A full moon splashed pale light through the rear window, sketching elaborate shadows on the ceiling and floor. One separated from the rest, moved, then fell back into place.

Bang. Bang.

Relieved, Eve released a pent-up breath. Just a loose shutter caught in the wind. She crossed to the window and opened it wide, a light breeze beading goose bumps down her arm. Feeling for the shutter, she pushed it in place, uncertain if the effort would secure it temporarily. It would have to do for the night. Tomorrow, she'd add it to the list of items she intended to broach with Caden. At least whoever had vandalized the house hadn't returned for a second round.

As she closed the window and stepped back from the curtains, her gaze was drawn by movement in the rear yard where her aunt's property ceded to a tree line. If not for the bright wash of moonlight, she might have missed it entirely. A shadow broke from the others, then flowed into the trees. A shadow that had been standing, watching the house. One that had likely seen her in the window.

Eve swallowed hard.

A shadow shaped like a man.

Chapter 2

It was hard sleeping after the disturbance. She tossed restlessly for the remainder of the night, dreaming of Aunt Rosie and Maggie when she was fortunate enough to drift off for brief periods. She had the strange sensation both wanted to tell her something, but each time they faded like mist.

When Caden arrived shortly after eight, she was on her third cup of coffee and jittery from a caffeine high. One cup was usually her limit before switching to decaf, a regime she should have stuck with that morning.

The man who stood on her doorstep looked nothing like the lanky eighteen-year-old she remembered. That Caden had been brash and daring to her twelve-year-old eyes. A free spirit who played guitar and took risks, like drag racing at the TNT or climbing the trestles of the K&M Railway Bridge. He and his friends had once seemed like demi-gods, hanging at the theater, smoking, doing all the things the cool kids did. In her schoolgirl mind, she'd envisioned him part knight, part gypsy pirate.

"Eve?" He smiled hesitantly, his gray eyes crinkling at the corners. His hair was the same coal black as Ryan's, but thick and straighter with a loose scatter of bangs. Every bit as tall as she remembered, he towered over her by a good six inches, his body lean and toned like a track athlete. "You look different." He offered his hand.

"So do you." Different but good. Good enough to be distracting. She shook his hand and invited him inside, feeling a bit like a twelve-year old girl crushing on a boy out of her league. "I guess Ryan told you about the vandalism."

"I knew about it—the whole town did—but I haven't been inside." He carried a metal case the size of a clipboard, the kind she'd often seen tradesmen use. He placed a piece of paper on top, then slid a pen from the back pocket of his jeans. "Do you want to point things out, or do you want me to do a walk through and give you an idea of what I think should be done?"

Straight to business, no small talk. That was interesting. "A walk-through sounds fine. Would you like some coffee?"

"No, thanks. I'll start upstairs if that's okay with you."

She watched him disappear up the steps, surprised by his reserve. Such a change from the boy who'd frequently teased Maggie and indulged his little sister. In school he'd talked about moving to LA, trying to make a go of it with his music. She'd heard him sing solo several times, usually at church, but once at a festival the summer before the bridge collapsed. It was amazing how she still measured time in Point Pleasant as before the bridge fell and after. It was simply the way of things.

In the summer of '67, Caden and a few friends had put together a makeshift band for a short performance at the fairgrounds. If she hadn't already had a horrible crush on him, hearing him sing to an audience would have been enough to seal her fate. She was certain every teen and preteen girl within hearing distance had fallen instantly in love with him. She'd gone home that night dreaming of a future where he moved away and became famous, then returned to Point Pleasant after she'd graduated high school. Within days, he'd fallen in love with her, declaring she was more important than fame and music, and he couldn't live without her.

Such schoolgirl silliness.

But her heart had done a little pitter-patter at seeing him again.

An hour later, she and Caden sat at the dining room table, just as she had done with Ryan, and he went over the list of suggested repairs.

"Some of the items are obvious." He slid the paper across the table for her to take a look. "Plaster repair and painting, the damage to the screened porch and kitchen door, but there are some others you might not have noticed."

"Such as?" Eve glanced down the list, a sinking sensation eating at her stomach. It wasn't the financial setback that would hurt as much as the time involved. Aunt Rosie's estate had been considerable, even if a good portion was currently tied up in equity. The biggest problem was she didn't want the estate hanging over her head.

"Some of the wiring has been exposed in the dark room. If I'm ripping out walls, that should be reworked and brought up to code. And the chemical spills have eaten through the finish on the hardwood floor by the closet. If your intent is to sell, you can market 'as is' or fix the items I'm suggesting and hope for a boost in resale value. I'll have to subcontract the electrical."

"You sound like you know what you're talking about."

He shrugged and stretched in the chair. "I've got a Realtor who calls me frequently when he needs repair work done on a client listing."

Another connection that would save time. "Can I get his name?"

"Sure thing. I thought you might be interested and brought a card just in case." He slipped it from the front pocket of his jeans and passed it across the table.

Eve glanced at the embossed gold letters: *James Dixon, River Real Estate.* "I'll call him." She wanted the house sold as quickly as possible. "Can you give me an idea what the repairs are going to set me back?"

"I'll work up an estimate and drop it off tomorrow. I'll break it out by item. That way if you don't want to do everything I suggest, you don't have to."

"That sounds fair. When do you think you can start?"

"Depending on what you decide, I'll probably have to pick up supplies, possibly order some lumber, but there are a number of things I can get started on right away." He shook his head. "Odd how most of the damage was to the dark room and your aunt's bedroom."

She'd thought the same. "Almost as if the rest was an afterthought."

Caden narrowed his eyes. "What does that mean?"

"Oh…nothing." She was likely being silly, but now that she'd had a chance to scrutinize each room thoroughly, she couldn't help notice the dissimilarities. Aside from the kitchen, which had been the point of entry through the screened porch, most of the other rooms had sustained minimal damage. It was almost as if the vandals had targeted the dark room and her aunt's bedroom, then hit the others so the damage wouldn't seem selective. "Ryan thinks it was kids having fun, but I'm not so sure." She bit her lip, thinking of the man she'd spied from her bedroom window.

Caden shifted uneasily, his posture relaying a hesitant thought.

She pounced on his silence immediately. "What aren't you saying?"

He frowned, tapping his pen against the table. Judging from the look in his eyes, he was uncertain how forthcoming he should be. At last he cleared his throat and dropped the pen as if reaching a decision. "I don't want to alarm you, but I've seen my share of damage before. Whoever trashed the rooms upstairs was either looking for something or did it in a fit of rage." He held up a hand as disclaimer. "Just my opinion."

Her heartrate increased. "Wouldn't your brother have told me that? He's a cop. He would have recognized—"

"Ryan might be in law enforcement, but he tends to see the best in every situation."

"Unlike you?" She wasn't sure why she'd said it, but staring at him across the table, she knew the observation was true. There was a hardness to his face that hadn't been there in his youth, a jaded coldness to his eyes that made him seem aloof.

He grimaced but inclined his head, acknowledging the comment. "I've learned to see things for what they are. Life rarely disappoints me."

"I'm sorry. I shouldn't have said—"

He held up a hand to forestall her apology. "I'm just making an observation based on experience."

"But Aunt Rosie didn't have any enemies." The idea was unthinkable.

"That you know of."

"You're scaring me."

"That's not my intention. Look, Eve, if I were a kid on a vandalizing spree, I'd do a lot more damage with a can of spray paint than tossing the place."

She thought of the black squiggle she'd seen upstairs. "There was only one wall marked with spray paint."

"To make it seem like vandalism." Caden leaned forward. "Kids like to make a statement. They spray paint words and symbols, not a simple line."

She swallowed hard. "Why are you telling me this?"

"Because even if you don't want me to do any of the work on this list"—he tapped the paper in front of her—"let me go to the hardware store and buy a deadbolt for the back door. I can shore it up far better than that piece of wood in place now."

"You're serious about this?"

He sat back in the chair. "Enough to share my thoughts with Ryan. This is the first time I've seen the damage."

"But you're suggesting someone did this deliberately."

"I know you want to believe your aunt didn't have enemies, but you've been away for fifteen years. A lot has changed. People change. Point Pleasant has changed."

"You've changed."

He balked as if she'd caught him off guard.

"You used to be so easy-going," she continued, venturing further. "I remember how Maggie said you—"

"Maggie's dead." He looked away. "That damn bridge."

"I lost my father on that bridge."

"You didn't kill your father."

"What?" Certainly, he didn't mean he was responsible for Maggie's death?

"Nothing." He shoved his chair back and stood. "I'll be back later today with an estimate for time and materials and to repair the back door."

"I didn't agree to that work." She was suddenly angry with him for cutting her off, for refusing to talk about Maggie. He couldn't just saunter into her home, work her nerves into a knot with theories about personal vendettas against her aunt, then close down and refuse to talk.

"I'm doing it, anyway." Without waiting for a response, he started for the front door.

"Caden." She trailed on his heels, the heat of anger warming her cheeks. "I'm not twelve-years old any longer, and I'm not your sister. That attitude may have worked on Maggie, but it doesn't on me."

He paused, his hand on the doorknob, and turned to stare down at her. "It only worked once with Maggie. And I wish to God it hadn't."

* * * *

Caden should have headed to his shop and started on the estimate he promised Eve, but guilt drove him next door. It had been at least two weeks since he'd visited his mother. The sight of Ryan's personal vehicle parked in the driveway told him his brother was working a later shift. Having his younger brother act as buffer between Caden and his mother would help if she spiraled into the past. Although she was fine on her own and went about her business as usual most days, there were times they worried about her driving or heading into town.

Oddly, she never talked to other people about Maggie, only them. It was as if their presence, especially his, triggered something that made her retreat into the past. To the rest of the world, she behaved as usual, a pleasant woman with a friendly smile and a soft-spoken demeanor.

"Ryan?" Caden stepped inside, setting his clipboard on a foyer table. There'd been a time he would have set his badge and pistol there, but his days in law enforcement had ended in a nightmare of blood and drunken screams. Even now, there were times his gut curdled thinking about Hank Jeffries and the Kline kid. The best thing he'd ever done was walk away from the police force.

"Back here." His brother's voice and the smell of coffee led him to the kitchen. The sight of Ryan seated at the breakfast table with a plate of scrambled eggs and bacon while his mother flitted around the stove resurrected memories of easy family mornings.

"You're just in time for breakfast, Caden." His mother smiled in his direction. Dressed in a rose-colored bathrobe, her blond hair secured in a low bun, she looked the picture of domestic bliss.

He bent and gave her a kiss on the cheek. "I'll just grab some coffee."

"Nonsense. I made far too many eggs. Someone has to eat them."

As he poured a cup of coffee from the pot on the counter, she served up a plateful of eggs and added a few strips of bacon. "There." She shooed him toward the table and set the plate in front of him. "Having both of my boys for breakfast. What a treat. I'll get you some silverware."

"Mom, sit down. I'll take care of it."

She seemed in good spirits, often a rarity. Caden steered her toward the table and got her settled with a cup of coffee. He located silverware in a drawer, then returned to his seat. "Did you already eat?"

She waved a hand over her coffee. "Don't worry about me. I'm not hungry."

From the corner of his eye, he saw Ryan give a slight nod, indicating she'd had breakfast earlier. Sometimes, she truly didn't remember; other times her protests were a bid for attention. Favoring him with a bright smile, she leaned across the table and patted his hand. "It's so nice of you to drop by, Caden. I haven't seen you in over a month."

Time for her to apply the guilt trip. She'd set a new record for speed. "It's only been a few weeks, Mom."

"Posh. I'm sure it's been longer."

"It just seems that way." He swallowed a forkful of eggs and exchanged a glance with Ryan. His brother was far more accustomed to their mother's flighty nature and her nosedives into fantasy. Guilt was something she rarely ladled on Ryan, a specialty reserved for her eldest son. As much as she claimed to love him, she'd never forgiven him for Maggie's death. It was a truth he'd carried in his heart for the last fifteen years.

The river had taken his sister's life, surrendering her body only after destroying her flesh. So each morning he woke in his small rented apartment overlooking the site where the Silver Bridge had stood, reminding himself he was at fault. Each night he closed his eyes on the view of that cold water, knowing Maggie's bones had lain trapped in the silt for six long months.

If only he hadn't convinced her to go out that night.

His mother nursed her coffee, eying him over the brim of the cup. "However long it's been, you look tired. Don't you ever sleep?"

Not well.

"Sometimes I have dreams," she continued, as if uninterested in his answer. "I had one last night."

Ryan cleared his throat, interrupting. Both brothers knew any mention of dreams would likely lead her down the murky corridors of the past. "I take it you saw Eve."

Thankful for the intervention, Caden nodded. "I told her I'd get an estimate to her this afternoon. There's a lot of damage upstairs. More than accountable by random vandalism."

"I always thought she was a sweet girl." His mother swirled a spoonful of sugar into her coffee. Turned toward the ceiling, her eyes held a faraway look. "It's so nice she came back to visit."

"I think she's just here to settle Rosie's estate, Mom," Ryan interjected. He returned his attention to Caden. "You didn't tell her that…about the vandalism?"

"She deserves to know."

Ryan gave a snort of disgust. "No one wants to scare her, Caden. It was probably nothing. Rosie didn't have enemies."

"But she had secrets."

Both brothers glanced to their mother at her strange pronouncement.

"What does that mean?" Caden asked.

His mother began to hum softly. Raising her cup to her lips, she took another sip of coffee. "Did you know Mrs. Aldridge is going to visit with me today when Ryan leaves for work? It's so I won't be lonely." She turned clear gray eyes on Caden. "Mrs. Aldridge says her husband still goes to the TNT to look for the Mothman."

"Mom." He didn't want to think about the Mothman. The creature had impacted his life in too many ways. "What did you mean about Rosie having secrets?"

"Mrs. Aldridge told me there's something in one of the igloos. You can't see it, but it's there and, if you ask it a question, it might answer." She blinked and set the cup down with a *thunk* as if a monumental realization had washed over her. "Do you think we should ask it why Maggie's body wasn't found with the others? It would have to be you, Caden."

His fork slipped from his fingers and clattered against his plate. "I was talking about Rosalind Parrish."

"She had secrets. Maggie told me last night."

"Mom, that's enough," Ryan snapped.

"Oh, dear, now I've upset you both." Her lips quivered.

Caden was amazed at how swiftly her face had crumpled in sadness. Fishing a tissue from her bathrobe, she sniffled and dabbed it against her eyes. "It's all so complicated. We should have listened to Maggie when she said she saw the Mothman. I think the creature was trying to warn us about the bridge collapse. Don't you remember how many people claimed to have seen it during the year leading up to the tragedy? It used them as messengers, and we were just too close-minded to see it." She shook her head remorsefully. "All those carloads of people in the TNT riding around with guns. I think we scared it off. Maggie might still be here if we'd only realized it was trying to help."

He wouldn't listen. He couldn't stay. "I have to go."

Her gaze speared him as he rose from his seat. "Why did you have to take her out that night? Why couldn't you leave well enough alone?"

"Ryan, I'll talk to you later." He was halfway to the door before he realized his brother was on his heels. Ryan wrenched him to a halt as he stepped outside.

"She's not in her right mind. You know it. She hasn't been since Maggie died. Don't let her get to you."

He grunted and laced a hand through his hair. Don't let her get to him? The woman had an uncanny knack of reminding him he'd been the one to coerce his sister out that night. All she'd wanted to do was stay inside, huddled in her bedroom, terrified after stumbling over the Mothman while visiting their grandmother.

"It isn't real," he'd told Maggie. "You only thought you saw something." He'd grinned, cocky and sure of himself, the one person his little sister had never been able to refuse. After three days of being cooped up inside, he'd wanted to shake the scare from her. She might have seen something, but not the creature. Of that he was sure. "Come Christmas shopping with me, and I'll protect you. I promise."

Only he hadn't protected her. No wonder his mother blamed him.

He wouldn't tell Ryan she was right. "Yeah, okay." Better to concede and let it go. "Look, I've gotta run. I've got some other estimates I need to work on, not just Eve's."

"Sure." Ryan clapped a friendly hand on his back. They were nearly the same height. Five years younger, Ryan was only an inch shorter.

His brother grinned in a clear effort to lighten the mood. "So, what did you think of Eve? She's really grown up, huh?"

He'd noticed. A little more than he wanted to admit. She'd been all arms and legs as a kid, coltish like Maggie, but the woman who'd greeted him at the house was shapely and trim. Her hair seemed lighter, still a rich chestnut that flowed around her shoulders, but threaded with gold. Had he been asked as a kid, he wouldn't have been able to say her eyes were green, but there'd been no mistaking that vibrant color as she'd sat across from him at the dining room table. It made him wonder what Maggie would have looked like grown up.

"Yeah. A marked change from pigtails." He started to turn away, then stopped, a niggling thought surfacing in the back of his mind. "I know most of what Mom says doesn't mean anything, but..." He hedged, uncertain how far to push his doubts. "Do you think she could know something about Rosie?"

Ryan closed the door behind him and stepped onto the porch despite the fact he was dressed in boxers and a T-shirt, wearing slippers instead of shoes. He'd probably been on late shift and had only recently crawled from bed.

"You're still hung up on that damage at the house, aren't you?" Ryan asked.

"I'm not a cop—not any longer—but I've seen enough vandalized properties to recognize one, and Rosie's house wasn't vandalized. Not in the normal sense of the word."

"You could be a cop if you wanted to." Ryan leaned against the railing. "Sheriff Weston would take his best sergeant back in a heartbeat."

"Ryan." He didn't want to go there, not down a path they'd trodden countless times before.

"All right." His brother backed away from the discussion. "What are you suggesting?"

"Maybe Rosalind Parrish did have enemies." Caden paused, thinking about what their mother had said. "Or secrets."

Ryan exhaled. "Okay, I'll buy it wasn't typical vandalism, but there's not a hell of a lot to be done. There was no one to report anything stolen, and the estate was in probate. We didn't even dust for prints." He shifted from foot to foot. "I'm more inclined to think someone was looking for money, couldn't find any, and made a mess to cover their tracks. Everyone in town knew Rosie was a wealthy woman."

Caden considered that. "When she died, an empty house became fair game."

Ryan nodded. "That doesn't mean you can't make things extra secure for Eve while she's here."

"I'm way ahead of you brother. I'm taking care of that back door later today whether she likes it or not."

Ryan grinned. "Looking out for little sister's friend?"

Caden shook his head. "Looking out for Eve."

Chapter 3

Amos Carter swatted a mosquito from his arm and took a drag off his Marlboro. Still early in the morning, the hush hanging over the TNT was heavier than usual. He didn't buy the legend of the Mothman, but sometimes the remote location gave him the creeps, even in daylight. It wasn't that he believed a giant winged humanoid haunted the place, but the vastness of the region didn't sit well with someone who liked noise. With over 3600 acres of nothing but overgrown trees, ponds, and old World War II ammunition igloos, it was too damn quiet, the silence broken only by the trill of a bird or the chattering of leaves.

Shifting, he settled against his car, bracing his back against the driver's door. The old '72 T-Bird was a hell of a gas hog, but it got him where he needed to go. Most of the time. This morning, the Ford had sputtered and coughed even on the straight flat of Potters Creek Road. He'd pressed deeper into the TNT, eventually pulling off the narrow road at the mouth of an overgrown trail cut into the woods. Hidden behind a rusted guardrail installed by the Army decades past, a tapered rut sliced between the trees—a footpath for anyone willing to brave chiggers, ticks, and the domain of the Mothman.

As a teen he used to get his jollies hanging out up here, drag racing or smoking weed. Then the damn creature had shown up, and suddenly there were carloads of people camped out waiting to spot "the bird." UFO fanatics came, too. Spiritualists, hippies, all sorts of whackos, even reporters. People used to ride around with guns like vigilante hit squads, waiting to nail the monster that had put Point Pleasant under a microscope. He'd done his share, tossing down a six-pack as he rode point with a loaded .30-06, best damn gun he ever owned. No one wanted to be caught off guard by the Mothman—especially since cars often stalled on the deserted stretch of road for no reason. Sure kept the cops hopping in those days.

Eventually, the crowds dwindled and the reporters went away. After the Silver Bridge fell, the Mothman disappeared, too. Now it was just birds, trees, grass, and abandoned ammunition igloos. A lot of the old WWII shells were still there, most in bad condition. Some of the bunkers had even exploded, causing temporary shutdowns. There'd been a few injuries, lots of bad press. People tended to stay away now. There was talk of contaminants and red water seepage, rumors the TNT was slated to become a government Superfund site. Local kids still hung out and curiosity-seekers went looking for the Mothman, but for the most part, the area was deserted.

Which is why the man he thought of as Reaper insisted on meeting there. He'd never call the bastard that to his face, but the name fit. The guy was like a leech, sucking life from everything he encountered. Too bad some of his nastier habits were about to blow up in his face.

Amos took another drag off his cigarette, then crushed it under his foot as a big car rolled in beside him. The mother never did anything small-scale.

Reaper got out of the vehicle, straightened his shirt, and walked around the front of the sedan. "You screwed up."

He hadn't expected an accusation, or the black look Reaper gave him. It wasn't his fault the guy hadn't given him enough information. Hell, Reaper hadn't even paid him much now that he thought about it. A couple measly hundred to toss the place and search for a photo negative. Reaper hadn't told him what it was, just said Amos would know when he saw it. Probably a shot of the guy getting his rocks off or balling someone's old lady. Whatever it was, Rosalind Parrish had held it over his head, and he wanted the damn thing back.

"I tore that cursed dark room apart." Amos jutted his chin to emphasize the words. He'd done his part. The guy wasn't getting no money back. "I trashed the house like you said to make it look like vandalism, but I couldn't find no film negative. It woulda helped if I'd knowed what I was lookin' for."

"Asshole." Reaper cracked him across the face.

Amos staggered, shocked by the abrupt violence. "What the hell do you think you're doing?" Spittle flew from his mouth. Ain't no way some puffed-up cretin was going to put their hands on him. Damn, it hurt. "No one takes a crack at me."

Before he could swing, Reaper hit him again. Open-palmed, as if he was slapping some worthless bitch. Amos gave a squawk when the third blow fell, driving him against his car. His ears rang, and his cheek burned with a powerful sting like bees had burrowed under the skin. He tried to catch his breath but Reaper hit him again. And again.

Oh, hell. He was getting the shit beat out of him like Doreen Sue when he smacked her around. This couldn't be happening. Not to him, not Amos Carter.

He raised his arms to protect himself, crumpling to his knees as Reaper rained blow after blow on his head and shoulders, using his fists now instead of his palm. The pain was excruciating. He couldn't even find the wherewithal to strike back.

"Who did you tell?" Reaper demanded.

"What?" Blood coated his tongue, making it hard to talk. A meager spark of hope sprouted in his gut. "What do you mean?"

Reaper kicked him in the ribs, sending new agony barrel-rolling through his chest. He groaned and tried to curl into a ball. "Who did you tell?" Reaper snarled. "Damn, you, I'll beat the shit out of you. Who did you tell?"

"No one!" He screamed the words, though he wasn't sure what he was screaming about. Reaper kicked him again and, for the first time, Amos started to think he might not come out of the beating alive.

"You can have the money back," he blubbered, uncaring that he cried like a five-year-old. Tears streaked his cheeks as fresh agony knifed through his belly with another kick. "Please! You can have the money back. I'll give it all back. I didn't tell no one nuthin'. I swear."

"I don't believe you, parasite."

Reaper withdrew. Oh, thank God, he withdrew! Amos was sure his ribs were broken, and several teeth had worked loose in his mouth. Maybe that's all the man wanted, his money back. He had to have hope. Let him get the hell out of here, and he'd lay off smacking Doreen Sue around. He'd make her work extra hours at that salon of hers until she earned enough money for him to pay back Reaper.

Sniffling, he wiped blood and snot from his nose. He could get up now, stand up like a man and face Reaper. They'd work it out. He looked up hopefully, trying to wedge his arms beneath him.

That was when he saw Reaper slowly and methodically pull on a pair of black gloves.

* * * *

She owned the place. It was a sobering thought.

Eve parked beside the Parrish Hotel. Behind her, the high flood walls that kept Point Pleasant safe from the waters of the Ohio River were broken by a wide gap. In the event of a potential flood, that gap could be filled with concrete inserts to hold the water at bay. An unlikely event given the last devastating flood had occurred in 1948, years before she was born. As a child, she'd often heard people talk about it, others going so far as to recall the colossal damage wrought by the floods of '37 and '13. Chief Cornstalk's curse in play, according to the old-timers.

By the time she was born, the Army Corp of Engineers had constructed flood walls around the city. Seventy-three hundred feet of concrete ranging from small obstructions to fifty feet in height. The grassy banks of the Ohio River lay behind that barrier, a place where she'd enjoyed many hours fishing, hiking, and bike riding. The waterway was now regulated by a lock and dam system that kept the once flood-prone city safe. Curse or no curse, her family's hotel was secure from the threat of overflow.

Her hotel.

Eve drew a breath. Three stories high with single rooms, suites, a parlor, ballroom, and café, it had been a second home while growing up. Her parents had rarely lacked lodgers thanks to Point Pleasant's location at the confluence of the Kanawha and Ohio Rivers, a junction commonly referred to as Tu-Endie-Wei in the Native American tongue of Wyandotte. She'd forgotten the rich history of the town, dating back to the time of George Washington and Daniel Boone. Chief Cornstalk was buried at Tu-Endie-Wei Park, his infamous curse blamed for everything from catastrophic floods to Mothman sightings and the Silver Bridge tragedy.

As she sat in her car staring up at the hotel with its wide front porch and bright blue awnings, an icy sensation crawled over her skin. Her great grandfather Clarence had burned to death, along with her grandparents, in a fire that took place at the hotel four years after she was born. Her great grandmother Sadie had died in the Influenza Pandemic of 1919 when she was just twenty-eight years old. Eve's own father had perished at thirty-four in the Silver Bridge collapse, and her aunt had died of cancer at forty-nine. Maybe there was something to the curse after all.

She shook the thoughts away. No, it was just superstition and silliness. Whatever memories lingered in Point Pleasant, they were only that—memories of the past. She had come to face the present, and that included coming to terms with the Parrish Hotel.

Eve entered through the front door into the lobby. The place looked much as she remembered with a large sitting area and a second floor balcony. An imposing staircase led to the second level, a wooden reception counter below. From the massive moldings to the thick brocade carpeting, Victorian furniture, gas lamps, and brick hearth, everything reflected the trappings of another era. This was a grand hotel modeled after a faded time in history when opera houses, afternoon tea, and horse-drawn carriages were the norm.

Eve approached the registration counter and offered a polite smile to the woman behind it. She seemed vaguely familiar with her straight blond hair secured in a ponytail and green eyes. Judging by her youthful appearance, they were likely close in age, which meant they might have gone to school together. Point Pleasant was only so big.

She extended her hand. "Hi. I'm Eve Parrish."

The girl frowned slightly but shook her hand before closing a ledger book that lay open on the counter. "We've been expecting you."

"We?"

"The staff." She tilted her head slightly. "You don't remember me, do you?"

Eve racked her brain. "I'm sorry. Should I?"

"We went to school together. I'm Katie Lynch."

"Oh!" The exclamation slipped from Eve's tongue before she could stop it. The Katie she remembered was the product of a broken family who lived on the wrong side of the tracks. Or, at least, that's what people had been fond of saying. Her mother had owned a hair salon and worked nights at a bar outside of town, which often ended up on police radar. Her older sister, Wendy, had a reputation for being "loose." Wendy had vanished shortly before the Silver Bridge fell, a rumored runaway, and to the best of Eve's knowledge, had never returned. Although she, Maggie, and Sarah had known Katie in school, they'd avoided her, often giggling behind her back.

"I, uh…" Tongue-tied, she wasn't certain how to respond. "It's good to see you."

Katie didn't roll her eyes, but the expression she gave Eve indicated she was tempted.

"Do you work here?" Eve asked.

Rather than answer, Katie motioned her behind the reception counter. "The office is this way. I assume you'll want to see the books."

"I… Yes. That would be good." Still flustered, Eve followed Katie into an office overlooking the rear parking lot. The view afforded little but a glimpse of river water tucked behind the flood walls. Despite the limited view, the room was bright and cheerful. Aunt Rosie had added personal touches since her parents had owned the hotel.

A maple desk and three wooden file cabinets were complemented by white eyelet curtains and a paisley rug over a wide-plank hardwood floor. Two visitor chairs with a small table between them occupied the wall across from the desk, and a large potted ficus tree basked in the light from two windows.

The tree brought a smile to her face, reminding her of the numerous plants she'd collected in her apartment at home. Hopefully, her mother was watering them as promised. A few more added to this office would make it feel more inviting.

"This was Rosie's office," Katie said. "I left the keys for the files in the top drawer of her desk. Guest receipts are to the left, employee and payroll records to the right. The cabinet in the middle is for vendors and expenses. I'm sure Mr. Barnett's firm would have gone over the figures with you, but should you like to review anything—"

"You seem to know an awful lot about my aunt's business dealings." Eve found herself on the defensive. How did this girl she'd once viewed with contempt know so much about Aunt Rosie? "Mr. Barnett told me there was an interim manager. I'd like to meet her."

"That would be me."

Eve blinked. "You?"

Katie's lips curled in a tight smile. "Surprised? Do you think I'm not qualified?"

"No, I…" She was turning into a stammering fool. This was ridiculous! She was the owner of the hotel. So what if she'd been caught off guard by a girl she'd once thought incapable of amounting to anything? It was time to reassert her position and the established pecking order from childhood. She'd never been one to hold herself above others, but Katie made her feel abruptly superficial. Gripping the strap of her shoulder bag tightly in her left hand, Eve pressed her lips together. "I simply wasn't aware of the protocols Aunt Rosie had in place. Her death was unexpected."

"To some."

"Excuse me?"

"Nothing." Momentarily flustered, Katie reclaimed her cool aloofness. "If you'd like a tour of the hotel, I can point out the changes your aunt made over the last fifteen years. I can also introduce you to the staff on site. I assume you'll want to speak with them as a group eventually."

"Eventually." She still hadn't decided what she was going to do with the hotel, but saw no reason in broadcasting her indecisiveness. "Let's go through the hotel. I'll look at the books later."

Though she didn't voice the thoughts to Katie, walking through the hotel resurrected a host of memories: running through the long hallways before guests checked in—her parents were always adamant she didn't disturb visitors—eating a PBJ with a glass of cold milk at the café lunch counter, helping her mother decorate the big Christmas tree in the lobby each December. So many memories dredged from the dust of decades she'd buried in the past. One February her parents had held a Valentine's Day dance in the ballroom, opening the hotel to the town. She remembered red hearts and streamers dangling from the ceiling, tables laden with finger hors d'oeuvres, and a giant ice sculpture in the shape of a swan. Her father had surprised her mother with a bouquet of pink roses and a diamond necklace that made her cry. She and Maggie had watched, hidden in a corner as her parents danced without music in the large ballroom before the guests arrived.

"We have a birthday party scheduled to take place the end of the month," Katie told her as they stepped into the ballroom. "Rosie rented out the ballroom for special events. We have a contract in place and can't cancel it, but—"

"That isn't an issue." Eve followed into the large room, conscious of the echo of her heels against the hardwood floor. It gleamed with several coats of wax, reflecting the glimmer of three chandeliers suspended overhead. A dozen circular tables draped in white linen surrounded the dance floor, a raised dais at the front of the room. In its heyday, the Parrish Hotel had hosted wedding receptions and banquets. "I don't want to change anything Aunt Rosie had planned." That much was true. "I'll need the details—time, vendors, planned events, employees who are scheduled to work."

"I can get you a list. Would you like to see the café now?"

She nodded, then followed Katie back to the street level. Presently closed, the River Café opened at 11:00 AM for the lunch crowd, followed later by dinner. According to Katie, it was mostly locals who came for lunch, the limited business rarely enough to warrant extended hours, but Rosie hadn't wanted to close her doors to the regulars. Dinner tended to be a larger draw, but far from the steady stream of patronage before the Silver Bridge collapsed. The smaller crowd aside, it was still the hotspot in downtown Point Pleasant on any given night.

Cozy and intimate, the café sported several large booths on one side of the room banked by a series of tables and an ornate wooden bar on the far right. The décor was an eclectic mix of antiques, hand-blown glass, and riverboat memorabilia. She remembered some of the pieces, like the large ship's wheel suspended above the bar, from childhood.

Katie introduced her to several of the employees who were present, then allowed her to wander on her own. Eventually, she wound her way back to the office and settled in her aunt's desk chair, thankful to be alone with her thoughts.

Adam Barnett had indicated if she wanted to sell the hotel, he might be able to connect her with a buyer. Her mother wanted her to settle matters quickly and return to Harrisburg. How easy it would be to leave everything in Barnett's capable hands and head home and wait for the arrival of a settlement check. She didn't need to be here, but her parents had once owned this hotel in partnership with Aunt Rosie. Her father had loved it, and her aunt had kept it solvent after the bridge collapse. Given everything she knew about Point Pleasant, that hadn't been an easy task.

She spent the next several hours sorting through ledgers, files and books. Katie returned once or twice to see if she needed anything, but basically left her on her own. When lunchtime rolled around, Eve abandoned the office, found Katie at the front desk, and suggested they have lunch in the café.

"You want to have lunch with me?" There was no mistaking Katie's look of surprise.

"I think we should talk. Is there someone who covers the desk when you go to lunch?"

"No, I usually close the lobby. Give me five minutes, and I'll meet you in the café."

She didn't seem overly pleased by the idea, but showed up as promised. They settled into a booth, ordered sandwiches off the menu, and quickly dispensed with small talk. Thankful to have the forced niceties behind them, Eve got down to business.

"How long have you worked for my aunt?"

"Since I was sixteen." Katie fiddled with the paper wrapper for her straw, smoothing it between her fingers. "I started part-time as a waitress after school, then went full-time after my son was born."

"Your son?" The revelation struck her like a thunderbolt.

"Sam is seven. The bus drops him off outside after school, and he stays for an hour in the lobby doing homework until my shift ends. Rosie didn't have a problem with that, but I'll understand if you want it to stop. School ends for the summer in a few days anyway, so I'll be making other arrangements for him."

It was hard wrapping her head around the idea of Katie with a child. She was tempted to ask about the father but feared the information might be awkward. What if Katie was an unwed mother? "Let's see how things go." She took a sip of the iced tea the waitress had left. "So you eventually made the switch from the café to the front desk?"

Katie folded her hands on the tabletop, her back straight, gaze unflinching. "I help out where I'm needed. After several years, I was managing the café for Rosie, doing the ordering, menu planning, and scheduling. Later, she asked me to help in the office, and I made the transition. Toward the end, when she grew sick, I took on more responsibility."

"She was sick?" Eve pounced on the idea. It had always been her impression the cancer came swiftly. "I thought everything happened quickly."

Katie glanced down at her hands. "She knew long before she told anyone. At the time, I didn't understand, but looking back, I can see her getting things in order. Your aunt never did anything without a purpose, Eve."

She felt a twinge of envy. "You sound like you knew her well."

"I did." No hesitation. "Most people in this town didn't want anything to do with me, but Rosie was different. She took a chance I'd amount to something."

Eve shifted uncomfortably. She'd been one of those people who'd formed an opinion of Katie based upon what others said. Her aunt would have admonished her for such narrow-mindedness, her parents, too.

As if conscious of her uneasiness, Katie steered the conversation elsewhere. "I'm thankful she didn't suffer. When the end came, it came quickly."

Eve's stomach did a small flip-flop. "I wish I'd been with her. I don't understand why she didn't tell anyone. I would have come back if I'd known she was sick."

The waitress, a young girl Katie had introduced as Nancy, arrived with their sandwiches, and for a time, they said nothing. When the girl left, and Eve had salted her fries, she found she had little appetite. She was a fish out of water in a town she'd deserted. At least, it felt that way. The girl seated across from her knew more about her beloved aunt than she did. The legacy of her family, the hotel, and the house her aunt had left her, felt like the trappings of a stranger.

Katie took a bite of her cheeseburger, then set it back on her plate and dabbed her mouth with a folded napkin. "You can't blame yourself." Her voice was softer than before, a trace of sympathy in her eyes. "I think Rosie was determined to suffer alone."

Eve glanced up, startled. "What does that mean?"

"I'm sorry. I shouldn't have said—"

"No, I want to know what you meant." Something resonated in her heart, prickling the hair on her arms. She'd be the first person to admit her aunt had changed over the years, the carefree spirit she'd once known becoming reclusive and sad. *That damn bridge. Why did it have to change everything?* "Aunt Rosie was well liked."

"She was."

"Many people would have flocked to her aid."

"If she'd allowed them." Katie bit her lip, clearly indecisive. "Look, I have no right saying this. It's just my opinion."

Eve nodded, urging her on. "Please." The walls she'd once felt for Katie Lynch crumbled. This woman plainly had a closer relationship with her aunt than she'd had over the last decade. Jealously lanced through her, but with it came the desire to set aside past prejudices. "If you know something—anything—I'd be grateful."

Katie fiddled with her fork, adjusted her napkin over her lap, then nodded firmly as if reaching a decision. "I don't pretend to know everything, but your aunt opened a door for me she closed on other people. These last several years, I probably knew her better than anyone in town."

The jealousy resurfaced, sharper this time, but Eve remained silent.

"My mother and I aren't close. We communicate, but that's about the extent of it." Katie raised her chin, a touch of defiance in her green gaze. "You know my sister took off before the bridge collapsed. Or, at least, that's what everyone would have me believe. That she got tired of life in Point Pleasant and ran away."

Eve offered a slight nod. The cruder gossip at the time had insinuated sixteen-year-old Wendy Lynch was knocked up and ran off to have an abortion. Everyone knew she slept around. The girl was fond of smoking, drinking, and drugs, with a weakness for boys and the backseats of their cars. "Easy" was what people had called her.

Katie pressed her lips together. "I've never believed it, but can't disprove it." She shrugged and shook her head, her ponytail bouncing behind her. "It doesn't matter anyway. All I know is that between my mom's reputation and Wendy's, everyone had me pegged."

Eve lowered her eyes, shamed by her own bias.

"If it hadn't been for your aunt giving me a job when she did, I'd probably be collecting welfare right now. Maybe I needed a strong female influence, and maybe she needed a daughter."

Or a niece, Eve thought guiltily.

"Whatever the reason, we connected, and I'm eternally grateful. She's been there for me throughout the years. I was at her side as much as she'd allow." A brief smile flickered over her lips. "Your aunt was closemouthed when she chose. She told me only what she wanted me to know."

Eve sat back, her lunch forgotten. She felt a closeness to Katie she hadn't expected. Had Aunt Rosie latched onto Katie because her own niece had left Point Pleasant? No, that was unfair. To Katie and to Aunt Rosie. Her aunt didn't choose people because she settled for second best. She befriended them because she saw promise in them, and she was rarely wrong.

"When did she tell you she was sick?" Eve had to know.

"Not until she couldn't hide it any longer. By then, it was just a matter of weeks." She bit her lip and looked skyward as if fighting tears. "I tried to convince her to do chemo, but she said it was too late. That she'd refused treatment intentionally."

"Why?" The idea was preposterous. How dare Aunt Rosie be so selfish! She should have realized she had people who loved her. *Who'd abandoned her, packed up, and left Point Pleasant fifteen years ago.* A sharp stab of guilt pierced her heart.

"Eve, I'm sorry. She…" Katie looked stricken. Taking a deep breath, she plowed ahead. "She said she deserved it. That the cancer was payment for something she'd done a long time ago."

"*What?*" Anger and outrage streaked through her. Her aunt never could have done anything to warrant such an unjust sentence. No, it simply didn't make sense. Katie was making things up. Baiting her, fearful she planned to sell the hotel and put her out of a job. The awful wretch was playing on her sympathy, trying to make her feel guilty.

"I don't believe you," she snapped.

Katie's gaze was level. "I didn't expect you to. But I was the one who sat by her bed when she was dying."

Eve drew back in shock. "You were with her?" Her heart fluttered and rolled over like a tumbleweed. When she spoke, her voice was small, a splinter of its normal volume. "At the end?"

Katie nodded. "They gave her morphine to manage the pain. She was in and out of sleep. Drifting, hallucinating, saying things that made no sense. She kept repeating how sorry she was for what she'd done, and how she prayed God would forgive her." Her brows knit in a puzzled frown. "Something about gray vines."

"Gray vines?"

Katie nodded. "That's what it sounded like. I tried to ask her what it meant, but she was delirious, too far gone. Eventually, she slipped into a deep sleep and never recovered. If it's any consolation, the doctor said she didn't suffer."

Eve exhaled, only then realizing she'd been holding her breath. All of her frustrations and doubts aside, a single truth weighed heavily on her heart. "Thank you for being with her. It means a lot to know she wasn't alone."

Their conversation veered into safer topics after that. What more could be said? Her aunt had elected to keep her cancer to herself until the last possible minute, had refused treatment, and then announced she deserved to die. Unsettled by the thought, Eve tried to imagine what would make her aunt surrender without a fight.

True, Aunt Rosie had never married and had chosen to live alone, but she'd once had an opportunity for happiness she'd allowed to fall by the wayside. Her behavior then hadn't made any more sense than it did now. Engaged to be married, she'd called off her wedding after the Silver Bridge collapsed, saying she'd been too devastated by the tragedy to consider her own happiness.

Eve's memory of that time was spotty at best—her father dead, her best friend missing and presumed drowned, the town in a state of shock and grief—but she recalled Aunt Rosie's intended groom, Roger Layton, begging her to reconsider. Maybe events would have unfolded differently if Aunt Rosie had proceeded with her wedding. No doubt she would she have gotten help when she needed it, embracing the treatments that would save her.

It all came back to the bridge and the catastrophe that devastated Point Pleasant. The town had been broken, and although it had gallantly pieced together its tattered community spirit, the golden heydays of the past would never be seen again.

Nor would Aunt Rosie.

Somehow, Eve managed to choke down most of her lunch, but it settled like lead in her stomach. When the meal was through, she and Katie parted company, she with a kinder impression of the other girl. She hoped Katie felt the same.

Returning to her office, she immersed herself in files and ledger books, learning everything she could about the hotel's past and present operations. Many of the records and saved correspondence dated back to the time of her parents and grandparents. The sight of the old documents made her feel like she'd awakened slumbering ghosts. One folder in particular drew her attention. Dated by month, it was marked *December 1967.*

The month the Silver Bridge fell.

She transferred it to the desk and sat staring at it for some time. If she looked inside, would she find anything to indicate life had come to a screeching halt in Point Pleasant? That her world had imploded, leaving her at the mercy of an uncertain and disjointed future?

It made no sense to look at past reports when she should be concentrating on the present state of the hotel in order to determine its future. And hers.

Still, she couldn't ignore the folder. Setting it aside, she placed it with her purse, intending to study it when she had more time. She'd take it home and look through it tonight, something to keep her occupied through the long evening hours. She needed a break from sorting through the mess left by the vandals.

The remainder of the afternoon passed quickly, and shortly after three o'clock, she was drawn to the lobby by the sound of laughter. Katie stepped from behind the reception counter as a young boy with curly brown hair burst through the door and rushed to hug her.

"Hi, Mom." He grinned as he looked at his mother. "No homework tonight. Can we walk along the river and then watch *Happy Days*?"

"After dinner." Katie caught sight of Eve at the same time the boy did. "Sam, say hello to Ms. Parrish."

He had pine green eyes like his mother and an infectious grin that immediately warmed Eve's heart. "Are you Mom's new boss?"

She flushed. "I—"

"I told him you were coming," Katie explained, "and that he had to behave if he wanted to hang out in the lobby until I'm done with work."

"I do homework if I have it," Sam volunteered. "When I'm done, I read or do puzzles." He displayed a Batman comic as proof. "No homework tonight 'cause school's almost out. Just a few more days, and I've got the whole summer."

"I remember how that felt." Summer was fun and freedom. Swimming in the river on hot afternoons, eating sun-sweetened watermelon and downing cold lemonade on the grassy banks. In the evenings, she, Sarah, and Maggie chased fireflies and told ghost stories, watching as bats launched from the trees behind Aunt Rosie's house. "It's nice to meet you, Sam. You can call me Eve."

"Mom says I should call you Ms. Parrish."

"Oh. Well, you should do what your mom says." It felt odd to be the boss and the grown-up. The last time she'd stood within the walls of the Parrish Hotel, she'd been twelve years old.

"Mom, Sarah and I just want to walk down the street."

"Don't be long," her mother had called from behind the reception counter. *"Your father will be back from Gallipolis soon. I have chicken at home for dinner."*

Katie seemed to recognize she'd focused on something else and quietly suggested Sam settle in the lobby with his comic book. After some more small talk, Eve retreated to her office.

She thought about her job back in Harrisburg—a secretarial position with a state agency that afforded her four weeks of vacation a year, two of which she was presently using. It simply wasn't practical for her to remain in Point Pleasant. Even her father and Aunt Rosie would understand that.

Resolved, she picked up the phone and dialed Adam Barnett's number. The sooner she started the ball rolling, the sooner she could wrap things up and head home. His secretary put her through, and he answered within seconds.

"Hello, Mr. Barnett? This is Eve Parrish. I thought about what you said regarding the hotel, and I'd like you to put out some feelers for a prospective buyer. I believe you mentioned you had some inquiries."

"Why, yes, Miss Parrish." He sounded delighted to hear from her, even more by the subject. "Only one, actually, but I believe the party is sincere. He knew I represented Rosalind's estate and approached me some time ago. I told him you were undecided with your plans."

"That hasn't changed." She continued to waffle over the decision, unable to make up her mind and break ties to a town that had brought her nothing but grief. "But I'm not averse to entertaining offers. I'm planning on contacting James Dixon of River Real Estate about selling, but wanted to give your contact an opportunity."

"I can work with Mr. Dixon. Perhaps you'd like me to make a discreet inquiry of the potential buyer and have him offer a figure? I'll handle the settlement, and Mr. Dixon can handle the contract. No signs, no advertising, no marketing."

She bit her lip, worried she was making a mistake. "Why don't you run it past your buyer and see what he's willing to offer. Please keep everything confidential, especially until I have a chance to speak with Mr. Dixon. I don't want word spreading I'm going to sell the hotel."

"Naturally."

After she hung up, Eve debated the wisdom of what she'd done. It was just an old hotel, not flesh and blood. It shouldn't bother her to sign on the dotted line, wash her hands of the structure, and tuck the proceeds into her bank account. But she had people counting on her for employment. People like Katie and Nancy and the other employees she'd met that afternoon. At the very least, whatever her decision, she would look out for them.

* * * *

When four o'clock rolled around, Katie and Sam left. A short time later, Eve packed up her folder and headed for her car. Main Street was mostly deserted when she stepped outside, the lack of vehicles the norm with traffic diverted to the new Silver Memorial Bridge at the opposite end of town. The strange quiet preyed on her nerves, an eerie sensation that prickled her skin like the shroud hanging over a ghost town. It was strange to see the streets empty, yet hear the hum of passing cars a few blocks away. With that simple rerouting of traffic, the world had elected to pass by Main Street, relegating it to a shadow of another age. An antiquity.

Eve slid into the car and set the folder on the passenger seat. She was in the process of inserting her key into the ignition when she spied a slip of paper pinned beneath her windshield wiper. Opening the door, she reached to the front of the vehicle, pulled the note free, and sank back into her seat.

Typed in the center of the page was a single sentence that sent a chill cascading down her spine. *You should leave before you get hurt.*

Chapter 4

With shaking fingers, Eve dialed the number on the business card, relieved to hear a masculine "hello" after the third ring. "Caden, this is Eve Parrish. I'd like you to repair the back door on my property. How soon do you think you can do it?"

Maybe she was being paranoid, but the note had left her shaken. There'd been no one about on the deserted street, but she imagined the author lurking behind a building waiting to see her reaction. Frightened, she'd rushed inside the hotel to her office, fished Caden's business card from her purse, and quickly dialed.

"I already started it," he said.

"You did?" She wasn't sure if she should be cross or grateful. "When?"

The man, annoyingly short on words, exhaled a perturbed breath. "I told you earlier I would take care of it today."

"But I didn't agree."

Silence.

She twined the phone cord in her hand and paced from the desk to the window. "How did you get in?"

He uttered a soft grunt. "Through the screened porch. It's not secure, remember? Neither is the kitchen door. I've already got most of the work done. I just came home to grab a few tools before heading back to finish. Do you want it completed or not?"

"Yes. Of course." Isn't that why she was calling? So what if he'd started the job without her approval? The important element now was that he finished. "And...I'd like to talk to you." He seemed to have firm ideas about the vandalism and Aunt Rosie. Ryan had brushed it off as kids, but Caden had denoted it as something sinister. In light of the note, she wanted to know more. "Have you had dinner?"

He paused as though surprised by the question. "I was going to grab a cheeseburger from McDonalds."

A typical male food staple. Though he couldn't see her, she rolled her eyes. "Don't bother. I'll grab something from the café for both of us. I'd like to talk with you about Aunt Rosie. Do you have time?"

He hesitated again, the silence filled with marked reluctance. She sensed it had little to do with the idea of them having dinner together and more to do with the past. Aunt Rosie was part of that, as was Maggie.

His answer came slowly. "Yeah. Okay."

"Great." She chose to overlook his uncertainty. "I'll meet you at the house. Just give me time to order something from the café."

Feeling slightly better she wouldn't be walking into the mammoth two-story alone, and anxious to show him the note, Eve detoured toward the River Café and flagged down the cook. There were definitely perks to being the owner.

* * * *

Caden had to admit the batter-fried chicken, mashed potatoes, and green beans were far better fare than the standard fast food he'd planned on eating. The company was considerably better than the drone of his TV, far prettier, too.

Eve had arrived at the house as he was installing the double bolt lock he'd purchased for her new back door. She'd dumped a manila file folder and a bag marked *River Café* on the kitchen counter, then crossed to examine his handiwork. He'd expected her to complain he'd moved ahead with repairing the door but knew something had changed since they'd parted company that morning.

Now, seated at the dining room table eating fried chicken off Rosie's casual china, Eve clearly had more on her mind than the remnants of the dinner still on her plate. Her conversation was casual and light, but her manner tense. He'd brought a cold six-pack along as his contribution to the meal, but she'd insisted on pouring the beer into a fancy glass. Hers anyway. He drank his from the can.

Taking a swig, he watched her across the table. It was hard equating her with the coltish girl who'd been his sister's best friend. "So why the change?"

Absently, Eve poked her fork at the mound of mashed potatoes on her plate. "I was thinking about what you said. About Aunt Rosie and how the damage to the house didn't seem like routine vandalism."

He suspected there was more to it, but remained silent, biding his time.

"You seemed so sure." She set the fork down, creased the napkin she'd folded over her lap, then met his gaze. "I wasn't here for the last fifteen years, Caden. I saw Aunt Rosie on the occasional holiday when she drove to Pennsylvania. I wasn't even here for her funeral."

He wondered about that, but didn't have the audacity to ask. If it had been his aunt... "You knew her better than I did," she said, breaking his concentration. "When I saw her or we talked on the phone, it was trivial. How business was going at the hotel, whether or not I was seeing someone, or what was happening on *Falcon Crest*. I guess I lost touch with the important things in her life."

He wouldn't mind having the inside track on whether or not she was seeing someone. "What do you want to know?"

She wet her lips. "Earlier today you said whoever ransacked the house was either looking for something or did it in a fit of rage."

"In my opinion." Maybe he should have kept his mouth shut, but cop instincts died hard. There were times, infrequent as they were, that he almost missed the job.

She leaned forward, her gaze steady. In the amber light of the overhead chandelier her eyes were flecked with gold. "You said Aunt Rosie had enemies."

"I said *maybe* she had enemies." He shouldn't have been so bold.

"Do you know anyone who'd want to hurt her or her memory?"

"No." That was the downside of it. He took another swig of beer, set the can on the table, and rotated it in his hand. The Parrish name was deeply rooted in Point Pleasant history. How could he explain gut intuition? That ever since the bridge collapse, he wasn't so quick to discount a prickle of misgiving when it played on his nerves. If he'd paid more attention to that feeling fifteen years ago, his sister would still be alive.

"People respected Rosie," he said at last, "but she kept to herself. She was friendly, even generous, but there was something secretive about her."

Eve frowned. "I don't follow."

"She wasn't someone you could get close to." It was a survival trait he'd adopted himself, a means to keep others at bay. When you carried a sin or secret in your past, it was a safety measure to stay sane. Perhaps he'd recognized the habit in Rosie because it was one he favored himself. He understood secrets, and he understood guilt. "Rosie was friendly on the surface, but she kept people at arm's length when it came to anything personal."

"She seemed pretty close to Katie Lynch. At least, that was the impression I got after talking to Katie."

He thought he heard a hint of jealousy in Eve's voice. Katie was a girl full of surprises, so different from her sister, Wendy. He was sorry he'd treated Wendy like most other guys who'd grown up with her, hoping to cop a feel beneath the railroad bridge or in the back of his car. He'd never gotten further than second base, but that was his hesitation more than hers.

"Katie told me Aunt Rosie was delirious toward the end and kept repeating how sorry she was for something she'd done," Eve continued, unaware of his thoughts. "She prayed God would forgive her. She kept mumbling about gray vines."

"Gray vines?" Caden shook his head. "That doesn't make sense. Does it mean anything to you?"

"No."

"Probably the pain meds. People say all kinds of crazy things when they're under the influence of narcotics."

"So you don't think she had anything to hide?"

He decided to turn the tables around. "You tell me. Why the sudden change of heart about the deadbolt on your door?"

"Oh…that." Her gaze dropped to the table, and she fiddled with her fork. A slight flush tinged her cheeks and, for a moment, he was reminded of the twelve-year-old girl who used to grow awkward whenever he was around. "I, um…." She bit her lip. "Something happened today when I left the hotel."

He didn't say anything, but kept his gaze trained on her. It had to be freaking hard to walk into town fifteen years after your family set the bar. Difficult enough under normal circumstances, but Point Pleasant had changed drastically. Even he thought of Main Street as carrying the taint of a ghost town. If it weren't for the Parrish Hotel and the few businesses that kept it afloat, Main would be as deserted as the TNT. Ironically, it was that region and the legendary monster rumored to haunt there that fed a steady trickle of tourists and curiosity-seekers into Point Pleasant.

Eve left the table briefly, crossing into the living room to retrieve her purse from the coffee table. Through the open arch between the two rooms, he watched her fish through the bag. She located a folded slip of paper, then returned to the dining room and extended it to him.

"Here." Rather than resume her seat, she stayed at his side, arms hugged close to her chest as if to ward off a chill.

Caden polished off the remainder of his beer and set the can aside. Opening the paper, he read the typewritten words in the center aloud, "You should leave before you get hurt."

Eve shivered. "At first, I thought it was a prank, but then I remembered the vandalism and the man I saw outside."

"What man?"

She slid into the chair beside him, abandoning her earlier seat. Turning sideways to face him, she toyed with the thin silver links of her watch. "Last night I heard a banging that woke me from sleep. It turned out to be a loose shutter in Aunt Rosie's room, but when I looked out the window, I saw a man standing at the edge of the trees in the backyard. He was staring up at the house, just standing there in the dark."

"Could you tell who it was?"

"No." She shook her head. "It was too dark, and he stepped back into the trees. Originally, I thought I imagined it, but after the vandalism and finding that note, the whole thing has me uneasy." She shook her head, obviously embarrassed for bringing it up. "Maybe I'm just being silly."

"No, you're being careful." His gaze dropped to the note. There was always the possibility someone could be playing a trick. Point Pleasant was a small town, and people had undoubtedly heard she'd returned. The name Parrish was news. Bored teenagers with little else to do but haunt the TNT and linger at the Crowne Theater might think it fun to rattle the new girl. He was intimately experienced with the pranks of teenagers and how horribly they could backfire. There were times at night he could still see Hank Jeffries's face as he held the Kline kid cradled in his lap.

Scissoring the note between two fingers, Caden raised his hand in the air. "I want to show this to Ryan."

"Then you do think it's something I should take seriously?"

"I wouldn't ignore it." He stood and walked to the back door, then paused to double check the new lock. She trailed behind him, carrying their plates to the kitchen counter.

"Maybe I should get a dog." She grinned slightly, but her voice sounded tight. Placing the dishes in the sink, she braced a hip against the counter and turned to face him. "You're making me nervous, Caden."

"I'm just inspecting my handiwork." Damn, he hadn't wanted to make her anxious, but it bothered him to think someone had been watching the house. He owed it to Maggie to look out for her friend. Eve's vulnerability made him want to protect her. "You'll be fine."

Uncertain if he was convincing himself or her, he was more than a little troubled by the thought of her alone. Sunset was only an hour away, pleasant in early June, but not without its ghosts. Even something as simple as waning daylight resurrected unpleasant memories for him.

The glare of flood lights, the twisted mangle of bridge towers protruding in the dark like some obscene metal sculpture....the stench of fear, blood, and cold river water, the shouts of rescuers and the gut-wrenching sobs of victims.

"Caden?"

He blinked, abruptly wrenched back to the present. Eve stood at his side, one hand resting lightly on his arm, her gaze laced with concern. "Are you all right?"

Damn. He hated when he flashed back like that. Usually the occurrences were rare, but since Eve's return, he'd been doing it more frequently. He nodded brusquely and examined the door.

"You'll be fine. Just keep everything locked up. I can hang around if you'd like." If he was honest, he *wanted* to hang around.

"No, that's all right. I want to sort through more of Aunt Rosie's belongings, anyway. I'm still straightening up her room. How soon do you think you can start work on the other items that need repaired?"

"Tomorrow morning if you like." Earlier, during dinner, they'd gone over the estimate he'd provided, and she'd agreed to all of the work, deciding it was necessary to make the house sellable. She'd told him she was on a two-week vacation from her job and needed to wrap things up quickly so she could put the home on the market before leaving town.

"Tomorrow morning is great. Let me get you a key." She headed back to the living room and her purse. "That way you can come and go throughout the day if I'm not here."

Caden followed, still shaken by that unexpected flash of memory, but determined not to let it show.

"Mr. Barnett gave me several keys." Eve passed him a spare. "Any time after eight is fine." She hesitated. "Do you think I should talk to Ryan about the note?"

"I'll take care of it for you." He knew his brother. Ryan would brush it off as a prank, then try to make Eve believe the same. While Caden didn't want to alarm her, he also wanted her to be cautious and safe. Heading for the door, he thought of his empty apartment overlooking the river. He'd go home, sit in the dark, and stare at that brooding expanse of water beyond the windows, imagining his sister's body decaying in the muck.

If only they'd let him search for her that night. If only he'd made sure she was out of the car before he'd been pulled free. He'd only had a few seconds to react as the vehicle sank below the surface and that bony, gray hand had gripped his arm.

"Thanks for dinner." He opened the front door, pausing on the threshold. "I'll be back tomorrow. I want to see Ryan before I get started. Call me if you have any problems tonight. You have my card."

He felt funny leaving, as though he was abandoning her, the same way he'd abandoned Maggie. Had there been a flash of ginger hair in the water? So cold...so dark.

He couldn't remember. And that was his curse.

To never know if he could have saved her.

* * * *

"I knew you'd come back." Maggie pulled her knees up to her chest and dug her bare toes into the grass.

The sun felt warm on Eve's face, honeyed with the kiss of late summer. Aunt Rosie's backyard was a favorite place to play, especially at the edge of the stream where they might find tadpoles or pebbles polished smooth by the water. A breeze raced through the grass, tossing the leaves on the tree branches overhead and sending ripples across the surface of the small creek.

"I didn't want to leave."

She was twelve years old, yet her thoughts were those of a much older person. The adult in her body looked at her youthful suntanned legs, the bright pink polish on her nails, chipped at the edges as it had often been, and the friendship bracelet around her wrist. "My mother took me away. She said she couldn't live here anymore. Not after Daddy died. She said it hurt too much to be reminded of what happened."

Maggie nodded somberly. "I was scared."

"When the bridge collapsed?" Somehow Eve knew she was dreaming. The twelve-year-old girl dressed in shorts and flip-flops sitting on the bank of the stream was her way of connecting with Maggie. "Did it hurt?"

"I can't talk about that part." Maggie plucked a blade of grass. "You have to figure it out, Eve. That's what your Aunt Rosie wants. It will help Caden, too. He shouldn't blame himself."

"Because he took you with him that night?"

"It's more than that."

Eve thought about it for a moment. "I always had a crush on him."

"Caden?" Maggie giggled. "I knew that. I could tell by the way you looked at him. It's part of the reason you have to stay."

"In Point Pleasant?"

"It's your home."

"It was my home." She tucked her knees close, mimicking Maggie's posture. "I wish the bridge had never fallen." She looked at her friend,

*feeling a long-ago sense of loss. For their childhood and laughter. Death
had robbed them both in different ways. She smiled sadly. "I know this
isn't real, that it's just a dream."*

"Then ask me a question. Ask something you've always wanted to know."

"Did you really see the Mothman?"

"Your Aunt Rosie knows."

* * * *

Eve jerked awake, Maggie's words echoing in her head. The house
was silent and dark, yet something felt wrong. She lay in bed unmoving,
holding her breath, straining to hear. Moonlight streamed through
the bedroom windows, carving strange shapes and shadows from the
nightstand and the dresser. Her purse, discarded on a nearby chair, took
on the form of a night beast reawakened from childhood. She remembered
nights huddled under her blankets, listening to the wind moan outside.
The year before the bridge collapsed, so many people had spread tales of
the Mothman, claiming to have seen the creature.

It had left her afraid to be alone in the dark, fearful she would see
the fiery red eyes or hear the awful flap of its enormous wings. People
who saw the monster said it made them feel funny in the head, and Mr.
Elderman insisted it had carried off his dog. The poor animal had been
found hours later, dead on the side of a road, miles from his house.

Make believe. Stories.

Was the Mothman real?

Your Aunt Rosie knows.

She gasped at the unexpected *brrrang* of the phone. The shrill ringing
shattered the silence and broke through the eerie reverie playing in her
head. Fumbling for the lamp beside the bed, she caught a glimpse of the
clock. Two in the morning. Dread settled in the pit of her stomach as she
thought of her mother, home in Harrisburg. The only news delivered at
two AM was bad news. Heart pounding, fingers shaking, she switched on
the light and snatched up the receiver. "Hello?"

Silence. Oppressive and thick, like the silence of the house.

Hair prickled on the back of Eve's neck. "Hello," she repeated, louder
this time.

A second, two seconds of prolonged silence, then the line clicked dead
and a dial tone hummed in her ear. Her fingers tightened on the receiver.
Quickly, she dropped the phone in its cradle as if it carried the taint of
disease. If something had happened back home, the caller would try to
reach her again. If everything was fine and she called her mom, she'd
wake her from a sound sleep and likely set her to worrying. No, it was

probably just a wrong number. A night owl looking for a kindred soul who'd inadvertently dialed her line.

Did you really see the Mothman?

Your Aunt Rosie knows.

There was no way she could fall asleep now, not after the strange dream and the unsettling phone call. Wrong numbers happened all time. It shouldn't bother her, yet coming on the heels of the ominous note that ordered her to leave and the vandalism to the house, it left her shaken.

Sliding from bed, she found her slippers, then wrapped her robe around her and padded downstairs. Tea would help. She switched on each light as she went, flooding the house with brightness to chase away her fears. In the kitchen, she rummaged a kettle from the cupboard, then filled it with hot water and set it on the stove. As she waited for the water to boil, she replayed the dream through her mind.

"I knew you'd come back," Maggie had said. It was silly to think she'd actually been talking to her friend, yet the exchange had felt so real. Maggie wanted her to figure something out...something that would help Aunt Rosie and Caden, if she believed the dream.

When the water boiled, she made herself a cup of chamomile tea and carried it to the living room where she curled up on the couch. It was hard to believe Aunt Rosie had lived in a house this big all alone. She sipped her tea, trying to imagine Aunt Rosie doing the same.

Caden had called her aunt secretive, and Katie had said Aunt Rosie believed her cancer was payment for something she'd done long ago. But that was impossible. Her aunt had nothing to hide. Certainly nothing so awful that she considered cancer a just punishment.

Frustrated, Eve set her tea down and rubbed her temples. Her gaze dropped to the folder she'd brought from the hotel and discarded on the coffee table. *December 1967.* The month and year the world changed.

Apprehensively, she set the folder on her lap and began to sort through the contents. Bits of correspondence, old receipts, supply lists, and ledger pages comprised the bulk of information tucked inside. There was even an employment ad for a hotel maintenance worker clipped from the local newspaper and a brochure advertising printing costs from a company in Gallipolis. Nothing to indicate the world had come to a screeching halt on December 15th.

As she returned the folder to the coffee table, a piece of paper slipped free. A small square torn from a message pad. She was about to place it back inside the folder when her father's blocky handwriting caught her eye. Dated a week before the bridge fell, the note was addressed to her mother.

Faye,
Hank called spooked about the Mothman again. I'm headed over to his place to try to calm him down. If you see Rosie, tell her Roger Layton called.
I don't like him.
Ben

Eve blinked, trying to make sense of the strange note.

Who hadn't her father liked? Roger?

She couldn't remember him ever saying a bad word about Aunt Rosie's fiancé, but he certainly couldn't have been referring to Hank. Hank Jeffries—the only "Hank" she could think of—had been a close friend of her father. His home was one of the few to border the TNT, and once the Mothman was sighted, Hank went a little crazy in his small rancher. He swore up and down he'd seen the creature staring through the windows of his house at least twice. He'd even shot out the bedroom glass in an effort to kill it. Like many people in Point Pleasant, Hank had been terrified of "the bird."

But Roger Layton?

Setting the note aside, she sipped her tea, trying to remember her aunt's fiancé. He came from a family of dockworkers, a straightforward man who used to swing her up in his powerful arms whenever he saw her. He always had some pretty stone or water-smoothed piece of glass found in the river to give her. *Here, take this and go show your friends.*

Roger had laughed a lot and sometimes made crude jokes, but Aunt Rosie had loved him.

Eve returned to the slip of paper and the condemning declaration made by her father: *I don't like him.*

She set her tea on the table, then pulled her robe closer, but the chill had little to do with the temperature of the room. Her father hadn't liked Roger, and her beloved aunt had harbored secrets.

"Aunt Rosie, I wish I understood what was going on. I wish there was some way you could talk to me."

Silence greeted her, the same entombing silence that had hung in the air when she'd awakened from her dream. If there were answers, she wasn't going to find them sitting in an empty house wishing for something that could never be. Her aunt was gone. There was no changing that.

Eve carried her teacup back to the kitchen, then headed upstairs to her bedroom. In defiance of her nerves, she shut the lights off as she went, moving with growing familiarity through the dark.

For however long she remained in Point Pleasant, this was her home now, and she wouldn't be chased away by threatening notes or ominous phone calls. If there really was something Aunt Rosie wanted her to discover, she wouldn't leave until she got to the bottom of the mystery.

Chapter 5

Caden got started later than he'd planned the next morning. Ryan was on early shift, so the first thing he did was track his brother down at the sheriff's office intending to tell him about the note Eve found. He caught Ryan as he was headed out the door for his police cruiser.

"Sorry, I can't talk." His brother waved a greeting. "I've got to take a call."

"Anything serious?"

"Probably not. Early morning hiker said he saw something in one of the ponds at the TNT. Thought it looked like someone dumped something big there. Sheriff wants me to check it out."

"Mind if I ride along? I've got something I want to talk to you about."

Ryan grinned. "Hop in. Sheriff Weston would love to have you back in a car full-time."

Caden frowned at his brother but complied all the same. The nice thing about rural county police departments was a casualness that allowed such familiarity…mostly because he'd worn a uniform for eight years. He slid into the passenger seat, and a second later, Ryan eased the car into traffic, headed for the TNT.

"Is this about Mom?" Ryan shot him a glance as he stopped for a traffic light on Viand.

"No. Why, is there a problem with her?"

"Just the usual." Ryan shrugged. "She was wound up last night, talking about Maggie. You know how she gets."

Caden remained silent, preferring not to discuss his little sister. He needed a break from remembering, especially after the flashback he'd had during dinner with Eve. Last night, he'd dreamed of Maggie crying out for his help, but he hadn't been able to save her. Again.

When the traffic signal turned green, Ryan eased ahead, passing Pioneer Cemetery on Ninth. As if sensing his reluctance to discuss Maggie or their mother, Ryan changed the subject. "So what did you want to talk to me about?"

"Eve Parrish. I'm going to be doing some work for her."

"Good. I hate to see her sell the place, but I can understand she's got a life somewhere else."

"Yeah." The admission came reluctantly. He'd enjoyed their impromptu dinner last night and wouldn't mind exploring the attraction he felt further. Too bad he wouldn't get the chance. "You told her you thought the damage to Rosie's house was an act of random vandalism. Kids out to have fun."

"Sure. We've seen it before." Ryan palmed the wheel as he banked the police cruiser through a curve. "I didn't want her worrying about being alone in the house."

"Maybe she should worry." Caden told him about the note Eve found on her windshield, pulling it from his pocket to display as proof.

Ryan turned his gaze from the road briefly, then shook his head. "I hope you didn't work her up over that. A lot of kids are pranking right now. School's ending in two days, and they're soaring on adrenalin after being cooped up all year. Someone even TP'd old man Doyle's house last night. I'd bet money some kid stuck that note on Eve's car and didn't even know who it belonged to."

"Just like you think the vandalism to Rosie's house was routine?"

Ryan cast him a sideways glance. "What else do you want me to think? Nothing was taken, and Rosie didn't have enemies. I've lived here all my life, Caden, but I'm not one to dream up conspiracy theories or believe in hogwash like the Mothman."

Caden looked away, turning his gaze out the window.

As a kid, Ryan had pretended to believe Maggie about seeing the creature, not wanting to upset her. He'd later told Caden he thought the whole thing was make-believe. It was why Caden had never shared what happened the night his car plummeted into the Ohio River. When icy water closed over his head and he'd fought for air, his arm pinned in the wreckage.

A tingle of phantom pain coiled around his wrist. It had been fifteen years, but the bones had never healed properly. The winter chill of the water had been nothing compared to the frigid grasp of the hand that freed him, that left him branded with three distinctive red lines angled over his forearm. Exhaling, he shook the memory away.

"I want you to keep an eye out for her. Don't be so quick to write it off. That's all I'm asking." He kept his gaze trained on the blur of houses, trees and buildings on his right, waiting for his memory of the Mothman to fade. "You live next door. Keep an open mind and check in on her now and then."

"Sure. Whatever." Ryan shrugged. "Once I get a break, I want to ask her out for dinner anyway. We need to catch up on old times."

"A date dinner or a friend dinner?" He regretted the question as soon as he asked it.

"A friend dinner." Ryan grinned. "I didn't know it mattered."

"It doesn't." The protest came too quickly to be believable. Grimacing at the slip, Caden again turned his attention out the side window.

Ryan chuckled. "Anything else I should know, brother?"

"Such as?"

"Such as maybe you're thinking of dusting off your rusty dating skills?"

Caden told him where he could stick the idea, but it only served to make Ryan laugh harder.

Ten minutes later they entered the TNT, passing a graffiti-scrawled sign that proclaimed McClintic Wildlife Management Area. Caden hadn't been to the remote location in years but could well recall summer nights parked in one of the turn-off areas. If he hadn't been with a girl, he was with his friends as they guzzled six packs and went through cigarettes like candy. Stupid stuff, a rite of passage for teenage boys. He'd lost his virginity to Bonnie Filmore in one of those pull-offs when he was eighteen, glad she'd been experienced and too drunk to realize he wasn't.

Further down the road, they passed a groundwater treatment facility, bracketed behind barbed wire. He'd forgotten how oppressive the air was, nothing indicative of welcome. If anything, it screamed "Keep out." In many ways it was like entering another world, one of dense woodlands and overgrown foliage. There was something almost primeval about the unnatural hush, as if a thousand unseen eyes observed their progress.

Caden had always felt a sense of "something" lingering here. A slow awareness that seeped under the skin. He used to chalk it up to subconscious tension until he came face to face with the Mothman in the fall of '66. He'd never shared that experience with anyone and probably never would. There were times it still felt fabricated. A bizarre scenario he'd created in his head, but the scarred branding on his forearm told him differently.

"How far?" he asked.

Ryan nodded ahead. "The next pond."

Thirty-one ponds were scattered through the TNT, all but two open year round for fishing. Electric motors were allowed on the larger ponds, which offered facilities nearby with pit-type toilets. Not that it mattered. Fewer people came these days as rumors of toxic chemical seepage spread.

"A camper on an early morning hike filed the report," Ryan explained. "Drove into town to grab breakfast and said he saw something in the reeds on the opposite side. Couldn't tell what it was, but said it looked pretty big. Sheriff Weston asked me to check it out before we get Natural Resources involved. You know how people dump garbage up here all the time and don't think twice. Remember all the whackos that overran the place in '66?

"You were a kid then," Caden countered.

"Yeah, but I remember Mom and Dad talking about it. They used to freak because you'd come up here with your friends."

It had been crazy then. Mothman fever had gripped Point Pleasant, and he'd been a part of it along with his friends Glen Moore and Wyatt Fisher. Sometimes they'd dragged their girlfriends along, each daring the others to venture into the abandoned igloos in the dark.

"My car stalled once," Caden commented. "No reason, everything just went dead."

Ryan pulled the police cruiser off the road at the entrance to a large pond and killed the ignition. "Did you see lights in the sky? Little green men come to steal you away?"

Caden gave a good-natured cuff to his head.

"Hey! That's assaulting an officer of the law."

"Older brother privilege. " He popped the door and stepped outside. The musk of leaves and soil hung heavily in the air. It was a feral odor, whispering of something ancient. The unnatural hush he'd sensed earlier surrounded them like a shroud, its touch all but tangible. Together they walked back an overgrown trail cut between the trees. Weeds and ferns bent easily beneath their shoes, springing upright after they passed. Eventually, they reached the pond and Ryan took the lead, edging around the bank.

Caden followed, the ground soft and squishy beneath his heavy work boots. "I don't see anything."

"There." Ryan pointed across the bank where a dark lump was huddled against the edge.

Caden narrowed his eyes, picking out something that might have been someone's cast-off garbage or something far more unpleasant. An ugly premonition crawled through his gut. "I've got a shitty feeling about this."

Ryan was already working his way around the edge, a long branch clutched in his hand. Extending it, he poked the thing in the water, using the tip for leverage. With effort, he was able to ease it from a tangle of rushes where it had become ensnared.

It rolled over like a fish bobbing belly upright. A bloated white face popped to the surface, the mouth slack, eyes unblinking and staring heavenward as if beseeching help.

"Oh, hell," Ryan said. "That's Amos Carter."

Caden swore. "It looks like somebody beat the shit out of him. You've got a murder on your hands, brother."

* * * *

Eve called James Dixon, Caden's real estate friend, and made an appointment to meet with him later that afternoon. Because she didn't want to be in the way when Caden began work at the house, she headed to the hotel still wrestling with the decision to sell. Surely, her aunt would understand she had no knowledge of how a hotel should be operated, nor did she want to relocate to Point Pleasant. Perhaps it would be possible to keep the hotel and have someone run it for her.

Katie Lynch certainly seemed capable. From all appearances, Aunt Rosie had been grooming her to handle operations when she wasn't available. Maybe that was the way to go—at least temporarily until she had time to give the matter adequate thought.

As she walked through the front door into the lobby, she found Katie engaged in conversation with a blond-haired woman at the check-in counter. Although her back was turned, there was something vaguely familiar about her. An unabashed sassiness in the way she stood, the flare of her hip jutted at an angle, her hand lodged in the crook of her waist.

"It's not like him," the woman complained to Katie. She dabbed her eyes with a tissue and sniffled loudly. "I'm telling you, something's not right. Even if he went on one of his binges, he'd be home by now."

"Is something wrong?" Eve asked, fearing an issue with a lodger.

Catching sight of her, Katie flushed. "No, um…"

The woman turned and eyed her up and down. "I'm Doreen Sue Lynch, Katie's mother."

"Oh." That explained the familiarity. She'd only seen Mrs. Lynch a few times as a child, usually when her mom took her to Doreen Sue's hair salon for a trim. More often than not, it was one of the other stylists who clipped her bangs and got rid of her split ends, Doreen Sue busy mixing color or doing a perm.

Not much had changed about Katie's mom in the intervening fifteen years. She still had the same bleached blond hair and favored the same tight, revealing clothes she had when Eve was a child. Today, it was white leggings with stiletto heels and a snug leopard-print top. A white-spotted purse hung from her shoulder, forming a baggy leather sack.

"Mom, this is Eve Parrish," Katie introduced her. "Rosie's niece."

"I remember you." The hint of a smile touched Doreen Sue's lips. Like her fingernails, they were glossy and red. "Your mama used to bring you into my salon to get your hair trimmed."

Eve nodded. "You always had a bowl of hard cinnamon candy at the door, and I'd grab one on the way out."

"Gee, that was a long time ago." The faraway look of whimsy in Doreen Sue's eyes didn't last long. Almost immediately her attention returned to Katie, and she dabbed her eyes again. "I think I should go look for him, don't you?"

"Is there a problem?" Eve asked.

"It's Amos," Doreen Sue replied.

Eve glanced at Katie for understanding. Surprisingly, her employee looked low on patience. Despite her mother's sniffling and tears, there was little sympathy in her eyes. "Mom's boyfriend," she explained.

"He's gone missing," Doreen Sue interjected. "He didn't come home last night, and I'm worried."

Out of her realm, Eve hedged. "Did you check with the police?"

Doreen Sue *pshawed* the idea with a wave of her hand. "Sheriff Weston and those deputies of his? They won't do anything. They'll tell me Amos is sleeping off a binge somewhere."

"He probably is, Mom." Frowning, Katie continued checking off items in a ledger book open on the counter. Seemingly uninterested in her mother's problem, she moved a pencil down each line, comparing entries against a typed list. "You know how he gets when he's had too much to drink."

"He promised me he wouldn't do that anymore. He said he was gonna change. What if he fell and hit his head or something?"

Katie sighed. "Mom, he'll be home when he's ready. For all you know, he might have found—" She bit her lip, stopping the thought before it could be uttered.

"What?" Doreen Sue pounced on the unfinished notion. "You were gonna say he might of found someone else to shack up with, weren't you? I know you don't like the man."

"No, I don't like him." Katie slammed the book shut. "He drinks too much, cheats on you, and treats you like dirt. Just like every other guy who came down the pike before him. Why do you think I don't like Sam visiting with you?"

Doreen Sue's face drained of color. "So now I'm an unfit grandmamma?"

Katie flushed and hugged the ledger to her chest. "I don't have time for this, Mom. The lobby of the Parrish Hotel isn't the place to air dirty family laundry." She gave a quick nod to Eve. "Excuse me."

Before Eve could manage a syllable, Katie disappeared into the office behind the counter, closing the door with a firm click. Eve wasn't sure if she was more mortified for herself, Katie, or Doreen Sue. Awkwardly, she looked at Mrs. Lynch, uncertain if she should say something to pacify the situation. "I'm sorry."

"Why? It's nothing to do with you." Doreen Sue dabbed her eyes again, smearing black mascara down her cheek. The sight made Eve feel sorry for her. In the right light, she would look pretty, if a little hard, but now she looked a mess. Tawdry and cheap standing there in her stiletto heels, bright red lipstick feathering at the corners of her mouth.

"Girl ain't never taken a cotton to me," Doreen Sue said with another dismissive wave of her hand. "Thinks she's better than me is what it boils down to." She fished in her purse, mumbling all the while until she produced a cigarette. "Damn, I can't find my lighter." She glanced up hopefully. "You wouldn't happen to have—"

"Sorry, I don't smoke."

"Just as well. Bad habit. Girl probably thinks I smoke around my grandson and gives him beer. Just 'cause she didn't have a proper daddy growing up don't mean I've got men traipsing through my bed."

Eve felt her cheeks color. "Mrs. Lynch, I really need to go."

"'Course you do. You tell that daughter of mine not to worry her head over Amos, 'cause he and I'll do fine without her. She's getting too big for her britches. Thinks because Rosalind put her in charge when she wasn't around, that she's some highfalutin executive now. Don't let her fool you." She waggled a finger in front of Eve's face. "All she really knows is how to wait tables. You'll see." Continuing with a litany of how Katie was an ungrateful daughter for all she'd done, and how anyone could see what a good grandmamma she was, she strutted for the door, heels click-clacking against the floor.

Eve felt like she'd stepped into a time warp. She'd forgotten the history of many of the families in Point Pleasant. Growing up, it hadn't simply been gossip about Wendy Lynch running off, or how Katie would turn out to be like her sister. The women had gossiped about Mrs. Lynch, too, discussing how "trashy" she was. Of course, that hadn't stopped them from visiting her salon or offering artificial smiles to her face. Maybe the woman was rough around the edges, but she'd always been nice to Eve, telling her how pretty her hair looked, even if it was one of her stylists who'd cut it.

Eve waited until the door swung shut behind Doreen Sue before heading for the office. She expected to find Katie immersed in work but discovered her pacing instead, hands on her hips as if trying to work off steam.

"I'm sorry," she blurted the moment Eve walked into the room. "That shouldn't have taken place in the lobby. It won't happen again."

Eve set her purse on the desk. "Your mom seemed pretty upset. Is it unlike her boyfriend to stay out all night?"

"A man like Amos? He does what he wants." Katie huffed out a breath and folded her arms across her chest. "I don't know why she can't see him for what he is. He's just like every other scumbag Mom let into her life, including my dad." She shook her head, tucking a strand of blond hair behind her ear. "I'm sorry. You don't need to hear this."

"If it involves you and affects your work performance, then it involves me. Especially when I have a proposal to make." She was surprised to hear Katie talk so candidly about her mother and father. Looking back on it, she couldn't remember a father ever being in Katie's life.

The girls in school used to say horrible things about Katie. How she let boys feel her up, and how she liked to steal her mother's whiskey and drink it under the bleachers at the football field. Eve had bought into the gossip at the time, even though the Katie she observed in the classroom was nothing like the image painted by the popular girls at school. She'd been part of that clique. With a name like Parrish, she'd been a shoo-in for popularity. Given her friends said those dreadful things about Katie with such authority, they had to be true, right?

Katie looked at her evenly. "Proposal?"

Eve motioned her to a chair across from the desk. Rather than take the seat behind it, she slid into the chair beside Katie, setting the tone for a casual conversation. "First, I'd like to say I'm grateful for all you did for my aunt. And I don't just mean at the hotel. I should have been the one at her bedside, comforting her when she was dying, but I didn't even know she passed away until after the funeral. Apparently, she left instructions with Mr. Barnett that I wasn't to be notified until after she was buried."

"She asked for you a couple of times."

Eve knew her face had paled, for Katie rushed ahead as if trying to soften the blow. "She was delirious. Sometimes she talked like you were there in the room. It was important to her that you continue the Parrish family legacy."

She'd suspected as much. "The hotel?"

Katie flushed. "I'm not saying that to keep my job, Eve. Rosie was more important to me than a paycheck."

"Perhaps a substitute mother?" she ventured softly.

Katie lowered her eyes, fiddling with a jade ring on her right hand. Brilliant green and oblong in shape, it was housed in an antique silver setting, surrounded by diamond chips. Expensive, old, and familiar.

"She listened when I had problems with my mom or Lyle," Katie answered her question.

"Is that Sam's father?"

"Biologically." She lifted her head, a flare of sudden anger in her eyes. "That's all the bastard is. When I told him I was pregnant, he said it wasn't his kid and told me to get rid of it."

Eve was horrified. "He doesn't help with Sam?"

"I wouldn't take a penny from that creep." Katie lifted her chin defiantly. "I don't want a man in Sam's life who'd deny his own son, even if it means I sometimes struggle. My dad took off when I was two, and my mom has been through a string of men ever since, each worse than the last. I want a better upbringing for Sam, and that includes keeping Lyle out of his life. Fortunately, he left town over a year ago and hasn't been back." She gave a soft laugh and shook her head. "It's probably stupid of me to tell you all of this. Who wants an employee with baggage?"

"Actually, I do." Eve smiled. Leaning forward, she put her hand over Katie's where it rested on her knee. "I know we weren't friends in the past, and we probably have a lot to learn about each other now, but my Aunt Rosie trusted you and that's good enough for me. I was hoping we could set aside past opinions and start fresh. I need an ally if I'm going to keep this hotel in the family."

Katie looked startled. "You're not going to sell?"

"I'm not sure." Saying it aloud was harder than she thought. Eve stood and paced to the rear window overlooking the Ohio River. The towering bulk of Point Pleasant's flood walls obscured most of the view, but a small expanse of water glimmered in the gap between opposing concrete barriers. Adam Barnett would call in the next day or two about his potential buyer. She'd set that ball in motion, but another part of her was starting to feel like she'd come home—back to the river town that held so many childhood memories. The tug on her heart may have been nothing more than nostalgia, but sometimes it felt like a true desire to continue her family's legacy.

"I need to take some time and not make a hasty decision. From what I've seen of the books, the hotel is solvent, but barely."

Katie nodded grimly. "It helps that Point Pleasant is located midway between Cincinnati and Pittsburgh. We've done pretty well with overnight guests who are passing through."

Eve didn't think the hotel would ever be the draw it was in the days when Point Pleasant was a booming river town but believed it had enough history and appeal to offer an alternative from the chain motels that had popped up across the river in Gallipolis. "If the Parrish Hotel is going to thrive, we need to play up its history and charm. Market it as a step back in time, not only in décor, but in service, too. Old fashioned service and a family-owned operation."

"You sound like you're keeping it."

It was what Aunt Rosie wanted. Apparently, Maggie did, too, if she was to believe her dream. "For now. I can't walk away from my family's legacy without taking the time to understand it first. I'm still going to explore my options, but even when I head back to Harrisburg, it can be business as usual for the hotel. Which brings me to the proposal I mentioned."

Katie sat straighter. She appeared poised for the worst, something that couldn't be further from the truth. "I'm listening."

Eve slid into her aunt's desk chair, assuming her position as owner. "I need to learn about the hotel. Not just looking at books and expense reports, but the ins and outs of every detail. I want you to teach me. I'd also like you to officially accept the position of manager." It was what Aunt Rosie would want, what she'd likely been grooming Katie for all along.

Katie blinked. "Manager?"

"With an increase in pay, of course. When I return to Harrisburg, I'll be relying on you to handle all responsibility in my absence."

"I—" Katie seemed at a loss for words. "I'm flattered."

"You'll accept?"

She nodded, looking a little stunned. "Thank you. Your trust means a lot."

"It's my aunt's trust."

"How can you be so sure of her faith in me?"

Eve nodded to the jade ring Katie absently twisted around her finger. "I remember that ring. My Aunt Rosie bought it on a trip she took to New York and never took it off. She loved that ring."

"Oh!" Katie flushed as if consumed by guilt and swiftly tugged the ring from her finger. Standing, she extended it to Eve. "Here. You should have it."

"No. Aunt Rosie obviously wanted you to."

"But it's wrong. You're her niece."

"I have plenty of things to remember her by. She gave it to you for a reason."

Katie bit her lip. "Eve, she was lonely."

"And you were her friend. Perhaps the daughter she never had." She saw it now. She and her mother had left her aunt alone. Perhaps Eve had only been twelve when her mother took her away, but as an adult she could have returned often. Instead, she'd allowed her mother's bias against the town keep her away. Aunt Rosie might have chosen not to marry, but that didn't mean she didn't long for companionship.

Katie's eyes glittered with tears. "She gave me the ring a few months before she died. I didn't understand why at the time, but now I realize she must have known she was dying. I didn't want to take it."

"But Aunt Rosie was stubborn." Eve smiled softly. "I'm glad you have something to remember her by."

"It belongs in your family." Katie tried to offer it again.

Eve shook her head. "You were family to her far more than I was these last several years. Besides, in her own way, I think she left it as a message for me."

Katie looked puzzled.

"So I would know I could trust you." Eve drew a breath, decision made. She was staying, at least temporarily. "And now that we have that established, I'd like to learn more about the hotel."

* * * *

Eve was manning the front desk later that afternoon when Sarah Sherman strolled into the lobby, released an ear-splitting squeal, and extended her arms for a hug.

"Sarah?" Eve could barely believe her eyes. "Is it really you?"

"In the flesh."

Eve darted from behind the counter and gave her friend a tight hug. "You look fantastic!" It wasn't a lie. Sarah's coppery hair and dark-chocolate eyes accentuated the becoming touch of rose on her cheeks. "I can't believe it's really you." She'd been meaning to look up Sarah ever since she'd returned to town.

"Ryan told me you were back. I'm on lunch break and took a chance you might be here." Sarah held her at arms-length for a few seconds, soaking in her features, then hugged her again. "Why has it taken so long?" She blinked owlishly as if realizing what she'd said. "Oh, I'm sorry, Eve. I shouldn't have said that. I know how upset you must be about Rosie. I didn't mean—"

"I know you didn't." Eve smiled. It felt good to see her friend again. Even with so many years between them, the bond she'd once shared with Sarah remained strong. "What are you doing here?"

As she asked the question, Katie walked down the steps from the upper level. Eve recalled her saying something about checking on the progress of maintenance work in the ballroom. There was still a lot of prep to do for the birthday party the hotel had on the books for the end of the month. Spying Sarah and Eve together, Katie nodded hello. "Hi, Sarah."

"Katie." Sarah was ready to dismiss her, her attention absorbed by Eve when her face abruptly drained of color. "Oh!" Shock bled through the exclamation. "You haven't heard, have you?" Her attention was solely on Katie now.

"Heard what?" Katie walked closer, joining them in the center of the lobby.

"About Amos Carter. Wasn't he living with your mom?"

Katie exchanged a glance with Eve, no doubt remembering the conversation they'd had earlier with Doreen Sue. "What about him?"

"I'm so sorry. I was at the courthouse when Ryan came in. He said he and Caden found a body out in the TNT, badly beaten. He was pretty sure it was Amos. News is already spreading through town."

"Are they certain it was Amos?" Katie covered her mouth with her hand, shaking her head. "My God, I couldn't stand the man, but I wouldn't wish him dead."

"Ryan sounded certain. I think they found ID on him."

"My Mom's going to fall apart when she hears this."

"She probably already has if she's at the salon," Eve inserted. "You better go check on her."

"I can't leave."

"Don't worry. I've got things covered. Your mom is going to need you. You saw how she was this morning."

"You're right." Katie shot her an appreciative glance. "Thanks, Eve. I'll be back as soon as I can."

After she left, Eve sat with Sarah on one of the couches in the lobby. Sunlight streamed through the windows, brightening the area, but she felt chilled, thinking of Katie and her mom. Amos must have treated Doreen Sue horribly. Sadly, that often didn't matter to a woman dependent on a man. "Doreen Sue was in here this morning, worried because Amos hadn't gone home last night," Eve explained to Sarah. "She was afraid something might have happened to him, but Katie thought he was sleeping off a binge somewhere. Her mom's going to be devastated."

Sarah shrugged apologetically. "He really wasn't the kind of guy you wanted hanging around, anyway. I've seen Doreen Sue cover a black eye with make-up plenty of times. Interesting that someone used their fists to put an end to his miserable life."

Eve was shocked by her bitterness. "You sound angry."

"He tried to grab me once in your café. I stopped by for a sandwich—it's a close walk from the courthouse—and he must have already downed a couple of six packs. I can't say I have fond memories of him."

"Katie doesn't like him either." *Didn't*, she amended.

"If you're lining up people with a grudge against him, that would be half the women in town. But I don't think any of them could have beaten him to death."

Eve shuddered. "I think I need a lighter topic. Would you like to have lunch with me and spend some time catching up?"

Her friend smiled. "That sounds wonderful."

* * * *

The man paced. He knew the little shit he'd beaten to death had called him Reaper behind his back. The idiot had let it slip once when they were downing beer. Fitting, considering he'd put an end to Amos's pathetic life. Besides, he liked the name. It made him feel powerful, a sensation he needed now with everything teetering on a precipice, ready to tumble.

Why did Rosie have to go and grow a damn conscience on her deathbed? All those years she'd kept his secret without his knowledge. That was the real mind blower—to learn she'd known about his crime and had never said a word. Not even to him. She could have blackmailed him, made sure he rotted in a jail cell, or set him up to die in the electric chair. Instead, she'd held her silence, sending him a letter just before she died. Her secret, her confession—along with a photo that captured his crime in ugly black and white.

Do the right thing, she'd pleaded in the letter.

As if.

He'd been elated when she died, thinking the threat removed. With her out of the equation, he should have been in the clear. Except the negative to that incriminating photo was still out there.

Somewhere.

Too many people came and went from the hotel—employees, café patrons, guests—Rosie would never have kept it there. It had to be in the house. He was sure of it, even though Amos, incompetent jerk, had come up empty.

The problem was the girl, Eve. The longer she stayed, the greater the risk she'd stumble over it tucked in a drawer or hidden in a cupboard somewhere. And then what? He'd never be able to weasel free of the crime with photographic evidence staring him in the face. No, he had to send her packing. Whether that happened gently, or not so gently, would be up to her.

He was done using underlings for dirty work. As it stood, he had to figure out who Amos had talked to. He was sure the son-of-a-bitch would have spilled his guts and fessed up rather than taken a beating, but Amos had insisted he hadn't told a soul.

Not possible.

Someone had found out. Someone was making phone calls to him. Weird shit with high-pitched noises, long silences, and strange shrieks. It had to be related. If Amos hadn't blabbed to someone about the negative, then Rosie had lied in her letter. She must have told someone the truth before she died.

So why wasn't he in jail?

He ground his teeth. He'd go crazy thinking about it. On the plus side, without the negative, there was no proof he'd committed a crime. All he had to do was find the damn thing and destroy it.

Which brought him back to Eve Parrish and how to get rid of her.

* * * *

It was almost six o'clock by the time Eve made it back to Aunt Rosie's house. Sarah had taken an extended lunch break, and they'd spent a good two hours catching up. Katie had returned sometime near three, saying one of the stylists at Doreen Sue's salon had taken her mom home and planned to stay with her until Katie got off work.

Eve found Caden in the dark room, measuring a sheet of drywall placed across two sawhorses. Dressed in jeans, a gray T-shirt, and work boots, he used a level to mark off a straight line as he bent over the sheet. Plaster dust peppered his black hair, and a tool belt hung from his hips. Three stark red gashes, the middle slightly longer than the others, were wrapped around his forearm. Scars of some sort, but they looked too vivid to be old.

"Hi," she greeted. From the looks of things he'd been busy tearing the room down to the studs. "How's it going?"

Caden glanced up. "On schedule." He drew a quick line along the level, then slipped the pencil behind his ear. "Don't let the look of things fool you."

Things looked rather good, especially him. "You're the contractor. I trust you completely." Folding her arms, she leaned against the doorway. "By the way, I heard you were with Ryan earlier today."

"You mean you heard about Amos Carter?"

"I was with Katie Lynch when I found out. Her mother was at the hotel, worried because he hadn't come home last night. Sarah Sherman showed up later and told us the news. It hasn't hit the paper, but I think it's all over town."

"Figures." Caden scowled. "I went to see Ryan early this morning to tell him about the note you got. He was headed out on a call, and I rode with him. I wasn't a fan of Amos, but someone definitely had it in for the guy. When I left Ryan, he was headed out to see Doreen Sue."

"Breaking the news couldn't have been easy." She paused, remembering some gossip Sarah had shared. "I hear some people think the Mothman is back."

Caden set his level aside. "The Mothman never hurt anyone."

"Oh?" Eve made no attempt to mask her surprise as she stepped away from the door. "What about the Silver Bridge? Some people think it caused the collapse."

Caden removed his tool belt and dumped it in the corner. "That's hogwash. If anything, the monster tried to help."

Interesting. "You sound like you know that for a fact."

He shook his head. "I'm just saying I don't think it caused anything. The bridge was old and couldn't support the weight of all that backed-up traffic. One of the eye-bars failed. Everyone knows that."

"So you *do* believe in the Mothman?" Why was that suddenly important to her?

"That's not what I said. A lot of people will do anything to fuel superstition in this town. I saw Amos Carter—or what was left of him. Someone beat him with their fists, plain and simple."

She flinched, unwillingly conjuring the sight in her head. As a child, she'd always thought Point Pleasant a safe haven. Murders didn't happen in the small river town. Domestic disputes, minor assaults here and there, even an occasional break-in, but not murder.

She decided to change the subject. "What did Ryan say about the note?"

"The same as before…not to worry. He thinks it was probably a kid playing a prank." He sounded as though he didn't buy it. She wasn't sure she did either, but in another week or so she'd be gone, and none of it would matter.

"I think I'll knock off for the night and start early tomorrow." Caden interrupted her thoughts. "I told Ryan I'd check on our mom since he's going to be stuck on a double shift. I just need to clean up a few things."

She nodded, finding it curious he'd chosen not to answer her question about the Mothman. "I'll see you downstairs."

When he wandered into the kitchen ten minutes later, he seemed in a better mood. "I'm sorry if I was short earlier. Sometimes the mentality of the town gets to me…the past."

Eve turned from the cupboard where she'd been scrounging up the makings of a meal. "You mean because of the bridge? Maggie?"

"Something like that." He cleared his throat, ending the subject. "So how have you found Point Pleasant since you've been back?"

She smiled. "Different, but the same."

"Have you been to the riverfront yet?"

"I haven't had the chance." She and Maggie used to love hanging out there as children, watching the large riverboats chug up and down the waterways pushing barges of coal. In the summer, there were fishing and boat rides, followed by school events and festivals in the fall.

Caden shifted. "There's a concert tomorrow night. A few friends of mine on guitar. I thought you might like to hear them."

It sounded like he was asking her out. "I'd love to." She offered a smile and couldn't help adding. "Do you still play? I remember you sometimes performed at the fairgrounds."

He shook his head, looking awkward. "Not much these days. I'm surprised you remember."

"I remember a lot of things, Caden. I had a terrible crush on you when I was a kid." Inwardly she cringed, shocked she'd blurted the truth. It was becoming far too easy to talk to him.

"Seriously?" He grinned. "You were what—six years younger?"

"That hardly made a difference." Stumbling to recover, she grasped at the first thing she could think to say. "All the girls liked you. Maggie used to say you could charm her into doing almost anything."

A shadow crossed his face at the mention of Maggie. "I should go. My mother's alone."

Something she'd said had obviously upset him. "Of course." They'd talked about Maggie before, if only briefly, so it couldn't be that. Bewildered by the change in his personality, she followed him to the front door.

He paused on the threshold, indecision in his gaze. "Look, I didn't mean to cut you off. It's just…"

"Maggie?"

"Yeah." He exhaled a tired breath, the fatigue reflected in his eyes. "I have good memories, but other times, all I think about is that night on the bridge."

"Maybe you should talk about it."

"Not now." He managed a weary smile. "I'll be back in the morning to continue work. Maybe we can grab dinner before heading to the riverfront and the concert."

She brightened with the idea. He *was* asking her on a date. "That's sounds great."

She followed him onto the porch, then waved goodbye as he headed across the yard to his mother's home. As she watched his retreating form, she was struck again by the change in his mood.

Like so many people in Point Pleasant, Caden Flynn had secrets.

* * * *

Caden tried to shove the discussion with Eve behind him as he walked into the living room of his mother's home. He *had* charmed Maggie that night, smiling and cajoling until she agreed to go out with him. Afterward, he'd been puffed up and proud for accomplishing something no one else in the family had been able to do. Maggie had looked up to him, even idolized him a little, and he'd used that adoration to manipulate her. The truth stung.

He found his mother seated on the couch, a pool of red yarn in her lap, a pair of wire-framed spectacles perched on the end of her nose. She divided her attention between *Wheel of Fortune* on the TV and the puddle of yarn that was slowly transforming into a scarf.

"Oh, Caden." She glanced up with a smile, a short fluttery laugh escaping her lips. "I thought you were Ryan. Isn't he coming home?"

"He got held up in town."

"Is it because of the murder?"

"You know about it?" He eased into a seat across from her. Mrs. Aldridge would have stayed through most of the day, leaving just a short while ago. But even if Mrs. Aldridge had heard the news, it was doubtful she'd have shared the information, fearful it would upset his mother.

"A man was found in the TNT." She spoke casually, her attention on the series of loops and stitches she skillfully produced. "I don't know who he was, but I know he was murdered."

Not possible. "How could you have heard?"

"You're dusty dear. You look like you've been rolling in plaster dust."

Distracted, Caden glanced down at his jeans, the denim dotted with a few clinging flecks of white powder. A neat freak, his mother would notice. Absently, he swatted the residue away. "Mom?"

"Maggie told me."

Not this again. He exhaled in frustration. "Mom, Maggie is gone."

His mother shot him a sharp look from above her glasses. "That doesn't mean she can't talk to me."

"Whatever." He stood, knowing arguing would do no good. "Ryan will be home later tonight. I'll get dinner started for you." The kitchen would be an escape from discussions about Maggie.

His mother continued as if she hadn't heard. "How else do you think I found out about the murder?"

Halfway from the room, he paused. Maybe someone had phoned to check up on her or shoot the breeze. She had plenty of friends in town, and Eve said word had spread about Amos's death. That made far more sense than his dead sister communicating with her. Enough was enough.

"Mom, this has to stop."

"She's only trying to help, you know."

Irritated, he scuffed a hand through his hair. Ryan handled these things far better than he did. His younger brother had patience he lacked. Then again, Ryan didn't carry the burden of Maggie's death. "All right. What did she say?"

"That you should go to the bunker and ask questions."

"The bunker?"

"In the TNT. The one where the Mothman was seen."

The hair on the back of his neck stood on end.

His mother set her knitting down and focused on him. Her gaze was direct, nothing clouded or hesitant to indicate fragility of mind. "Maggie said you know about the Mothman. From a Halloween night long ago and from when the bridge fell."

Caden felt the color leave his face. He'd heard enough. Between the discussion he'd had with Eve and his mother's crazy ramblings, he had to get away. Pivoting, he turned on his heel and stalked from the room.

Even then the memories hounded him. But it wasn't the Mothman he remembered. It was Maggie and the last moments they'd shared.

* * * *

"Are you cold?" Caden cranked the heat in the car, noting his sister sat slouched in the passenger's seat, huddled into her jacket. She'd grown solemn, especially after his last minute detour to the gas station for a pack of Marlboros. He'd run into Wyatt Fisher and ended up bullshitting for fifteen minutes while Maggie waited in the Chevy.

"I just want to go home," she said in a small voice.

His gut twisted. He thought was doing a good thing, getting her out of the house. For the last three days, she'd done nothing but hide in her bedroom, fearful the Mothman would steal her away if she ventured outside. She'd eaten little and broken into hysterics when her parents tried to force her into going to school. Doctor Pullman hadn't been able to find anything wrong with her, only that something must have given her a terrible fright.

His parents had been at wits' end not knowing what to do. Eventually, he'd managed to coax her from the house with the promise of helping her choose a Christmas gift for their mother and father. The holiday was only a little over a week away, and he wanted his sister to enjoy it. "I won't let the Mothman or anything else harm you," he'd vowed. He knew about the Mothman—more than most—and had no fear of the creature.

In Gallipolis they'd visited two stores before she settled on a keychain for their father and a pretty silver locket for their mother. After that she'd been ready to head home, growing increasingly anxious the closer it drew to sundown.

"It's going to be dark soon," she said.

"I told you I wouldn't let anything hurt you."

Caden turned down the volume on the radio. The station had switched from Christmas songs to contemporary music, blaring "Never My Love" by The Association. He came to a stop in the middle of the Silver Bridge, swearing softly at the back-up unspooling in front of his Nova. Traffic had been crawling, but now it was at a standstill. He shouldn't have stopped for the damn cigarettes. If he hadn't made the detour, they'd probably be home already. He hoped his mom was making something hot for dinner. It was fricking freezing outside.

He peered through the windshield, noting how many birds had accumulated overhead. He'd never seen so many flying together this time of year. Normally they roosted on the bridge. It was almost as if they didn't know where to land.

"Weird." Two vehicles ahead of him, a tractor-trailer rolled forward a few feet before stopping. Caden inched closer, then hit the brakes. "Damn. I can't see shit with that truck in the way."

"You shouldn't swear," Maggie said.

"You're right, I shouldn't. At least not in front of you." He grinned. "I'm glad you went out with me. Maybe tomorrow you'll go somewhere with Mom and Dad."

She looked down at the bag on her lap that contained brightly colored packages inside. The clerk at the store had wrapped both gifts in festive red and green paper, a sight that had made her smile. He wished she'd smile more.

"I don't like going outside," she whispered. "He's outside."

"The Mothman?"

She nodded, but kept her head down. "I was so scared Caden. I think he wanted to kill me."

He frowned, wondering if he should confide in her about his own experience. Maybe telling her about what happened to him at the TNT over Halloween might lessen her fear.

No.

He chewed the inside of his cheek. It was better to pretend the creature was a myth. Myths had no power to harm.

On the radio The Association continued their melodic song about eternal love.

"No one's going to hurt you, Maggie, but you have to let go of this—" A strange tremor buffeted the car. It felt as if the bridge shifted. "My God!"

The tall rocker towers on either side of the bridge swayed with a sickening lurch, and the headlights in his rearview mirror dropped abruptly into empty space. One second there, the next gone. Someone screamed, igniting a bone-chilling chorus of frantic cries. A sound like metal grinding against metal exploded in his head. Beside him, Maggie let out an ear-piercing shriek, but he only had time to gulp a breath before the world fell away.

Chapter 6

Lillian Layton was not at all as Eve expected. Perhaps it was the lilt of her name, conjuring images of a singer or stage actress, but she had anticipated a striking, stylish woman. Rather, the woman who met with her the next day at the Parrish Hotel was understated, plain in appearance. She wore no make-up and had secured her graying blond hair in a tight bun. A sensible button blouse and baggy slacks hung shapelessly on her stick-thin figure. Seated across from Eve, she perched primly on the edge of her chair and held her handbag—square brown leather—like a shield on her lap. Her nails were chewed to the quick.

"Thank you for seeing me on such short notice," she said.

"It's certainly not a problem, Mrs. Layton. I was planning on contacting you next week to make sure I was familiar with everything you'd like for your husband's birthday celebration." She smiled warmly, trying to ease the stilted air. The woman reminded her of a stereotypical church lady who didn't have time for shenanigans. "Fifty is a big one."

"Yes, well…" Mrs. Layton's gaze flicked away briefly. "I appreciate your time nonetheless. I know it must be difficult after your aunt's passing. And please, call me Lillian."

"Thank you. I'm fine with Eve as well."

"Do you remember my husband?"

"Vaguely." An image of Roger Layton flashed into her mind as she recalled the words her father had penned to her mother—*I don't like him.* Something must have happened to change Aunt Rosie's opinion of him, too. Why else would she end their relationship? "I know my aunt was engaged to him for a time."

"Yes." Lillian's mouth puckered in displeasure, but she didn't comment further. Rather, she took a sip of the coffee Eve had offered earlier, pausing briefly before returning the cup to its saucer. "Roger is well thought of in Point Pleasant," she ventured at last. "My family owns the bank, and he operates it as Vice President. I thought it was fitting his birthday be celebrated in style."

Interesting. He'd gone from a dockworker when Aunt Rosie had known him to a bank VP. That was definitely a step up in position. "Is it a surprise?"

"Oh dear, no." Lillian parted with a fluty laugh. "Roger expects the hoopla and would have it no other way. My husband enjoys being the center of attention. Fortunately, he's permitted me to handle all of the preparations. I wanted to talk to you about the menu."

"Of course." Eve had been prepared for that and removed the banquet order from a file on her desk. "You requested a pasta buffet with lasagna, spinach tortellini, and meatballs. We'll include the usual sides—salads, several breads, and antipasto, as well as a dessert bar." She ran a finger down the page. "I see you also requested hot hors d'oeuvres and an open bar."

"Yes." Lillian shifted, clutching her handbag more tightly. "I've been rethinking the menu, however, and would like to switch to a split entrée if the option is still available."

"Certainly." It would mean securing more servers since the menu would switch to a sit-down dinner, but the pricing on entrees was higher and the hotel could use the revenue. There was also the up-charge for a split entrée which would help defer the cost of the additional staff. "Would you like to see a banquet menu or did you have something in mind?"

Lillian opened her purse and withdrew several creased sheets of paper. "Rosalind gave these to me earlier." Unfolding them, she read from the printed list. "I've already reviewed them and would like to go with the prime rib and stuffed chicken breast. Greek, for the salad, I think, and I'd like to add a bottle of your middle-shelf Merlot and Riesling to each table."

Eve scribbled notes as the woman rattled off the list of changes. She'd have to get with Katie and her kitchen manager to make certain everything was ordered in plenty of time. The event would test their resources. The idea of leaving Katie to handle it alone while she was in Harrisburg suddenly felt like a cop-out. Maybe there was a way she could extend her stay through the end of the month.

Returning her attention to the events folder, she flipped through several pages. "The changes won't be a problem. The only thing I seem to be missing is a count, which you can supply later, and a final on centerpieces for the tables. Will you be providing floral arrangements or would you like us to handle that?"

"I'll have the town florist deliver them that afternoon. Yellow carnations." She smiled slightly and returned the papers to her purse. "They're my favorite."

That was interesting. Someone had put yellow carnations on Aunt Rosie's grave. "And the band?"

"Someone should be in touch with you early next week, if not today. I believe they'll need to be in around noon to set-up their equipment. That should cover everything." She stood abruptly, ending the meeting, and extended her hand. "Thank you again for seeing me on such short notice."

A little taken aback by the swiftness with which she'd concluded things, Eve stood as well. Lillian's handshake was firm, a match for her no-nonsense personality. "It was good to meet you."

"And you. I'd stay longer, but my son is waiting for me in the lobby. I promised I'd take him to a matinee at the Crowne Theater." Her face softened at the mention of her son. So different from the stiff business demeanor she'd displayed while discussing her husband's birthday celebration. There'd been no glimmer of anticipation or excitement over the party in her voice. How odd.

"I'll walk you to the lobby."

Stepping from the office, Eve spied a thin boy seated on the couch in front of the windows, a book open on his lap. When he spied his mother behind Eve, he immediately scrambled to his feet.

"Ready, Mom?" His expression was eager as he raced across the lobby.

"In a minute. Jeremy say hello to Miss Parrish."

"Hello, Miss Parrish." The boy smiled politely. He had the same straw-colored hair as his mother, his eyes a darker blue. Eve guessed his age around twelve, though there was something about him that made him seem older. A seriousness in his expression and the way he carried himself. "Mom's taking me to see *Raiders of the Lost Ark.* I never get tired of it."

"That sounds like fun." She'd seen the movie last year when it was originally released and had noticed the Crowne Theater was rerunning it as a matinee. "I hope you both enjoy yourself."

Lillian turned to face her. "Please don't hesitate to call if there's anything else you need in relation to Roger's party."

"I'll do that." Eve walked them to the door, then said goodbye. When she turned back into the lobby, Katie stood behind the reception counter, shaking her head.

"What?" Eve asked.

"You've met the ice queen."

Eve crossed to the counter. "She didn't seem that bad. Just…" She searched for the right word. "Serious."

"Stiff," Katie corrected. "If she cracked a smile, her face would split."

"I take it you don't like her."

Katie shrugged indifferently. "Let's just say she doesn't have a high opinion of me. I'll be glad when her husband's birthday bash is over."

"Well, she just switched the order from a buffet to a split entrée, and I need to talk to you about the changes. Let's chat out here. It's nicer than my office. I'll get the paperwork." She started to turn away, then stopped. "I forgot to ask…did you hear from your mom today?"

Amos Carter's murder had made the front page of the *Point Pleasant Herald* and was the talk of the town.

Katie nodded. "She's doing as well as can be expected, holed up at home with a box of tissues and a carton of cigarettes. I'm trying to be sympathetic, but I don't know why she loved Amos so much when he cheated on her and beat her up."

Eve flinched. She couldn't imagine any woman staying with a man who treated her so horrendously.

"I think she just liked the security of having a man around," Katie said with a disgusted shake of her head. "As if she can't make a go of it on her own. My mom's always been that way. She needs a man in her life, but somehow she always manages to attract the ones who treat her like dirt."

"I'm sorry."

"Not your fault, or your problem." Katie often came bluntly to the point. "I'd rather forget about it and concentrate on the changes Mrs. Layton wants."

"I'll get the paperwork." Eve felt a sense of relief. She didn't plan on staying in Point Pleasant for any length of time, and thus couldn't afford to become involved in the emotional complications of others, but she felt badly for Katie. The girl had obviously led a hard life and had a rocky relationship with her mother. Too bad Wendy had taken off all those years ago. Having her sister as an ally would have been a buffer for Katie and her mother.

As Eve stepped into her office to gather the folder on the Layton party, she couldn't help wonder if Wendy might someday return.

* * * *

Eve finished the afternoon by meeting with James Dixon of River Real Estate. The appointment gave her a chance to introduce herself and get his opinion of the real estate market in Point Pleasant. Between the lingering recession and high interest rates, few people were buying.

James conceded she had valid worries about the market, but felt strongly the house had enough history in the community to draw serious prospects. He suggested she contact him again after Caden completed all the necessary repairs. In the meantime, he'd "comp" other properties in the area for recent sales, though he cautioned there would be few. They discussed the hotel, but she remained on the fence about selling. Adam Barnett hadn't contacted her again, which made her wonder if his buyer had fallen through. Perhaps it was for the best.

By the time she reached the house, Caden had finished work for the day and left. She discovered Aunt Rosie's former dark room completely drywalled and taped, ready for spackling, sanding, and paint.

Returning downstairs, she dropped her purse on the kitchen table, then searched in the refrigerator for a soda. The phone rang as she poured a one-calorie Tab into a tall glass filled with ice.

"Hello?"

"Hello, Eve. This is Adam Barnett."

"Oh." Stretching the phone cord to the table, she sat down with her soda. "I was just thinking about you. I met with James Dixon, and we discussed the hotel."

"I'm glad to hear that. I spoke with my client and have a generous offer for you. I think you'll be quite pleased."

"Really?" Then why did her stomach clench? She twisted the phone cord, listening to him rattle on about the unlikelihood of finding a buyer able to raise the necessary capital for so large an investment. His client, however, was preapproved and would have no problems delivering on the loan. Wasn't she lucky?

When he told her the price his client was willing to pay, her heart gave a skip of alarm. Granted, she didn't know the going rate for an operation like the Parrish Hotel, but the offer seemed incredibly generous. Far more than she'd imagined.

"Eve? Miss Parrish?"

Awkwardly, she cleared her throat. "Yes. I, uh…"

"I realize you'll probably want time to consider."

"I do." *And then some.*

"That seems fair. I should warn you, however, that my client is looking at multiple business opportunities in various areas. The Parrish Hotel is only one of those. I can't guarantee how long he's willing to wait."

"I understand. Truthfully, though, Mr. Barnett, I'm having second thoughts about selling."

The pause that unraveled across the line felt weighted with displeasure. "I thought you were going back to Harrisburg?"

"I am. I may." Wedging the phone between her shoulder and neck, Eve dug a pen from her purse and scribbled the offered price on a paper napkin. "That doesn't mean I can't maintain the hotel from a distance. I've hired Katie Lynch as my manager, and I'm learning the operations. There's a chance I may elect to keep it."

"This comes as quite a surprise." Annoyance crept into his voice.

"I realize that, and I'm sorry for any trouble I've put you through, or any false hope I may have given your client. Give me a few days to think it over, and I'll get back to you. I'm not decided either way."

"Very well, Miss Parrish. Do consider carefully. I don't believe you'll get another offer in this price range."

"I understand. Thank you again."

After she hung up the phone, Eve sat for a moment pondering the proposal. Why *would* anyone make such a generous offer? There was no question the hotel was a landmark, but she hadn't thought it near the price Adam Barnett's client was willing to pay. Perhaps Mr. Barnett's buyer was a business savvy entrepreneur who saw hidden opportunity in the property.

She sighed and took a sip of her Tab, knowing Aunt Rosie and her father would frown on the sale.

Carrying the soda with her, she stepped onto the screened porch overlooking the rear of the property. A pleasant June breeze perfumed the air with the candied scent of honeysuckle and sun-warmed grass. White wicker furniture with plump pink cushions made the screened-in area inviting. Despite the vandals using the porch as their point of entry, there'd been little damage to the furniture, the trespassers more intent on the house.

Farther away, the rear yard ended at a small creek bordered by a wooded copse. How she and Maggie used to love to play along that streambed, splashing through the water in the summer, ice-skating on the narrow ribbon in the winter.

As she stood contemplating the scene, a flicker of movement passed between the trees. Someone walked along the creek bed, then paused to face the house. The person was too far away for her to decipher their features, but she saw a shape—tall and broad-shouldered, wearing a dark gray or green shirt.

A prickle of cold danced up her spine as she recalled the person she'd caught watching the house her first night in Point Pleasant. The man—

for surely it was a man—waited several heartbeats before continuing away from her. By that time, her hands were damp with sweat, her heart hammering a staccato beat.

It was probably just someone out for a stroll.

In Aunt Rosie's backyard.

The shrill ring of the phone made her jerk in fright before she identified the cause of the interruption. Probably Mr. Barnett again. With a nervous laugh over her jumpy nerves, she returned to the kitchen and lifted the receiver. "Hello."

For several seconds there was nothing but silence, then the ominous stillness was eaten up by a high-pitched shriek. When the innocuous looking instrument spewed a burst of static and clacking, she slammed it into the cradle.

"This is ridiculous." She wasn't certain who she spoke to, only that her heart had lurched into hyper-drive and she was shaking.

Kids.

Ryan had said the same about the note on her windshield. School was almost out and kids were playing pranks as if it were Halloween. Or maybe it was just a wrong number with electronic turmoil caught up on the line. Tomorrow, she'd insist the phone company check her service to be sure nothing was wrong.

Biting her lip, she considered the man she'd seen watching from the woods. He couldn't possibly have reached a phone and made a call that quickly. The whole thing was just a coincidence. He'd been out for a stroll, maybe followed the creek into Aunt Rosie's backyard from farther down the stream, and the phone call was a malfunction in the line.

That made sense…far better than the alternative, which meant she had not one stalker, but two.

* * * *

Eve put the incident from her mind when she met Caden later that night. He wore jeans and a plain white T-shirt, the red marks angled across his forearm plainly visible. When they arrived at the River Café, several people waved or called greetings. It seemed most everyone knew him, the casual familiarity making her feel as if she'd stepped under a spotlight. She tried not to count the stares as they slid into a booth near the bar. Small towns and gossip went hand in hand.

"You seem quite popular," she said after Betty, their waitress, took their drink orders and left them to look over the menu. Eve already knew it by heart.

Caden apparently did, too. He barely glanced at it before setting it aside.

"You must do a lot of remodeling jobs," she commented.

He shook his head with a thin smile. "I only started the business eighteen months ago. Before that I worked for the sheriff's department."

"Like Ryan?" Surprise slipped into her voice. It seemed odd he'd given up a steady career in law enforcement for a business that was subject to the ups and downs of the economy.

"We used to share a car," Caden confirmed. "I went through the police academy first; he followed when he was old enough. It worked for a while." He trailed off, leaving her with the impression he didn't want to continue.

From the bar, she overheard snatches of conversation as three men discussed Amos Carter over draft beers. "TNT...heard someone made soup of his face...catch the bastard...weird shit out by those ponds..."

She tuned it out, still unnerved by the thought of murder in the quiet town.

"Why did you leave?" she asked.

He shrugged indifferently. "Bad call." Tension crept into his shoulders, and the corner of his mouth tightened with the shadow of a grimace.

Waffling on whether or not she should pry further, she glanced at the three blood-red lines angled across the forearm Those marks, so odd in coloration and appearance, might have had something to do with his "bad call."

He caught her staring and tilted his head to indicate his arm. "From an accident a long time ago."

Her gaze flashed to his face. She could think of only one accident that defined life in Point Pleasant. "The Silver Bridge?"

He nodded. "My wrist was trapped, pinned under the seat."

His wrist. Yet the marks were on his forearm. Before she could prod further, the front door banged open and two men spilled into the café, jabbering excitedly between them. In their mid-twenties, one with copper-colored hair, the other brown, they quickly claimed spots at the bar.

In no time, the three men who'd been discussing Amos Cater were glued to the newcomers' every word. The one with copper-colored hair gestured animatedly with his hands, talking rapidly. Eve overheard "Mothman" and "TNT."

"What do you think that's about?" she asked Caden.

"I don't know, but I intend to find out. Hey, Duncan—over here." He motioned to the young man with red hair, waving him to their table. Without hesitation, the man bounded to Caden's side, his face ruddy from excitement.

"What's going on?" Caden asked.

"You ain't heard?" Duncan ping-ponged a glance between Caden and Eve. "Me and Donnie were out at the TNT. Wanted to try some fishing. Thought maybe we'd hook into a giant mutant fish with all the talk about contaminants and a Superfund site. You know…screwed up genetic shit the government wants to keep off the radar." He talked swiftly, gulping air.

Something definitely had him rattled. Eve bit her lip. The US Government was mired in the mysteries and legends of Point Pleasant every bit as much as the Mothman, Chief Cornstalk, and the countless UFOs once rumored to haunt the area. Some people even believed the Mothman was an alien brought to Earth by a government experiment gone haywire. Secretive "men in black" had frequently haunted the streets of Point Pleasant after the Mothman first appeared, but they'd vanished as mysteriously as the TNT's infamous bird once the Silver Bridge fell.

"What did you find?" Caden titled his head, skepticism in his gaze. "A two-headed fish?"

"Hell, no!" Duncan's voice lurched up an octave, cracking with enthusiasm. "We saw the Mothman."

Caden blanched. "What?"

Duncan nodded empathically. "Donnie saw it, too. We were about to call it quits. Headed back to the car. Wanted to grab a beer in here, you know? Then we heard it…kinda like, I don't know…a windstorm or something. There was a funny buzzing in my head. I looked back and saw it coming straight at us with those glowing red eyes. Thought I'd shit myself."

"Maybe some kind of big bird, huh?" Caden ventured, his voice strained.

"No way." Duncan gave another vigorous shake of his head. "It flew over us and disappeared into the trees. Once we got our act together, Donnie and I tried to track it, but we couldn't find anything. I'm telling you, Caden, the Mothman is back." With a triumphant grin, Duncan smacked his hand on the tabletop, then quickly bounded back to the bar where Donnie was still engrossed in sharing their story.

"Great." Caden rubbed his eyes. "Just what we need. Sheriff Weston and Ryan already have their hands full looking for Amos Carter's killer. Now they're going to have every lunatic with a gun scouring the TNT like they did in '66."

"You really don't think people will take them seriously?" Eve asked.

"With enough enthusiasm and stupidity, there'll be plenty of takers."

Betty returned with their drinks—beer for Caden, white wine for Eve—and asked if they were ready to order. After writing down their selections, she gathered up the menus with a shake of her head. "I guess you heard all that fuss Duncan and Donnie Bradley are making."

"You don't believe it?" Eve asked.

"Honey, I wouldn't believe those two if they said President Reagan was handing out free cash to any bum with a wallet." A fiftyish woman who'd worked at the café when Eve was a little girl, Betty tucked her order pad into the pocket of her apron with familiar ease. "I remember when they said Tom Park's dog got mangled fighting off some kind of an ape-creature. Turns out the poor thing blundered into a barbed wire fence. Anyway…" She smiled. "Welcome back to Point Pleasant."

Caden gave a weary exhale as she moved away. "I bet you didn't have UFOs, Mothmen, and ape-creatures in Harrisburg."

"I'm afraid the best we can manage is the Susquehanna River, but it doesn't even have a water monster." She took a sip of her wine. At the bar, Duncan and Donnie were still carrying on about their experience in the TNT. She'd actually missed that kind of hokeyness—the chatter and gossip spun from campfire legends and faded folklore. As fun and silly as it could be, she hoped any new rumors of the Mothman wouldn't cause problems for Ryan. And there was nothing remotely hokey about Amos Carter's murder.

After that they reminisced about events from childhood—watching boat launchings at Bruce Mechanical, visiting the soda bar at G. C. Murphy's, how they'd liked or disliked a particular teacher from school. The topics were general, what Eve considered safe. There was no mention of the Silver Bridge, Maggie, or Caden's mother. He avoided talking about why he'd left the police force, and she didn't press, sensing he preferred to keep the conversation light.

When dinner ended, they strolled the short distance to the riverfront, passing through a large opening between the flood walls. It unfolded on a long dirt path that stretched several hundred yards to Tu-Endie-Wei State Park at the southern end of town. As a kid, she remembered riding her bike with Maggie and Sarah, following that track along the river. Tonight, a couple dozen people meandered along the path and grassy riverbanks, several with dogs, a few women pushing strollers. A jogger passed them, and several boys on bicycles whizzed past. Farther up and off to the side, a group of kids tossed a ball back and forth. She noticed Sam Lynch and Jeremy Layton among them. The entire scene was casual and leisurely.

Glancing to the spot where the Silver Bridge had once stood, she experienced a flash of melancholy. It was strange not to see the towers erected against the sky. Muddy from rains upriver, the water carried a deep orange tint, reflected from the evening sun. A riverboat chugged down the waterway pushing two enormous barges laden with coal, destined for the Ohio side.

Eventually, she and Caden wandered to a flat area that housed a portable platform shaded with a blue backdrop. The stage was already set with guitars, sound equipment, and microphones. Nearby, a number of people had set up lawn chairs or spread blankets on the ground in anticipation of the coming concert.

Caden introduced her to Glen Moore and Wyatt Fisher, friends of his since high school. She remembered Glen, but Wyatt was a few years older. He'd already been in the workforce, hauling coal, when she was still in junior high.

"Got a couple of chairs set aside for you," Wyatt told Caden, earning a thumbs-up from his friend.

A half hour later, Eve settled into one of the chairs as the two guitarists launched into a set of acoustic music. She liked the mix—everything from Dan Fogelberg and Kenny Rogers to Bob Seger and Alabama.

"They're good," she told Caden after listening for a while.

Seated beside her, he nodded vacantly. Although he tapped the fingers of one hand lightly against his knee, he didn't seem to be paying attention. Several songs later when the duo launched into a rendition of "Never My Love," he stood and took her hand. "Let's go for a walk."

She was tempted to question if anything was wrong, but the look on his face made her hold her tongue. He led her back down the dirt path and through the opening in the flood walls toward the Parrish Hotel. "Caden is something wrong?"

He shook his head. "Do you mind if we just walk for a while?"

"Okay." It was certainly a beautiful night, the sun starting to set, shading Main Street in dusky strokes of antique gold. They turned the corner at the hotel where a few guests reclined in rockers on the broad front porch, then continued down the sidewalk toward the Crowne Theater. It was the same path she'd taken with Sarah Sherman the night the Silver Bridge collapsed.

"That song," Caden said. "'Never My Love' was playing on the radio when Maggie died. We were on the bridge, stuck in traffic. It was the last thing I heard before the bridge fell. To this day, every time I hear it, I flash back to that night."

"Oh, Caden, I'm sorry." What a dreadful reminder of a tragic event. Ryan had said he was plagued by guilt. If only he'd talk about that night, about Maggie.

"Little things set off my memory of that night, too." She hoped her honesty would help. "Even this walk toward the theater. Sarah and I were headed this way when we heard the bridge go down." Admitting it brought a knot to her gut. "I knew my father was coming back from Gallipolis and prayed he wasn't on it, but something inside told me he was. They found him in the debris pile on the Ohio side, his car crushed."

She looked straight ahead, watching the dancing flicker of lights from the Crowne's marquee. A few people stood in line at the ticket booth waiting to see the *Star Trek* movie, *The Wrath of Khan*. "Sometimes that night and everything that happened—the bridge and the screams. It seems like a dream." She turned to gaze up at him. "My life changed when that bridge went down. I understand what you're feeling."

He nodded somberly. "I forget that you lost someone, too."

"Maggie looked up to you, Caden."

"Not that night."

Somewhere on Viand, a horn blared. Caden released her hand and raked his fingers through his hair. The action was brisk and agitated. "I couldn't protect her. I told her I would. I promised nothing would hurt her."

"You couldn't stop a bridge from falling."

"I shouldn't have coerced her into going out."

"You couldn't foresee what was going to happen."

"You don't understand." He shook his head, stopping on the sidewalk to face her. "I got her out because I thought it was the right thing to do. She was terrified of the Mothman. She believed me when I said I'd protect her."

No wonder Ryan said his brother tortured himself with memories. She met his gaze squarely. "Caden, nearly everyone who fell into the water that night died. There were only a handful of survivors."

"And I was one of them." He snapped the words in anger. Exhaling, he lowered his voice. "I'm sorry, Eve. I shouldn't vent to you like this. I don't know why I am."

"I want to help you." She placed a hand on his chest, staring up into his eyes, gray like the twilight around them. "Maggie was my best friend. She wouldn't want you to feel guilty about what happened."

"You don't know all of it." He slumped against the building behind him.

"Then tell me."

He considered for a moment, his mouth a tight line. "All right," he agreed at last. She listened as he relayed what happened that night, then shook her head. "I don't understand what you want me to see."

"Isn't it obvious? If I hadn't stopped for cigarettes and spent those fifteen minutes bullshitting with Wyatt, Maggie and I would have been across the bridge before it collapsed. I haven't smoked a cigarette since that night and never will."

"Caden, stop it. You can't lay that kind of guilt on yourself."

"Why not?" He was suddenly bitter. "My mother does."

She flinched. "You don't mean…"

"That she blames me?" He laughed, a harsh sound. "She might not come straight out and say it, but the message is clear."

"But you can't go by that. Ryan said she hasn't been the same since Maggie died. That she imagines things. You don't even know if it's really her talking…in her right mind."

"So it seems you know all of my family's dirty secrets." He sighed. "Tonight hasn't exactly turned out like I'd planned. I promised you a nice dinner and a concert at the riverfront. Instead, we get gossip about the Mothman, and I dump my problems on you."

"I wouldn't say that." She tilted her head slightly, smiling slyly. "The stuffed chicken was good. Then again, I own the café."

He grinned and hooked an arm around her shoulders, steering her back the way they had come. "Let's go back to the concert. We can still catch the last hour."

She leaned against him, slipping an arm around his waist. It felt comfortable and natural. "I like the sound of that."

* * * *

Caden liked the way she fit into his side and the floral scent of her hair. She didn't over tease the style like many women today, loading it with hairspray until it was an over-processed mass. The more time he spent with her, the more he grew attracted to her. She was down to earth, sensible, and caring. Which was why he shouldn't have unloaded all that garbage about the bridge and Maggie.

His guilt had nothing to do with Eve. She'd been his sister's friend, nothing more. Maybe it was her tie to Maggie that had prompted him to spill his guts. That and bad timing. Glen and Wyatt hadn't known about the song—he'd never told anyone—but it had set him off, releasing an avalanche of old memories.

The best thing he could do now was to try to salvage the remainder of the night. It wasn't like Eve would be around much longer. Eventually, she would pack up and return to Harrisburg. There was no question he'd miss her. At the very least, he wanted to get to know her better in the time remaining.

As they rounded the corner of the hotel, heading down the side street to the river, Eve gave a small gasp.

"What's wrong?" he asked.

"My car." She pointed to a red Corolla parked a few feet away. "Not again."

He understood what she meant immediately. A slip of paper fluttered under the edge of a wiper blade where it was wedged against the window. "Stay here."

He raced toward the riverfront where a few people strolled through the gap in the flood walls. Nothing looked out of the ordinary. A young mother pushed a stroller, her husband at her side, holding the hand of their toddling daughter. The group of kids they'd seen earlier tossing a ball were camped around the corner, shooting marbles. A man walked his dog, heading up the other side of the street, and a group of women talked companionably several feet away.

Caden stopped, looking back toward Eve. She was already peeling the note from the windshield. "Hey kids," he called to the group of boys. "You see anyone strange around here? Anyone who might have been messing with the cars parked along the side?"

The boys exchanged a glance among themselves. "No, sir." The Layton kid, polite as hell and a little too mollycoddled by his mother. Probably why she and the other women chatted nearby where it was easy to keep an eye on their kids.

One of the other boys giggled. Sam Lynch, Katie's kid. He was younger than the rest, but they let him tag along. "We saw Fred Markle and some girl kissing over there." He pointed across the street behind the Post Office and made smooching sounds. "Looked like they were glued together. Does that help?"

"'Fraid not." No doubt the boys had enjoyed a good laugh about the make-out session. He flipped a wave in parting and sprinted back to Eve's side.

"I almost wish it were a parking ticket," he said. He also wished she hadn't touched it, likely smudging any traceable fingerprints.

Silently, she extended the slip of paper to him. He took it carefully by the corner, his gaze dropping to the typewritten words in the center: *If you don't leave, you'll end up like Amos Carter.*

"That's it." The game had turned deadly. "We're going to see Ryan, and this time, he's damn well going to listen."

* * * *

Eve was scared. She wouldn't admit it, but Caden could sense the change in her. Before, she'd been ready to believe the original note a prank. Even though she'd had him install a deadbolt on the back door, she'd clearly hoped it was an unnecessary precaution. Now, any remaining doubts had been tossed out the window. Even Ryan had to take the threat seriously.

Caden watched as she wandered away to pour a cup of coffee.

The sheriff's office was busier than usual. Duncan and Donnie's story had spread through town, prompting numerous phone calls from concerned citizens worried the Mothman had returned. Coupled with Amos Carter's murder, the rumors had the usually sedate office operating on double-time. Only a handful of desks compromised the work area, but each was presently occupied by a deputy or harried clerical employee, answering phones and relaying calls to dispatch. The air smelled of stale coffee, cigarette smoke, and typewriter ink.

Still seated by his brother's desk, Caden leaned forward. "Let me know if the lab is able to determine anything from the note. It's a long shot, but they might be able to lift a print or two."

Ryan nodded, setting the plastic evidence bag containing the note aside. "I'll keep you updated. I know you're worried about Eve." A glimmer of self-chastisement flickered through his eyes. "I should have been more attentive the first time. I really thought the whole thing was a prank." Expelling a breath, he slumped in his chair.

Caden knew he'd been working around the clock since Amos's body had been found. Murder in a small town like Point Pleasant put everyone on edge. Even worse, there was no information forthcoming to pacify the public. Toss in the Mothman, and the last thing the department needed were notes threatening more violence.

"I didn't want to say anything in front of Eve…" Caden looked across the room to make sure she was still occupied by the coffee pot. "But I'm starting to wonder if whoever wrote the notes could be the same person who killed Amos."

"Shit." Ryan scrubbed a hand over his face. "My gut would have me believe differently—it's just somebody using Amos's murder as an example of what could happen if Eve doesn't leave— but there's one thing that bothers me."

"Only one?"

Ryan grinned tightly, then leaned forward, growing serious. He lowered his voice. "Everything started when Eve came to town. I could just be reaching, trying to connect the dots. Maybe Amos getting offed has nothing to do with it, but the timing is awfully coincidental. And then there's the vandalism to Rosie's house."

"That happened before Eve came back."

Ryan seemed to consider. "If that's the case, it would mean the chain of events started with Rosie's death."

Caden thought about it. What could Rosie's death possibly have to do with Amos Carter?

"If the house wasn't vandalized, it means someone took it apart looking for something." Caden shot another glance across the room. Eve was still at the coffee pot, holding a Styrofoam cup as she talked with one of the female clerks. She looked tired, worn down. No wonder, considering they'd been at the station a good two hours. Outside, darkness had claimed the sky, night blanketing Point Pleasant in a thick charcoal cloak.

"Why would someone want to scare Eve away?" He was quiet for a moment before continuing. "Katie Lynch told Eve she was with Rosie at the end. She said Rosie kept mumbling she was sorry for something she'd done earlier in life."

Ryan frowned. "Such as?"

"That's the million dollar question. She was delirious. Katie said she mentioned 'gray vines' several times."

Ryan gave a disgusted grunt. "Sounds like gibberish to me."

"What if it means something?"

"Like what?"

"Hell, I don't know." He was getting irritated now. "You're the sheriff's sergeant. Figure it out."

"Caden."

"All right." He held up a hand, knowing he was dangerously close to crossing the line. Ryan was already stretched thin with Amos's murder. He didn't need attitude on top of it. "Sorry. We're both on a short fuse. All I know is I couldn't protect Maggie. I'm not about to let something happen to Eve."

Ryan glanced across the room as she approached, carrying her coffee. "Maybe the best thing you can do is convince her to leave."

And that was the hell of it. He didn't want her to go.

* * * *

Eve stood on the front porch of the Flynn home, Caden at her side, an overnight bag in her hand. A light breeze carried the scent of clover and sweet June honeysuckle, somehow muskier with the fall of twilight. Several streets removed, the drone of traffic kept up a steady hum in the night.

"I feel silly about this. Aunt Rosie's house is right next door," she protested. "I'll be fine."

"Probably, but why take chances?" He gave her a gentle smile, weakening her resolve.

Initially, Ryan had been the one to suggest she stay overnight at the Flynn home. He was going to be stuck at the station and needed Caden to stay with their mother. Eve had insisted she didn't need a babysitter, but eventually caved when Caden added his persuasion to Ryan's.

"What about your mom?"

"My mother will be fine with having a houseguest. She'll enjoy the company."

"You don't have to go to all this trouble for me." She felt her cheeks heat with warmth, thankful for the darkness.

"It's no trouble."

Taking her by surprise, he kissed her softly. The sensation sent a wave of pleasure through her, the kiss so unexpected, she froze.

Drawing back, he stared down at her. "I probably shouldn't have done that."

"No." A heady breath rattled her lungs. "I…I'm glad you did." A thousand butterflies took flight in her stomach, leaving her light-headed. "The truth is…I was hoping you would."

"That makes all the difference." His eyes were bright as polished metal in the moonlight. Raising his hand, he stroked the back of his fingers down her cheek. When he touched his lips to hers a second time, she sighed and folded against him.

For the moment, all her fears instilled by the note melted away.

* * * *

"I'm not crazy or even senile," Elizabeth Flynn told her ten minutes later with a matter-of-fact stare. Eve sat in the living room with the older woman while Caden left to carry her overnight bag upstairs and make a few phone calls related to his construction business. On the TV, Suzanne Somers and Joyce DeWitt traded innuendo with John Ritter on *Three's Company,* a buzz of chatter in the background overlaid with a muffled laugh track.

Eve had hoped to make small talk about the weather, but Caden's mother clearly had other ideas. The moment her son stepped from the room, she zeroed in on the subject of her deceased daughter.

"Caden and Ryan don't believe me." A book of crossword puzzles lay open in Mrs. Flynn's lap, her hands folded neatly on the dog-eared pages. Prim and proper, she appeared dressed for a summer tea party, wearing smartly pleated beige slacks and a cranberry blouse with pink speckles.

"Maggie visits me in my dreams. Sometimes she shares things. Like when she told me you were coming back."

Eve wet her lips, uncertain what to say. Caden would have her believe his mother was senile, but she seemed in perfect command of her wits. And even Eve had dreamed of Maggie her second night in Aunt Rosie's house. A tremor of anxiety prickled her nerves. It would be so much easier to prattle about the mild summer they were having or join in the frivolity of the laugh track on *Three's Company.*

She stole a glance at the TV, hoping John Ritter would do something outrageous to distract Mrs. Flynn. Instead, Caden's mother continued as though she had Eve's complete attention.

"She wants you to sort it out. Something is preventing her from passing to the next life. She's been trapped here so very long." Shaking her head, she dropped her gaze to her hands and fiddled with her pencil. Her fingers were bony and bird-like. Maybe she wasn't crazy, but she looked frail to Eve, as if a strong wind would blow her away.

"It took them six months to find her body," Mrs. Flynn said, a catch in her voice. "And then…and then she just wasn't Maggie. My Maggie."

Eve was drawn into the discussion despite her reluctance. "I remember the searches." The Army Corp of Engineers had set up a basecamp, overseeing operations as search and rescue boats dragged the river. Even when the center eventually closed, local townspeople continued combing the icy waters with their boats.

"I kept hoping they'd find her." Mrs. Flynn spoke in a hushed tone as if her words reopened painful wounds. "After that first night, I knew she was never coming home, but I wanted my baby for burial." Tears bright in her eyes, she swiped a trembling finger beneath her lashes and looked at Eve. "Caden was determined to find her. As soon as he was able, he was there day and night, participating in the official search. When the Army left, he kept looking. I didn't think he'd ever stop. Finally, my husband made him quit. It was hard enough losing Maggie but seeing Caden tear himself up night after night…it was like we lost two children. He blames himself."

"He thinks you blame him, too." She was no doubt sticking her nose where it didn't belong, but couldn't let the opportunity pass. Not when Mrs. Flynn was talking so openly.

The older woman fiddled with her pencil, the thin yellow barrel riddled with teeth marks as though it had been chewed repeatedly. Sucking her bottom lip between her teeth, she refocused on the crossword puzzle book pillowed in her lap.

"A five-letter word for temperate," she said without looking at Eve.

"Mrs. Flynn?"

"Mild is too short, isn't it? Perhaps balmy?"

"Elizabeth?" Eve persisted.

Caden's mother met her gaze. "I did blame him for a time. I needed someone to be responsible, and he was an easy target."

Eve was tempted to ask how a mother could do such a thing, but restrained herself. Her expression must have betrayed her feelings.

"I know what you're thinking." Mrs. Flynn smoothed a hand over her slacks. On the TV, *Three's Company* had been replaced by a breezy sailboat inspired commercial for Hawaiian Punch. "How could a mother treat her son that way? I ask myself the same thing."

"You need to change it. He thinks you still blame him. You can ease his guilt."

The older woman shook her head. "No. Maggie said it has to be you. I've done too much damage for Caden to accept anything from me. It's up to you to find the answers."

Eve drew back, exasperated. It was far from easy conversing with a woman who believed she was in communication with her daughter's ghost. "What answers?"

"About what happened that night."

Eve thought back to what Caden had told her. "Caden took Maggie Christmas shopping. On the way back, he stopped at a gas station to buy a pack of cigarettes and ended up chatting with a friend while Maggie waited in the car."

"Fifteen minutes."

"You know the story?"

"Yes. He hasn't smoked a day since."

"Then you know they got stuck in traffic on the bridge. It collapsed and he blacked out." It felt unjustly apathetic to reduce such a horrific night to a few blunt images, but she plowed ahead. "He said he didn't see Maggie when he came to. He was in the water, clinging to debris when someone pulled him out."

"There's more to the story."

"What more could there possibly be?"

Mrs. Flynn twined her hands together. "I wish I knew. I only know what Maggie tells me in my dreams. You've dreamt of her, too."

Eve recoiled, knowing she hadn't shared that particular nugget of information with anyone.

"Maggie said it's all related," Mrs. Flynn persisted.

Perhaps the woman *was* crazy. "What is?"

"Caden, the Silver Bridge, the Mothman…even your Aunt Rosie. It all goes back to that night."

Eve felt like someone had punched her in the gut. There it was again—that strange connection. How was her Aunt Rosie involved?

Did you really see the Mothman?

Your Aunt Rosie knows.

"Mrs. Flynn, please. If you know something, you need to tell me. Someone has vandalized Aunt Rosie's house and left me threatening notes. I don't understand why."

"It has to do with the Lynch girl."

Eve gaped, blindsided. "Katie?"

"No. The other one. The one who ran away."

"Wendy?"

"Yes. I don't understand it myself. I just hear what Maggie tells me."

"Mrs. Flynn…"

The older woman yawned. Inhaling deeply, she smiled as if waking from a trance. "It's late, isn't it?" She closed her crossword puzzle book. "I should probably head upstairs and call it a night."

They'd just spent ten minutes talking gibberish. Wendy Lynch had disappeared when Eve was twelve years old. Coincidentally, around the same time everything else happened—Maggie seeing the Mothman in the Witch Wood and the horrible tragedy of the Silver Bridge. How did Wendy running off tie in with the other events, and especially with Aunt Rosie?

Before she could ponder the matter further, Mrs. Flynn stood and patted her hand. "Talk to Katie. Maggie said that chat is overdue."

Chapter 7

Three days passed before Eve worked up the nerve to talk to Katie about her sister. During that time, she had dinner with Caden, enjoyed a girls' night out with Sarah, and made a firm decision to extend her stay in Point Pleasant another week. Her work supervisor in Harrisburg granted the leave without grumbling, but her mother was less amicable.

"I hope you're not entertaining the notion of staying in that dreadful town permanently," she'd lamented when Eve called to relay the news.

The two notes she'd received were proof someone plainly wanted her to leave—why, she had no idea—but she was starting to grow comfortable with her routine at the hotel. In reviewing the books, she realized she could pay herself a weekly salary almost equivalent to what she made as a Commonwealth employee in Pennsylvania. Toss in the fact the mortgage on Aunt Rosie's house was paid and she didn't have the worry of monthly rent. That more than compensated for her reduction in income. If she'd ever wanted to radically change her career path and future, Aunt Rosie had supplied the wherewithal to open a fresh door.

And then there was Caden. Their relationship was new and tenuous, but she wanted the luxury of time to explore their growing closeness.

He'd stayed at her home each night, camped out on the couch when she retired upstairs. Finally, she told him his over-protectiveness was silly. Ryan had found nothing new from the note, the only fingerprints lifted by the lab belonging to her and Caden. The strange phone calls she'd been receiving had stopped, and the phone company had reported they could find nothing wrong with her line. She'd intentionally avoided telling Caden about the calls, fearing he'd think them related to the notes. In her opinion, both were looking more like random pranks. Either way, she couldn't continue to worry about threats that might never materialize. Tonight, she planned to stay by herself. In the meantime, she wanted to talk to Katie about her sister.

Eve found her new friend and hotel manager in the ballroom.

The space looked lovely, a throwback to the days when Eve's parents had rented it out for wedding receptions and galas. A shower of sunlight spilled across the freshly waxed dance floor, trapped and reflected by the fiery crystals of the chandeliers overhead. Cream-colored linens adorned the tables, complemented by a swirl of butter-honey in the thick paisley carpet. She could almost envision her parents twirling across the floor, her mother laughing delightedly over her father's campy dance moves. How sad that her mom had once loved living in Point Pleasant, only to loathe the town and all it represented now.

"Roger Layton's party is still a week away, you know," she said as she entered.

Katie turned her attention from the notebook in her hand and offered a smile of greeting. "I know, but I wanted to make sure there was room on the stage for a podium. Lillian called earlier and added it to her new requests."

"There's more?" Eve slid into a seat at the nearest table.

Katie nodded. She wore her blond hair loose this morning, the straight locks tinted a becoming gold in the wash of sunlight streaming through the windows. "Podium, microphone, a champagne bucket for the head table, and two champagne flutes for her and Roger."

"Sounds like someone is going to be offering the birthday boy a toast," Eve commented.

Katie made a face. "With only the king and his queen getting a taste of the high-end stuff."

"You sound like you don't care for him."

"Don't get me started." Katie waved the observation aside. "What are you doing up here anyway? I thought you'd be in the office. Did you see I came up with a rotation schedule to keep the front desk covered even over lunch?"

Eve nodded. Katie had wasted no time in streamlining operations, ensuring business ran smoothly and professionally. No wonder Aunt Rosie had placed such faith in her. It was a shame Doreen Sue didn't realize her daughter's potential.

"You did a great job with that. Sharon's covering right now." Eve fingered the silky edge of a tablecloth, tempted to explore Katie's reaction to Roger—her father's note still bothered her—but decided to save that conversation for later.

"Why don't you sit down?" She motioned to a seat beside her.

"Uh-oh." Katie flashed a smile. "Don't tell me you're second guessing your decision about making me manager?"

Eve shook her head, appreciating the humor. Given their rocky start, it was surprising they could joke so easily. Even more surprising how wrong she'd been about Katie as a child. "I wanted to ask you about Wendy."

Katie blinked. "My sister?"

"Yes." She feared risking their newfound friendship, but decided to tell Katie everything that had happened to her.

"I know this is going to sound crazy." Taking a deep breath, she stepped off an imaginary cliff and relayed her experiences since returning to Point Pleasant—the odd phone calls, notes, even the shadowy figure of a man she'd glimpsed in the backyard on two occasions. She finished by relaying her conversation with Mrs. Flynn. "So, between the notes and the vandalism, I feel like someone is trying to scare me away. I wouldn't ask about Wendy—I know the memories have to be painful—but I'm running out of places to turn."

Katie swallowed hard, her fingers tightening around the notebook in her hands until her knuckles were white. At least she hadn't suggested Eve be committed to an asylum.

"Why would Mrs. Flynn say my sister is connected?" she asked. "Do you really believe she talks to Maggie?"

Eve hadn't wanted to go there. "I don't know, but I'm getting desperate in my attempts to understand what's happening…how Aunt Rosie was involved. I'm willing to try anything."

"What about the igloo at the TNT?"

"The what?"

"I'm surprised you don't remember." Katie wet her lips as if uncertain how her suggestion would be received. "The bunker where the Mothman was seen."

"I thought he was seen at the north power plant? Out by the fairgrounds?"

"The first time, but after that he haunted the igloos, too. Don't you remember how people used to flock to the area?"

Eve hadn't been to the TNT since she'd returned, but knew the old WWII igloos were recessed in the ground, their domes covered with grass and briars, many crowned by trees. They'd been constructed so the webs of foliage camouflaged them when viewed from the sky should an enemy plane breach US airspace. From what she understood, most were now accessible to the public; a few of the bunkers still housed archaic shells.

Caden had told her that occasionally one exploded, prompting the army to close that area of the TNT temporarily.

"What about the igloo?"

"Maybe you can find an answer there." Katie set her notebook aside, leaning forward to converse more urgently. "Eve, I'm worried about you. Especially after what happened to Amos. What if his murder is connected?"

She bit her lip, a sensation of dread unraveling in her stomach. "I've thought of that." More than she wanted to admit. God forbid if her mother ever learned the details. She'd insist Eve pack up and head home at once.

"Then you need to do whatever is necessary to stay safe," Katie persisted. "I know Caden and Ryan are looking out for you, but don't discount the igloo because it sounds silly. A lot of people believe there's some type of supernatural force or being inside."

"The Mothman?"

"No, something else." Katie looked thoughtful. "Connected to the Mothman, perhaps. A few local photographers, including Rosie, have taken shots that clearly show floating orbs."

"Are we talking ghosts?" The idea that her aunt had participated in what was, for all intents and purposes, a ghost hunt seemed absurd. Aunt Rosie was a free spirit—at least she had been before the Silver Bridge fell—but she'd never been one to embrace superstition or the supernatural.

"Maybe." Katie twisted the emerald ring on her finger. "I never wanted to examine the idea too closely. All I know is what I've heard. If you go inside and ask a question, 'something'" —she made air quotes with her fingers—"might answer."

"Did you ever go?"

Katie hesitated. Finally, she nodded. "I asked about Wendy. I never believed she ran away."

"Did you get an answer?"

"No, but I'm not sorry I made the effort."

Eve thought back to what she knew of Wendy. The girl had been sixteen when she vanished. She'd taken off once before, only to be brought back by the sheriff. Eve hated to ask, but had to state the obvious.

"What makes you think she didn't run away?"

Katie frowned. "My sister got in her share of trouble, but she would have told me if that's what she had planned. The first time she ran away, she confided in me. She said she was going to miss me, but was tired of all the men Mom trotted through the house. Of the way we lived. She said she had to get away. When she disappeared the last time, it was different. *She* was different."

"How so?"

"She was happy, upbeat. She hinted around about a new boyfriend, but said it was too soon to share the news. The next day she vanished."

"Did you tell the sheriff that?"

"Of course I did." Katie waved the notion aside in disgust. "But he'd already made up his mind about Wendy, just like everyone else in town. Sure, he and his deputies made a show of sniffing around and asking questions, but after a few days, they wrote her off as a runaway."

"Maybe it's possible she really did take off." That was a better alternative than thinking something might have happened to her.

Katie sucked on her bottom lip. "She would have tried to contact me by now. A letter or a phone call. Something. I can't even talk to my mom about her because she's convinced Wendy ran away, too. So last year I drove to the TNT and stood in that bunker night after night for a period of two weeks, asking the same question—'Where is my sister?' If there is something supernatural in the place, it didn't answer."

"And you still think I should go?"

Katie shrugged. "What will it hurt? If you buy into the idea Maggie is talking to her mother through dreams, and that your aunt and my sister are connected, why not give it a try? It's no more bizarre than anything else you've said."

That was the hard, crazy truth. She really had nothing to lose.

As she thought it over, the whir of a vacuum cleaner sprang to life in the hallway. Someone from housekeeping sweeping the carpet. No doubt they'd be poking their head into the ballroom, too.

"I'll go with you," Katie offered.

"Seriously?" The thought of having someone tag along made the prospect far more appealing. The TNT had always creeped her out as a kid. She hadn't been looking forward to venturing there alone, and she certainly couldn't tell Caden or Ryan. A tentative smile crossed her lips. "You'd really do that?"

Katie nodded. "I know what it feels like to be up against a wall, and I do believe your aunt was hiding something. As much as I loved her, Rosie had secrets."

"The gray vines."

"I'd forgotten about that." Katie laid her hand over Eve's on the table. "It has to be connected to the notes on your windshield. We need to find out what it means."

"We?"

Katie smiled. "I think we're in this together now."

* * * *

It was dark inside the igloo, the shadows in direct contrast to the afternoon light streaming from beyond the roughly hewn stone walls. Eve crossed the threshold, followed closely by Katie. A dank odor reminiscent of old metal, black earth, and mold greeted them. A shiver ran down her back as she thought of the ammunition once stored there and the contamination that had leached into the ground.

There were legends, too, folklore she'd heard as a child. It was said even George Washington had encountered strange phenomena when surveying these grounds prior to the Revolutionary War. It made her wonder if some ancient power lingered in unseen ley lines that crisscrossed the TNT.

Thankful she'd thought to bring a flashlight, Eve played the beam around the bunker, picking out splotches of graffiti—crudely scrawled names and dates, a reference or two to the Mothman, strange symbols she didn't recognize. Hopefully, they weren't satanic in origin. Blown away by the idea of Katie venturing here at night, she turned to her friend, impressed by her courage.

"What do we do?" The eerie hush of the surroundings caused Eve to whisper and sent a string of goose bumps scampering down her arm.

"Ask your question." Katie spoke just as quietly, as if she, too, was affected by the unnerving silence.

Uneasily, Eve raised her eyes to the darkened dome that arched above their heads. Even with the doors open, there was something claustrophobic about standing inside the bunker. She tried not to think of the creeping, crawling, and slithering things that might be lurking in the corners. Pitching her voice to carry, she addressed whatever manner of creature called the igloo home.

"I need to know about my Aunt Rosie." Her heart thundered a loud drumbeat in her ears.

No answer.

"A question," Katie whispered. "You have to ask a question."

Apparently even in the supernatural realm there were rules. Eve thought for a moment, focusing on the secret everyone seemed to think Aunt Rosie had taken to the grave. "What was my Aunt Rosie hiding?"

Silence reverberated through the dome. She waited, holding her breath, every muscle in her body tensed for flight should some malevolent power suddenly appear.

Katie looked at her wide-eyed. "Try something else."

Exhaling, she nodded. As creepy as it was, the visit was starting to feel like a waste of time. Did she really think she was going to receive an answer from a disembodied voice in an abandoned World War II ammunitions bunker? Still, she'd been desperate enough to entertain the notion, driving up here and trekking through the woods. She couldn't back out now.

"Maybe you're being too specific," Katie suggested. "Try something more general."

"Okay." Eve thought a second, then spoke in a clear voice. "Was my Aunt Rosie hiding something?"

Ten seconds of silence passed. She was about to brand the whole thing useless and suggest they leave when something moved behind her. Spinning, she stumbled backward with a gasp.

"Yes".

The voice was in her head, a rasping grate like dry wood scraping over pitted stone. The sense of *something* in the igloo grew, a presence that clotted the air and weighted her beneath a heavy shroud. A single glance at Katie revealed her friend felt it, too.

"Did you hear that?" Katie whispered, her eyes enormous in the darkness. "It said 'yes.' The answer was in my head."

"Mine, too." Her heartbeat ratcheted higher.

"Ask something else. There's something in here with us."

A fat slug of fear crawled to life in Eve's belly. Fresh goose bumps prickled her arms. If she dwelled on the unseen presence for any length of time, she'd end up shrieking and fleeing in terror.

Pretend it's a Ouija Board...like you used to play with Maggie and Sarah.

Rooted to the spot, she tried to quell the jackhammer thud of her heart. Aunt Rosie had hidden something, taking her secret to the grave. It had to be related to the vandalism.

"Is something hidden in Aunt Rosie's house? Something related to the secret?"

"Yes."

The answer came quickly this time, delivered in the same scratchy murmur.

Stifling a mushrooming bubble of terror, Eve forced herself to continue. Not only had the air grown thicker, it had grown colder, too. She feared her teeth would chatter and make her appear more frightened than she was. "Is it still there?"

"Yes."

Would the being share more than a single word answer? "Can you tell me what it is?"

Silence.

Katie touched her hand, mouthed the words *my sister*.

"Was Aunt Rosie's secret related to Wendy Lynch?" Eve asked.

"Yes."

Beside her, Katie made a choked sound and raised a hand to her mouth. "Did my sister run away?" she blurted.

Silence. When it dragged on for ten seconds, Katie nodded to Eve. "You ask it."

Was it possible only one person could speak to the entity at a time? Dear God, *what* had they summoned? "Did Wendy Lynch run away?"

The silence dragged, all-encompassing, like a weight pressing from above. It built in Eve's chest, sparking a sickening realization. If Wendy didn't run away, only a single alternative remained. She hated voicing it, but Katie deserved to know one way or the other. "Is Wendy Lynch alive?"

"No."

Katie gave a choked cry. "What?" She gripped Eve's arm, her fingers tightening in hopelessness and fear. "That can't be." Panicked, she looked to Eve.

"I'm so sorry. But it explains what you said about Wendy." She tried to soften the blow. "You said she was different those last few days, excited about her new boyfriend. A person like that doesn't pick up and run away."

Katie looked desperate, tears glimmering in her eyes. "Unless that boyfriend asked her to leave with him."

Eve wrapped an arm around her shoulders. Her friend was shivering, too. "I'm sorry, Katie. I don't think that's the case." The air thinned as if the thing in the bunker prepared to withdraw. The sense of pressure diminished, the air warming with its departure.

"Don't go," Eve cried. There was so much more they needed to know. Somehow Aunt Rosie was tied to Wendy Lynch and her death. What had she been hiding? What had she known?

"Was Wendy murdered?" If the girl was no longer living and hadn't run away, odds were she'd either died accidentally or was killed. Maybe Amos Carter's death was too fresh in her mind, or maybe she was just traumatized by the thought of speaking to a supernatural entity, but Eve immediately latched onto the uglier possibility.

The air thickened again and an icy finger of cold swirled around Eve's throat. The silence lasted barely a second.

"Yes."

At her side, Katie wept softly, one hand pressed to her lips to choke back sobs. Eve tightened her arm around her friend. Aunt Rosie couldn't have been caught up in something as heinous as murder. "Was my Aunt Rosie involved?"

"No."

Thank God for that. "Did she witness Wendy's murder?"

"No."

She tried to think, unable to fathom what tied the two together. "Did she know Wendy was murdered?"

"No."

Growing frustrated with the seemingly impossible web being spun, she bit her lip. Katie, at least, seemed to be pulling herself together. She straightened, her eyes watery, but tears no longer falling.

"Eve, maybe it has something to do with Maggie. Wendy disappeared right before Maggie saw the Mothman in the woods. Do you think the two could be connected?"

Had Maggie really seen the Mothman?

Your Aunt Rosie knows.

Somehow all of the events had to be linked. Even Mrs. Flynn had said as much. Unfortunately, she couldn't think of a question that would result in a yes or no answer.

Katie pressed her lips together, looking grimly determined. "Ask it if Maggie saw Wendy's murder."

"No."

The voice spoke for the first time to Katie's question. She exchanged a startled glance with Eve. There was no doubt it was a strange experience to ask something of the air and have it answer. Her mind conjured images of the thing they couldn't see—an extraterrestrial. A demon. A ghost.

More goose bumps rolled down Eve's spine. "If she didn't witness Wendy's murder, how can everything be tied together?"

"Something happened that day to frighten Maggie," Katie reasoned. "If she didn't witness a murder and she didn't see the Mothman, she saw something else. Something that terrified her so badly she wouldn't leave her bedroom for three days."

"And only then because Caden coaxed her out." Eve felt the phantasm's withdrawal, an increased thinning of the air that told her the entity was leaving. "Don't go," she pleaded. "We need answers."

The presence became a bare whisper on the edge of her mind. In desperation she shouted one last question, the only thing she could think to tie three lives together. "Is Wendy's body in Point Pleasant?"

"Yes."

A crackle thrummed through the air, gone as swiftly as it started. The presence lingered a second longer, then wafted into a realm beyond their reach. In the natural silence that followed, Eve glanced at her friend. Within seconds, she became conscious of the trill of birdsong deep within the TNT, the creak of branches as a gentle wind agitated the trees. She felt drained, yet oddly wired with adrenalin.

"Are you thinking what I'm thinking?" She scuffed her hands against her arms. The unnatural chill was fading.

Katie swallowed. "If Maggie didn't see the Mothman and she didn't witness my sister's death, she must have seen her body."

"But she said something was in the Witch Wood."

"The Witch Wood?"

"Just a name we had for the thicket behind Nana's house." Eve shifted as the memory washed over her. "Maggie said something chased her. Something gray that had red glowing eyes."

"Maybe she just thought that. Maybe she was so scared, she turned whatever she saw into the Mothman. Everyone was talking about the creature. It makes sense she'd latch onto that, turning whatever—or *whoever*—she saw into a monster. She was just a kid."

Eve followed the thought to its logical conclusion. "You think she saw Wendy's killer?"

"Maybe."

The pieces were starting to fall into place, yet a key element remained missing. How was Aunt Rosie involved? "Then your sister's body could still be there…in the Witch Wood. We have to go back to the place where Maggie saw the Mothman."

"And do what?" Katie looked stunned. "Are you suggesting we dig for Wendy's body?"

"Not *we*." Eve gripped her by the elbow and steered her from the igloo. "I know it sounds horrible, Katie, but you want to find out what happened to her, don't you?" She drew a deep breath. "This is starting to become more than we can handle, but I have an idea."

* * * *

It took two days before Eve could get Caden and Ryan together for dinner with her and Katie. Ryan's work shift was at fault, but eventually he rotated onto a daylight schedule, and she was able to set up a casual dinner for all of them at her house.

She was in the kitchen preparing a tossed green salad to go with the chicken she had baking when she heard a thump outside. Craning her neck, she glanced out the kitchen window but didn't see anything amiss in the yard. Discounting the noise as inconsequential, she located a roll of plastic wrap in the nearest drawer, tore off a section, and fit it over the salad bowl.

Another thump.

Frowning, she opened the door to the screened porch, then exited to the yard where the lawn unfurled in sun-dappled patches of green. She'd hired a neighborhood boy to take care of mowing and edging, but he wasn't due back for another two days. Maybe he was banging around in the gardening shed. Although, from what she could see, the door was closed and appeared to be locked.

Thump. Thump.

Keying in on the location of the noise, Eve circled the side of the porch and immediately recoiled.

Oh, God.

A horrified gasp tumbled from her lips when she spied the poor creature floundering on the ground. Whatever manner of animal had caught and mauled the crow had shredded the bird's wings until only ragged tips remained. Trapped in a death throe, it banged against the house with every failed attempt to fly.

Eve stumbled backward, bile rising to her throat. No animal could have done that. Not to both wings, leaving the torso intact. That meant a human perpetrator. Nervously, she glanced around, fearful whoever committed the atrocity lingered nearby. But there was nothing remotely sinister in the shower of sunlight spilling through the trees or the gentle skip of wind through the grass.

The bird made one final heartrending attempt to fly, flopped to the ground, and was still. Tears burned Eve's eyes. School pranks were one thing, but to sadistically mutilate the crow indicated a frighteningly dark nature. She couldn't leave it there, broken and abandoned like a thing of no value. Driven by equal parts anger and horror, she jogged back to the house, intent on locating the key to the shed. She would find a shovel and bury the bird. It deserved that much.

Before she'd taken two steps into the kitchen, the phone erupted in a jarring ring.

Eve pressed a hand to her chest to compose herself, rattled by the senseless slaughter of the crow. She wasn't certain if it had managed to flounder into her yard or someone left it there in another deliberate attempt to scare her off.

Swallowing hard, she picked up the receiver. "Hello."

Two seconds of silence preceded an inhuman screech that made the hair on the back of her neck stand on end.

Schreeeeeeee...eeeeee...schreeee...

Eve slammed the phone down, her legs abruptly weak. She pressed her hands to her face, muffling a cry. She'd thought she was done with the calls and was suddenly weary of looking over her shoulder for a stalker. For all she knew, the mysterious caller could be the same person who'd butchered the crow. "Eve, are you in there?"

She jumped at the sound of a woman's voice, but a cautious glance through the back door revealed Doreen Sue Lynch on the stoop of the screened porch. She stood with her hand raised as if to knock.

Eve exhaled in relief. "Doreen Sue, what are you doing here?" She quickly crossed the porch to open the door to the yard.

The woman looked better than the last time Eve had seen her. Her make-up was fresh, expertly applied, if a little gaudy, her blond hair sprayed and teased to perfection. Dressed in denim shorts, spiked sandals, and a bright fuchsia top, she hardly looked like someone in mourning.

"My last appointment at the salon canceled, and I had some time to kill before I pick up Sam for the movies tonight. I hope you don't mind." Doreen Sue bit her lip as if uncertain of her welcome. "I know I didn't make the best impression at our last meeting, so I thought I'd drop by and say hello." She smiled awkwardly. "Hello."

When Eve didn't immediately respond, she tried again. "I rang the bell at the front door but no one answered. I thought maybe you were in the yard."

Eve touched her neck as if waking from a trance. "I'm sorry. I was out back earlier. And I understand you were upset when we met before. Please, come in." She held open the door and stepped aside for Doreen Sue to enter.

"Did I come at a bad time?"

"No, I'm just a little distracted."

In the kitchen, she offered Doreen Sue a soda. The woman declined but slid into a seat at the table, making herself at home.

"Something smells good."

"I'm baking chicken with a cranberry glaze." Eve sat across from her and attempted a smile, but her mind was still on the dead crow and the strange phone call. "How have you been? I mean...since Amos?"

"Better." Reaching into her purse, Doreen Sue removed a pack of Virginia Slim menthols. She tapped the top against her hand as if preparing to eject a cigarette, then seemed to recall she wasn't at home and absently waved the pack in the air. "There's been nothing new from the police, but everyone has been so kind. The girls at my salon. My customers. Even Katie."

"Why would that surprise you?" Eve was genuinely taken aback. "She's your daughter."

Doreen Sue frowned, the press of her lips revealing age lines at the corners of her mouth. "We do all right, but I've always had the feeling she doesn't approve of me. My lifestyle."

Eve bit her lip, uncertain if she was qualified to comment. Katie Lynch had become a good friend in a short time, and she didn't want to jeopardize that relationship. At the same time, her heart went out to Doreen Sue. Even as a little girl, Eve had thought the woman genuine despite her faults.

"Katie just wants what's best for you."

With a disdainful roll of her eyes, Doreen Sue tossed the cigarettes into her oversized purse. "Katie wants what's best for her, and that includes a mama who's less colorful." She shook her head. "It doesn't matter. She lets me see my grandson, and right now that's all I care about. Now tell me—what has you upset?"

Eve opened her mouth to deny anything was wrong, but before she could utter a word, Doreen Sue waggled a bubblegum-pink fingernail in her direction. "Don't tell me there's nothing wrong. I've been around women—stylists and customers—all my life and could write a book on the nuances of body language and facial expressions. Ha! Bet you didn't think I knew that word nuances, did you? I'm a lot brighter than Katie gives me credit for."

Eve clamped her mouth shut. She hated to hear the woman put herself down, especially belittling herself in her daughter's eyes. "Mrs. Lynch, I never—"

"Doreen Sue," she said, patting Eve's hand. "Now, tell me what's wrong."

She thought about denying her uneasiness again, but relented after a few seconds. Maybe Doreen Sue had seen the mutilated crow when she walked around the back of the house. Or maybe she would say it was the signature prank of some horrible neighborhood boy and Eve could stop worrying that someone was threatening her with omens of harm.

"What a dreadful prank," Doreen Sue said after she'd finished sharing the tale. With a horrified grimace, the older woman fished through her purse and emerged with a pack of spearmint gum. She offered a stick to Eve who shook her head.

"You shouldn't worry about it. All this pranking will die down now that school's out and the kids can burn off their energy with swimming and ballgames." Looking thoughtful, Doreen Sue folded a bright green rectangle of gum into her mouth. "You'd think they'd have learned from that mess with Hank Jeffries how pranks can backfire."

Eve sat straighter, not liking the sound of what she heard. She'd thought about contacting Hank several times since returning to Point Pleasant, but wasn't sure he would remember her. "I know Hank. He was a good friend of my father's. What about him?"

"Oh, you poor thing." Doreen Sue patted her hand again. "You probably don't know he died."

"Died?" Eve drew back, the breath rushing from her lungs as if she'd been punched. "But…" Bewildered, she could only stare. "How?"

Doreen Sue settled in her chair as if preparing for a long tale. "Maybe I will take that soda after all."

Eve nodded numbly, her mind spiraling in a million directions. Had her mother known Hank was dead? Aunt Rosie? How long ago had he died? As she poured a Tab into a glass for Doreen Sue, she flashed on the image of a square-jawed man with deep brown eyes and a scruff of beard. He'd shown her how to fly a kite and where to look for tadpoles in the creek behind Aunt Rosie's house.

"He was afraid of the Mothman," she said as the memory surfaced in her mind. Returning to her chair, she slid the glass in front of Doreen Sue.

"Not afraid." Doreen Sue sipped the soda and set it aside. "Terrified. He'd seen it not long before the bridge fell. Messed him up something fierce. Lots of strange things happened near his house through the years. Or so he said."

Eve thought of the note she'd found from her father to her mother. Part of that had been about Hank.

Hank called spooked about the Mothman again. I'm headed over to his place to try to calm him down.

According to Eve's father, Hank had spent many sleepless nights with a loaded shotgun at his side. Maybe his obsessive fear had finally gotten the better of him.

"Heart attack?" she guessed.

Doreen Sue shook her head. "Not even close. Hank liked to drink, you know." She raised her glass as if toasting his memory, but set it down without taking a sip. "Got worse as he got older. Not a lot to do around here, especially for a man like Hank. He lost his job when Bruce Mechanical closed up shop. After that, he drifted from odd job to odd job, always looking over his shoulder for the Mothman. Everyone knew he was paranoid about the creature. It was kind of a joke."

Eve felt bad for Hank. In a small town, gossip was the pinnacle of entertainment. Hank's obsession with the Mothman would have made him a running punch line, the butt of countless gags and ridicule.

"Two summers ago, the Kline boys got it in their heads to play a prank on Hank." Doreen Sue tapped her fingers lightly against the table as she recounted the story. "I heard they swiped some of their daddy's beer, got liquored up, and went looking for fun. I guess they chose Hank because he was an easy target. Tim sprayed himself with gray body paint—you know—the kind they sell for Halloween. He even sprayed his hair. Then he nicked two road reflectors to use as eyes. Red, like the Mothman's." Poking a finger into her glass, Doreen Sue swirled the ice cubes against the sides. With her eyes lowered, her mascara-blackened lashes made spiky spider webs on her cheeks. "Anyone sober would have never mistaken him for the Mothman, but Hank had been drinking. A whole bottle of Jack Daniel's, according to what Sheriff Weston found later."

Eve's stomach rolled over. She had a nasty sense where the story was headed. "I remember hearing Hank shot up his house once when he was drunk. He thought the Mothman was outside his window."

Doreen Sue nodded. "Only this time when he shot the place up, he hit Tim Kline square in the face with a shotgun blast. The boy was just eighteen years old."

Eve gripped the edge of the table, repulsed and saddened by the story. A prank gone horribly wrong. She wasn't certain who she was angrier at—the Kline boys for doing something so stupid and cruel, or Hank for feeding his irrational terror with booze.

"When he realized his brother was dead, Parker Kline took off running." Doreen Sue shook her head, slowly turning the glass in her hand as if looking into a crystal ball. "Hank was a basket case, at least that's the story. When he realized what he'd done, he called the cops, blubbering and sobbing. Polly, the dispatcher—she comes to my salon to have her hair done—told me she could barely understand him. By the time Caden Flynn arrived on the scene—"

Eve hitched down a startled breath. "Caden?"

Doreen Sue's gaze flicked to her face. "You know he used to be a sergeant with the sheriff's department, right?"

"I didn't realize he was a sergeant. He told me he quit because of a bad call."

"Hank Jeffries," Doreen Sue confirmed. "When Caden got to his place, Hank was outside, wailing his head off, Tim Kline in his lap like some broken doll. I heard the boy's face was gone. Real grisly, if you know what I mean. And there's Hank screaming he's gonna end it all, that he can't live knowing he killed the kid. Caden tried to talk him out of it, but by that time, Parker Kline came back. The sheriff figures he ran to his truck about a mile down the road."

Doreen Sue cocked her head, visibly rethinking the matter. "Well, actually, his daddy's truck. Apparently, the boys had grabbed it for the night without telling their father. I know for a fact Floyd kept a gun under the seat. Not legal, but he did it anyway. I dated him for a while after his wife died, and he told me 'You never know when you'll be forced to shoot a snake.'" She shook her head. "I didn't think he was talking about a reptile, so I broke it off. My men aren't always gentle, but I won't put myself in harm's way of a bullet."

"That's smart, Doreen Sue." Eve tried to move the story along. She admired the woman for setting standards—even if they could be considerably higher—but wanted her to get back to Caden and Hank. "What happened when Parker got there?"

"Can't you guess? The boy was all torn up with grief. Caden said he kept shouting it was a prank, just a stupid prank. He blew Hank away, and poor Caden had to shoot him. He didn't kill the kid, but it was touch and go for a while. Enough to make Caden turn in his badge."

Eve's stomach had congealed into a mass of tightly constricted knots. No wonder Caden had walked away from a job with the sheriff's department. "What happened to Parker?"

"He recovered." Doreen Sue shrugged. "Physically, but not in the head. Turns out the whole prank was his idea. Knowing he was responsible for getting his twin brother killed reduced him to a nutcase." She tapped a tapered pink fingernail against her temple. "The last I heard, he was in the state mental hospital for criminals. He thinks he can talk to UFOs now."

"What a dreadful story."

"That's why kids shouldn't play pranks." Doreen Sue finished off her soda and glanced at her watch. "Do you mind if I use your phone? Martin

Ward asked me and Sam to meet him for ice cream after the movie, and I haven't had a chance to get back to him."

"The phone's on the wall." Eve pointed toward the rear of the kitchen by the screened porch, dazed from the story she'd heard. Caden would have known Hank, maybe even had an occasional beer with him at the Riverside Café. And he would have watched the Kline brothers grow up, probably saw them every Sunday in church along with their parents, or at local baseball and football games. After all the grief he'd experienced— the Silver Bridge tragedy, losing Maggie, his mother's unstable state of mind—it was unfair he should suffer this, too.

"Martin's such a sweet guy," Doreen Sue offered pulling Eve from her thoughts. "He's been checking in on me now and again ever since Amos died."

"That's nice." It obviously hadn't taken long for Martin to come calling, but according to Katie, Martin Ward was a hard worker with good ethics. Unlike most of the men Doreen Sue dated in the past, Katie actually approved of him.

"The phone might be on the fritz," Eve said as she carried Doreen Sue's glass to the sink. "I've been getting a lot of strange calls with screeches and clicks. I had the phone company check it out, but they couldn't find anything wrong with the line." Whatever their verdict, she still wasn't convinced the odd calls weren't the fault of an electronic malfunction.

"Screeches and clicks?" Doreen Sue paused mid-dial, pressing the receiver to her chest. "I've heard that happens sometimes when a family member dies."

Eve rinsed the glass with water, then set it in the drain board to be washed later. Something cold slithered down her back. "Excuse me?"

"Your Aunt Rosie." Doreen Sue bobbed her head as if the answer was obvious. "She might be trying to communicate with you."

Eve started to laugh, then quelled the instinctive reaction when she noted Doreen Sue's expression. The woman wasn't joking.

"Spirits often try to converse through electricity and everyday instruments like TVs, lights, and phones. I know it sounds silly, but I follow all of that stuff…horoscopes, psychics, UFO theories." A wave of her hand said she took only half of it seriously. "I've seen some strange things around here, especially by the TNT. I've never seen the Mothman, but I remember reading an article about a medium who was convinced her dead husband tried to communicate with her through phone calls. She heard things like amplifier feedback, insect noises, and strange clicks whenever she answered the phone."

Eve felt her face drain of color. After talking to a disembodied "thing" in an igloo at the TNT, she should have no problem believing her dead aunt was reaching out to her. She'd sat in the living room only days after arriving and voiced that wish aloud. *Aunt Rosie, I wish I understood what was going on. I wish there was some way you could talk to me.* The phone calls had started not long afterward. Fluke or answer to her request?

"It could just be a problem on the line," she said at last.

"Probably." Doreen Sue pressed the hang-up button and redialed. A second later her voice turned playful and sultry. "Hi, Martin. It's Doreen Sue. Sam and I would love to have ice cream with you after the movie."

Listening to the purr of her voice, Eve turned and gazed out the rear window. She thought of Hank Jeffries, Caden, the Kline brothers, and pranks. The dead crow was still in her yard. If the bird had been intended as a sick prank to scare her away, then the culprit must be the same person who'd left the notes on her windshield. In all likelihood, her personal ghoul was letting her know he'd moved past written threats.

She wouldn't be surprised to see someone lurking beneath the trees in the distance. A shiver of fear swept through her despite the frivolous play of sunlight on the grass, a lightly cloud-scaped sky overhead. What happened when her stalker decided slaughtering birds wasn't enough? When he came after her?

Closing her eyes, she listened to Doreen Sue prattle on in the background. Aunt Rosie had hidden something in her house. The being in the igloo had told her the item—whatever it was—was still here. Somehow, the unknown thing and her stalker were tied to Wendy Lynch, Maggie, and Aunt Rosie.

At all costs, she and Katie needed to convince Caden and Ryan of that critical truth.

Chapter 8

Eve slid a shovel beneath the dead crow and wriggled it to the center of the spade.

"That is so gross." Katie held a black plastic trash bag as far away from her as she could, her face twisted in revulsion. "I want you to know I'm doing this under protest."

"So you said."

"I still think we should tell Caden and Ryan about that thing the moment they get here." Katie made a gagging sound, more than a little green as Eve dropped the mutilated bird into the bag. "Why do you have to bury it anyway?"

Setting the shovel aside, Eve took the bag from her, careful to hold the revolting thing at arm's length. Drawing a breath of clean air, she tried to banish the stench of carrion. "It deserves that much."

"It's evidence. Evidence shouldn't be buried."

"We don't know that it was left deliberately. It could have been mauled by a cat."

"You don't believe that any more than I do."

Now wasn't the time to argue the point. Caden and Ryan would be arriving any moment. Fortunately, Katie had shown up early, shortly after her mother left, giving her the chance to talk to her friend alone. Eve had led Katie outside and shown her the butchered crow. Horrified, Katie insisted she leave the bird where it was and show it to Ryan when he arrived.

But Eve wouldn't hear of it. She needed Ryan *and* Caden focused solely on Wendy Lynch tonight. A discussion about the crow would send them all off track. Enlisting her friend's help, Eve decided to dispose of the crow temporarily, bagging it and hiding it behind the shed until she could bury it later.

Katie picked up the shovel and followed her. "I can't believe anyone could be so sick," she said after Eve deposited the bag out of sight behind the small gardening shack.

Eve pulled off her gardening gloves. "I'll try to bury it tonight after everyone leaves. Otherwise it's going to stink and attract animals."

"You should show it to Ryan after we've told him about Wendy," Katie countered. "He's a cop. Don't discount this. It isn't a kid's prank."

She was right. The vicious mutilation of the bird was far more sinister than the usual end-of-school-year shenanigans. "Let's just see how things go," she said as the two walked back to the house.

Inside, they both scrubbed their hands thoroughly with hot water and soap, then Eve poured them each a glass of Pinot Grigio. Standing with her back to the sink, she swiped a hand across her brow. "I should probably go freshen up. I'm sure I look a mess." If nothing else, she felt grimy and sweaty after toiling with the bird.

"You look fine," Katie assured her, "but go ahead." She sipped her wine, then set it on the kitchen table. "I can take care of whatever you need done down here."

Eve had already set the dining room table with Aunt Rosie's fine china and crystal stemware. She hoped she wasn't being too ostentatious for the guys, but had wanted to make the table look pretty. Another time she'd have everyone over for pizza or hamburgers on the grill, but tonight was all about presentation—right down to what she and Katie planned to share with them.

"Would you?" She smiled at her friend, realizing how much she'd miss her if she ever went back to Harrisburg.

If?

In the past it had always been *when*. Lately, she seemed to be thinking as though she planned to remain in Point Pleasant.

Eve pulled two boxes of flavored crackers from the cupboard and pointed out a few serving platters. "I was going to set out some cheeses and dips before dinner," she explained. "Everything is on the center shelf in the fridge. The cheese just needs to be cut up."

"Go freshen up." Katie shooed her toward the doorway. "I'll take care of it."

By the time she returned ten minutes later wearing a fresh blouse, her hair neatly brushed, Katie had the cheese, crackers, and dips arranged on two platters. When Caden and Ryan arrived a short time later, she gave Caden a kiss and Ryan a hug.

"Will your mother be all right by herself, or do you have someone staying with her?" she asked.

"She'll be fine." Caden kept his arm linked around her waist with casual familiarity. "We try to make sure she isn't alone overnight, but don't always worry so much during the day. Sometimes Mrs. Alderidge stays with her, other times she's on her own. She told me to say hello."

Eve smiled, remembering her last conversation with Mrs. Flynn. Everything the woman said had been reiterated by the being in the igloo. She was starting to think Mrs. Flynn was in full control of her faculties and Maggie really was speaking to her through dreams. "I'll have to take a dinner plate over to her later."

"She'd like that," Ryan said, appearing relaxed.

Initially, she'd been worried how he might view the dinner invitation, fearing he would think she was trying to set him up with Katie. But her childhood friend seemed happy to be included and had already stolen more than a few glances in Katie's direction. Maybe that hadn't been such a farfetched idea after all.

After some chit-chat over drinks and appetizers—the guys opting for Miller Genuine Draft instead of wine—she served dinner in the dining room. Cranberry chicken and wild rice with a green salad and corn muffins. She was far from a gourmet cook, but the meal was a hit. Afterward, they had Katie's homemade dessert, a decadent chocolate cake with peanut butter icing. Eve made a full plate with a little of everything, including dessert, and ran it next door to Mrs. Flynn. By the time she returned, the guys were relaxing on the screened porch and Katie had cleaned up the kitchen.

"You didn't have to do that," Eve told her friend, finding her finishing up at the sink. Katie had put away all of the dishes, a sign she had probably been a regular dinner guest of Aunt Rosie's and was intimately familiar with the house.

"I know, but I wanted to expend some nervous energy." Drying her hands on a dishtowel, Katie shook her head. "I can't believe we're going to tell a sheriff's sergeant and an ex- sheriff's sergeant that we need their help to dig up a body."

It sounded absurd when voiced that way, but Eve knew however anxious she felt, the sensation had to be magnified tenfold for Katie. Not only had her friend recently learned her sister had been murdered, her body buried somewhere in Point Pleasant, but a killer had taken Wendy's life and gotten away with the crime.

"Come on, let's do this." Steering her friend outside, Eve led Katie onto the porch. It was almost nine in the evening, but the sky remained light, brushed with the first tentative strokes of twilight. The days had lengthened, creeping toward evening as the official start of summer loomed near and fireflies shyly materialized for the first time.

Eve joined Caden on the glider, their usual seat on the porch, while Katie and Ryan reclined in matching wicker chairs across from them. For a while they talked casually, the discussion ranging from the Challenger shuttle launch with Sally Ride, the first woman in space, to Reagan's Star Wars plan, and how much everyone missed *M*A*S*H*. Sooner or later, Eve knew she would have to broach the topic simmering at the back of her mind. It was the reason she'd orchestrated the dinner, craving a laidback environment when she and Katie outlined their recent experiences. Sending her friend a measured glance, she guided the conversation to the TNT. It took only a few minutes to explain how she and Katie had poked around the igloo, though she purposefully neglected mentioning Mrs. Flynn had directed them there.

"So we thought we'd ask a few questions since we were there anyway. You know..." Her hands grew sweaty as she tried to manipulate the conversation in the needed direction. "See if there was any truth to the rumors about an entity lurking inside."

Ryan gave a derisive snort. "Do you know how many people have fallen for that hogwash? I wish I had a dime for all the idiots who trudged up there and asked questions only to come out looking like an ass—uh, fool." The swiftly voiced correction was tangled up with an apologetic glance for Katie.

Eve's friend didn't seem to realize Ryan had tempered his language for her. Interesting. If she weren't so focused on the root cause for broaching the conversation, Eve might have dissected his behavior in more detail.

"What if I told you something *did* answer our questions?"

Caden shifted uncomfortably. He'd been sitting with his arm draped over her shoulders, but drew free, facing her with a serious expression. "What do you mean—*something*?"

Wetting her lips, Eve exchanged a glance with Katie. "Do you want to tell them or should I?"

"You do it." Katie's face was white, her hands clenched tightly together.

"All right." Rapidly, before she could lose her courage, Eve relayed the encounter she and Katie had with the being in the igloo, sharing everything it told them. Caden was silent when she was through, his expression grim, but Ryan looked ready to burst with the absurdity of the idea.

"You expect me to believe Wendy was murdered based upon feelings you had in an old World War II bunker?" He gave an incredulous shake of his head.

"They weren't feelings." Katie spoke sharply, her lips thinned to a white line. "We heard a distinctive voice. You know as well as I do supernatural events have taken place there, Ryan."

"What I know is that I have a dead body—Amos Carter's—and that's the murder I'm concerned with. Not hearsay about something that might have happened fifteen years ago. However much you want to believe differently, Katie, the odds are your sister ran away."

"No." Anger flashed in Katie's eyes. "I refuse to believe that after what I heard in the igloo. I've never believed it."

"So what are you suggesting?" Ryan's gaze held unmistakable challenge.

Katie waited three pulse beats before tossing out the plan she and Eve had devised earlier. "We have to go to the Witch Wood. To the spot where Maggie saw the Mothman. I think Wendy is buried there. That must be what Maggie saw that scared her so badly."

"That's freaking crazy." Ryan shot to his feet and paced a short distance away in agitation.

Eve rushed to her friend's defense. "Ryan, I agree with Katie."

"It doesn't matter. I'm a sworn officer of the law." The lighthearted friend she remembered from childhood had been replaced by an icy professional. "I'm not about to go digging around in the woods, looking for a potential murder victim, based on a conversation you two had with the bogeyman. You might as well ask me to believe in the Mothman."

"I do." Caden spoke quietly, venturing into the conversation.

Startled, Eve glanced in his direction. Since stepping onto the porch, she'd been walking a mental tightrope, determined to convince Ryan and Caden about what happened in the igloo. Having her boyfriend as an ally was a situation she hadn't foreseen. Interesting he'd chosen this moment to take a stand about Point Pleasant's notorious monster.

Ryan stared at his bother like he'd lost his mind. "You believe this supernatural bullshit?" No tempering his language now.

"I do."

"Caden, be serious. It's bad enough Mom—"

"Listen, Ryan." Caden spoke swiftly, cutting him off mid-sentence. "I don't know what scared Maggie in the woods behind Nana's old house, but something did. I don't know if she saw the Mothman, but I know what happened to me when the Silver Bridge fell. That's enough to make me believe there might be something in that igloo. Something that talked to Eve and Katie."

Ryan regarded him silently. Judging by his expression, Caden rarely spoke about the bridge disaster or his impressions of that night.

"Go on," Ryan prompted.

Caden shifted. It was obvious he didn't like being the center of attention, just as obvious he couldn't back out now. Motioning for his brother to sit, he drew an uneven breath. To Eve it looked like he prepared to spin back a mental clock.

"It was cold in the water." The first words out of his mouth were strained, tangible tension mirrored by his body posture. "I thought I was going to die. I would have if the thing hadn't freed me."

Ryan eased into a chair, his gaze never leaving Caden. "What thing?"

Eve sensed the answer even before Caden spoke.

"The Mothman."

* * * *

The impact of the car hitting the water tossed his body like a limp ragdoll. His head cracked against the driver's side window, and he blacked out.

When he awoke, it was to a world of dark and cold, filled with pain. The fire in his lungs forced him awake, the building pressure alerting him he was running out of oxygen. Everything around him was dark, a nightmare world of freezing water and twisted metal. The car had completely submerged.

Maggie! Oh God, where was Maggie?

He tried to move and felt an answering spike of pain ricochet from his wrist. He would have screamed if he'd had the air and the strength. The icy water quickly sapped what little stamina he had left. With effort, he forced the door open. Thank God the pressure had equalized enough for that. Something cut through the darkness—headlights from another car that had sunk nearby. He tugged at his arm, trying to free it, but it was pinned below by something he couldn't see. Pain splintered into his elbow, pushing him close to blacking out again. It was too cold, too freaking cold, and he needed air.

A wave of panic crashed over him, every bit as suffocating as the darkness. He thrashed in the grip of fear, convinced he was going to die, powerless to save his sister who must have been carried away in the icy current. The cold wet would kill him within minutes if he didn't find a way free of its grasp. Already his consciousness waned.

A discordant buzzing grew in his head, jerking him back to clarity. It was a sound he'd heard once before. Images assaulted him, resurrecting the memory of an inexplicable encounter on Halloween night.

Did he remember? Yes. Would he forget over time? Never.

A scarlet glow seeped through the water, edging closer. As it neared, he pinpointed the source of the strange illumination—two unblinking red eyes. The same eyes he'd spied on a brisk autumn night in the TNT.

Long gray fingers coiled around his arm, the touch more frigid than the entombing water. The buzzing in his head grew, pulsing against his temples. He caught a glimpse of a face framing the eyes, of wings folded behind the creature's back. There was nothing remotely angelic about it. Rather it looked like a being born of sulfur and chaos, a grisly nightmare come to life.

In that second when it hauled him free and propelled him to the surface, he knew its name. A name that would resonate in his head and memory for years to come: Mothman.

He broke through with a gasp, tried to find the lungs to scream, but could only cough and sputter, hacking up river water. Flotsam was everywhere—parts of vehicles, the busted panels from the semi that had been ahead of him, headlights angled up from the water like searchlights. Packages and bags, glittery Christmas presents bobbing among the debris.

Maggie. Where was Maggie?

He grabbed one of the panels. Clung to it and tried to haul himself from the water. Lacking the strength, he dropped his head against the wet panel, hot tears mingling with the icy water on his cheeks. "Mag—" He tried to call her name but only managed a hoarse croak. Loud splashing sounded behind him, and a gruff hand closed on his collar.

"Hurry!" someone yelled. "This one's alive. Help me haul him out."

* * * *

Caden had never told anyone the tale, but he shared it now, the way it unfolded in his head. They let him speak without interruption, and when he was through, he waited for judgment. Ryan, practical as camouflage during turkey season, would say he was a dipshit in need of a shrink. Katie, who he'd known peripherally for years, would politely reserve judgment, and Eve…

He glanced at the woman he'd grown attracted to, noting a marked glimmer of gratitude in her eyes. She'd needed him to do this. He saw she was proud of him for sharing a private and difficult moment in his life.

Reaching across the glider, she took his hand. "Thank you," she mouthed softly, words meant only for him.

He would have kissed her if not for the others. Already he could feel Ryan's cutting gaze.

"You think the Mothman freed you that night?" his brother challenged.

"I don't think. I know." Caden lifted his arm, displaying the three angry red lines angled across his forearm. "How do you think I got these? It's where the Mothman gripped me." Turning his arm over, he indicated the middle line, longer than the rest. It wrapped around to the inside of his wrist, just as fingers might do.

Appearing uncomfortable, Ryan shrugged. "I thought they were the result of an injury from that night."

"Do they look like scars to you? An injury would have healed. This is a brand, a permanent imprint that will never fade." The marks on his arm hadn't changed in fifteen years, as vivid and red today as they'd been in '67. Ryan couldn't deny that.

"And the memory you're not to forget?" his brother asked. "What's that about?"

Caden released Eve's hand, stretching to wrap his arm over her shoulders. Surprisingly at ease, he used his heel to coax the glider into motion. Outside, twilight had thickened, creeping within the confines of the screened porch in velvety nests of shadow. Crickets harmonized on the night breeze, the musty smell of damp earth and growing things wafting from the creek at the edge of Rosie's property.

Eve's property, he corrected. It was her home now. Hopefully, she'd stay.

"It wasn't the first time I encountered the creature," he admitted.

"I'm listening." Ryan's expression remained unreadable, his voice cop-neutral. For a moment, it felt like Eve and Katie weren't there. That it was just him and Ryan, brother to brother, debating the probability of unlikely events.

Time to spill his guts. If Ryan wanted to label him a nutcase, that was his choice.

"It was October before the bridge fell. Halloween night. I went to the TNT with Wyatt, Glen, and some girls we'd met in Gallipolis." He stole a sideways glance at Eve, uncomfortable talking about the date he'd been with that night, but she didn't seem to mind. "The girls had heard about the Mothman and wanted to check out the TNT. We figured if we were going to catch a glimpse of the creature, Halloween was the best time. So we went up there with some flashlights and a lot of stupid ideas."

He paused, remembering the giggles of the girls as they'd piled into Wyatt's battered green station wagon, him and a redhead named Julie squished in the backseat with her friend, Tina. Glen had climbed in the rear, Wyatt's girl getting the privileged passenger's seat up front.

They'd hiked into the woods after parking, the girls clinging to them in the dark, chattering and giggling, snagged between a sense of excitement and fear.

"Earlier, we'd come up with a plan to scare the girls. It was Wyatt's idea." He could still remember the dumbass stunt and how they'd thought it was going to be the epitome of fun. "After we got to the igloo where the Mothman was seen, I was supposed to say I had to take a leak and sneak off into the woods. I'd wait a few minutes, then scream my head off like something happened to me."

"That's awful." Eve gave him a soft punch to the ribs.

"Hey." He grinned, remembering the stupidity of it. "I was eighteen. What do you expect?"

"Did you go through with it?" Katie asked.

He shook his head. "No. I headed into the woods like we'd planned, but after a few feet…" His voice trailed away as he thought back to that night. The crunch of dried leaves beneath his sneakers, the air cold against his face, the girls' voices dwindling behind him. "I heard a humming." The noise was hard to describe, a sound that had seemed to come from *inside* his head as much as originate in his surroundings. "Instead of going back to the igloo, I took off deeper into the woods. I'm not sure how far I ran, but the noise kept growing louder. And then I saw it."

Ryan scowled. "The Mothman."

Caden nodded, noting his brother didn't voice it as a question. "It was crouched on the ground. I remember I couldn't see its face, only the eyes. A piece of wood had punctured its right wing and was impaled in the flesh, high up, near the middle of its back. It looked like a broken branch."

"Like it got tangled up with a tree?" Katie appeared riveted to the story, hanging on every word. She, at least, seemed to believe him.

"Yeah. Because of the way it was positioned, the creature couldn't reach it."

"And you pulled it out?" Heaving a loud exhale, Ryan webbed a hand over his face. He watched Caden through his spread fingers. "You're yanking my chain, right?"

Caden returned his stare, saying nothing.

"What an amazing tale," Eve whispered at his side.

Two believers.

As if sensing he was outnumbered, Ryan shook his head and leaned forward, clasping his hands between his knees. "You didn't call for the others? Didn't want someone to validate what you'd seen?"

"No. I wanted it to get away." How could he explain what he'd felt at that moment? "I went up there, a dumbass kid looking for excitement, hoping to cop a feel with a girl I barely knew. But all of that changed when I saw the Mothman. People think of it as a freak of nature." He shook his head, irritated he couldn't articulate his thoughts better. He'd felt something that night, a piercing impression of the creature. Old, archaic, as if it had lived an eternity.

"I didn't feel like I was in danger. I didn't sense aggression from it, just—" He swallowed, not sure he could admit the rest.

Ryan waited a beat before prompting, "And?"

Memory washed over Caden. "Loneliness. Exhaustion. Confusion."

"Confusion?" Surprise echoed in Eve's voice.

"Yeah. Like it was in turmoil or something. I *wanted* it to take off without being seen."

Eve appeared breathless. "You got that close to it?" her eyes were wide, touched by an unmistakable glimmer of awe. "What was it like?"

"That's just it. I can't tell you." He'd tried countless times to remember. To conjure an image of reaching for the impaled wing…placing his hand on that strange alien flesh and exerting pressure as he ripped the branch free. In his mind, he knew he'd done all those things, yet his memories were nothing more than impressions. The being had cluttered his mind with an outpouring of melancholy and extreme fatigue that had almost reduced him to sobs. It was something he tried not to think about.

"Did you see its face?" Ryan asked. "Its claws? How big was it?"

"I don't know. Probably around seven feet like everyone says, but all I remember—" He bit off the words, unwilling to recall the wretched gloom he'd felt. He shook his head. "Just…confusion. It was tired."

"Tired?'

Caden nodded.

As if realizing he wasn't going to get any further with his interrogation, Ryan blew out a breath. "So you got the branch out of its wing and never told anyone about it." He had reverted to his cop-neutral tone. "And that's why it freed you the night the Silver Bridge collapsed."

Caden stared until Ryan looked away, the answer obvious.

"But no one else saw the Mothman that night." Katie sounded disappointed, forced to point out the obvious.

"There was a lot of chaos when the bridge fell." Ryan appeared thoughtful. "I remember hearing about all the birds in the air. People said the bridge collapse upset nature. Some people reported seeing the Mothman, but we'll never know how many." He shifted his attention to Caden. "Whether I believe you or not doesn't matter. However you survived that night, I'm grateful. What I question is the idea of traipsing around the woods looking for the body of Wendy Lynch, a girl who probably ran away."

Katie sat straighter. "What would you do if it had been Maggie? Wouldn't you want answers? Wouldn't you want to know for sure?"

"Katie…" Ryan's protest was silenced by the determination on her face.

Caden couldn't blame her. How long had he been tortured by the thought of Maggie's body at the bottom of the Ohio River, buried in the muck and sediment of an unmarked grave? She'd lain there for six months before being properly laid to rest. Before he was able to weep over her casket and tell her how sorry he was for not protecting her. Katie had no doubt felt the same torture for years, wanting to know what became of her sister.

"I say we do it." Caden made his decision, directing his next remark to Ryan. "You've been scoping out the TNT, looking for clues to Amos's murder. Do you think it's a coincidence he died right after Rosie's house was ransacked?"

Ryan frowned. "What are you suggesting?"

"Exactly what the thing in the igloo wanted Eve and Katie to know—the events are related, and it goes back to what happened fifteen years ago. To whatever it was Maggie saw in the woods."

"Are you nuts? Amos didn't have anything to do with that."

"Maybe, maybe not. What's it going to hurt to poke around?" Caden sent his brother a challenging grin. "If I'm wrong, you can rub my nose in it for the next fifteen years."

When Ryan swore softly, Caden knew he had him. Eve and Katie seemed to sense it, too.

"I know where Maggie was when she saw the Mothman," Eve said. "Near the large sycamore shaped like a woman with legs. I remember how we used to hang out there when we were kids and pretend it was a witch."

Caden nodded. "It sounds like a plan. Tomorrow night."

* * * *

The next day as Eve waited for Sarah Sherman to arrive for lunch, Ryan made an unexpected appearance in the lobby of the Parrish Hotel.

Dressed in uniform, his dark hair still blessed with the wayward curl of youth, he looked a cross between the childhood friend she remembered and the law officer who'd been evident last night.

"Hi, Eve." He nodded a greeting before focusing on Katie who stood behind the front desk. "Katie."

Eve's friend nodded in return, though her gaze quickly strayed to the guest registrations she sorted. Busy work.

Prior to Ryan's arrival, the atmosphere had been relaxed, a pleasantness mirrored by the honeyed dusting of sunlight in the lobby. Outside on Main Street, an occasional car passed, offering a visible reminder the older areas of Point Pleasant hadn't been entirely forsaken by the rerouting of traffic to the new Silver Bridge. Metallic paint, chrome, the glint of a windshield reflecting afternoon rays of sunlight. With a bit of imagination, she could almost visualize the gleaming muscle cars and sleek sedans of yesteryear cruising past, the doors open to a summer breeze as her parents manned the check-in counter, and guests lounged in high-backed rockers on the front porch. But now it was only Ryan's sheriff's car outside. Ryan shifted awkwardly as he watched Katie sort through the stack of guest registrations. If Eve didn't know better, she'd think he was tongue-tied, an odd occurrence for the cavalier boy she remembered.

"Nice to see you, Ryan. I hope this isn't an official call," she said.

"Not entirely." He shook his head, appearing grateful for her comment. "I just got back from the TNT. We found Amos's car."

Katie glanced up sharply. "Where?"

"Near the old north power plant off Fairground Road."

"Didn't you look there before?" Eve asked.

"We did, but just a quick once-over. The search was concentrated mainly to the areas off Potters Creek Road since that's where Amos's body was found. We would have spotted his car if it had been at the power plant."

"So you're saying it just turned up?" Katie sounded doubtful. "Out of nowhere?"

"I'm not sure what I'm saying." He frowned, his brows drawing down over his eyes. "The weird thing is we couldn't find any tire tracks around it, almost like it had been dumped there. Or dropped."

"How could that be?" Eve had an inkling but hesitated voicing the thought.

"We're still trying to figure that out." Judging by his expression, he was baffled by the anomaly. "The roof was caved in like something had landed on it. Something big."

She couldn't resist sharing her suspicion any longer. "The Mothman?"

"I didn't say that."

"But there have been more sightings." She wasn't entirely sure where she stood on Point Pleasant's infamous monster, but couldn't ignore the rumor mill that kept the Mothman front and center. "I heard Duncan and Donnie Bradley aren't the only ones who saw it. When I stopped at the drugstore this morning, the woman behind the counter told me a friend of hers saw it near the public boat launch."

"I heard that, too," Katie confirmed. "And Sam said his friend's sister spotted it near the fairgrounds."

"Yeah. And a cab driver saw it near the county airport." Ryan sighed, his expression weary. "I've heard all the reports. We're getting hammered at the sheriff's office trying to sort legitimate calls from the crazies."

"So you think some of the reports are true?" Eve asked.

His frown twisted deeper. "What I think doesn't matter. As a cop, it's my duty to investigate any claim. Unfortunately, we've got a mass of whackos in the mix. Besides, why would the Mothman bother with Amos's car?"

"Maybe it was trying to help." The more Eve considered the possibility, the more she believed the likelihood. "It could have dropped the car in a place where it thought it would be found. It helped Caden before. Maybe it isn't the evil monster everyone thinks."

Ryan's expression reflected doubt. "Maybe." However skeptical, he was apparently too polite to disagree completely.

"Um, look, the reason I'm here…" Fidgeting noticeably, he focused on Katie.

Before he could say anything further, a pair of guests wandered down the stairway into the lobby. Eve recognized them as a married couple who'd checked in the previous afternoon for an overnight reservation—George and Glenda Whitmore. A few hours ago, they'd called down and asked to extend their stay. She'd been more than happy to accommodate them.

"Oh, hello." Glenda, a skinny redhead who sported a slouchy top à la Jennifer Beals in *Flashdance* approached the desk with a twittering giggle. "Sure hope you can help us. George and I wanted directions to that munitions site. You know…" Glancing over her shoulder, she waved to her husband. "What's it called again, George?"

"The TNT area. Like dynamite." George, a thick-chested man with a mullet, scratched at the ridge of light stubble on his chin. "We heard some people in the café yesterday saying the Mothman was back. Thought we'd drive out to that wildlife area and check it out before we head home."

Eve smiled pleasantly. The Mothman had been a continued draw for tourists to Point Pleasant. Having the legend revived was hardly bad for business. "Where's home?"

"Gettysburg."

"I'm not far from there. Harrisburg." They chatted for a few minutes about familiar landmarks in Pennsylvania, then Eve asked Ryan to supply them with directions to the TNT. She thought about telling the woman she might want to change her cork wedged sandals for sneakers but decided against it. Once the woman got a look at the trails in the TNT, she probably wouldn't venture from the car.

Ryan shook his head after they left. "I guess we should be grateful for tourist dollars."

"And the Mothman." Eve plunked an index finger against his chest. "Now, tell us why you're here."

"Oh, um…" He offered a one-shouldered shrug, looking out of his element. "I wanted to apologize to Katie."

"To me?" Katie blinked in surprise. "What for?"

"Last night." Another shrug as Ryan worked the words from his tongue. "I know I was belligerent…the whole idea about looking for Wendy's body. If I came across like a bulldog, it had nothing to do with you."

Katie plainly hadn't expected he'd given the matter a passing thought, much less that he'd offer an apology for his behavior. Clearly, he was more than a little smitten with Eve's friend and apparently didn't want Katie to think badly of him.

"Uh…thank you." A flush of color touched Katie's cheeks. Lowering her eyes self-consciously, she fiddled with the registrations on the counter. Seconds later, a horn blared in the distance, shattering the awkward moment.

"That doesn't sound remotely official," Eve pointed out to Ryan, recalling his reference for the visit.

"You're right. I also wanted to ask about Amos." Growing confident with a shift to law-enforcement mode, Ryan focused on Katie again. "I've talked to Doreen Sue a few times, but she hasn't been able to shed any light on someone who'd want to kill him. Whoever did it left him with his wallet, two credit cards, and forty-eight dollars in cash."

"Not a robbery." Eve had a sense where he was headed. "So you think he knew his killer?"

"It's a good possibility."

"A lot of people knew him, but he didn't have many friends." Katie's mouth pinched into a frown. "Mostly drinking buddies. He liked women, alcohol, and shooting pool, and couldn't be bothered with fishing or hiking. I have no idea why he would have gone to the TNT."

A touch of sympathy colored Ryan's gaze. Reaching forward, he laid his hand over hers where it rested on the counter. "Doreen Sue's better off without him." The contact lasted only a second before he withdrew. "Amos either met someone at the TNT, or someone jumped him while he was there. We haven't ruled out a vagrant. Someone passing through who killed for thrills."

Eve had noted the touch as well as the flush that rose in Katie's cheeks. "If that was the case, you'd think Amos's wallet would have been missing." She studied him openly. "Why not take the spoils?"

"Exactly. Which brings us back to Amos meeting someone. Probably someone he knew."

"I've got another suggestion." Katie looked uncertain whether or not she should venture the idea. Lowering her eyes, she fingered the registration slips spread out on the counter, then shoved them aside as if arriving at a decision. "If you want my opinion, I think Amos's death is related to what happened at Rosie's house."

Eve raised her hand to her throat. "You mean the vandalism?"

"If that's what it was. You said someone used black spray paint."

"Yes. On the second floor."

Ryan appeared skeptical, waiting for her to continue.

"Amos was out late that night," she explained. "Sam and I stayed with my mom because she wasn't feeling well. I remember hearing Amos come in somewhere around three AM. The next morning, I saw his shirt in the laundry room, and it had black paint on it."

Ryan remained cautious. "It could be a coincidence."

"No." Katie shook her head. "Amos was allergic to paint. It did something to his gut and made him sick. He could only stomach it in small amounts, otherwise he'd throw up."

"There was hardly any spray paint damage," Eve murmured, recalling the single squiggle on the wall in Aunt Rosie's dark room. A light bulb flashed on in her head. "What if the person who ransacked the place *was* searching for something?" She built on her friend's scenario. It was what Caden had been saying all along. "What if the spray paint was an afterthought to make it look like vandalism?"

Ryan drummed his fingers against the counter but said nothing.

"And the person doing the vandalism couldn't stomach the odor, so they barely used any paint at all." Katie quickly took up the thread. "They were clumsy with the can because it was something they never used. As a result they—Amos—ended up getting paint on his shirt."

Drawing a breath, Ryan relented at last. "You two make a good argument, but even if I buy it, it's still coincidental. And it fails to address the most important issue. The basis of the whole theory."

Eve titled her head questioningly. "Which is?"

"What was Amos looking for in Rosie's house?"

The answer hit her like a fist to the gut. "Gray vines."

Unfortunately, Eve was no closer to understanding the meaning now than when she'd first heard the phrase.

Her aunt had taken that secret to her grave.

Chapter 9

Reaper waded through a snarl of weeds and thistles, hoping for a glimpse of shiny metal. The sky was partially overcast, but there was enough sun that the damn money clip should cast a reflection. He hadn't even realized he'd lost the thing until the morning after he'd dumped Amos's body in the pond.

The loss stung, but he'd decided to write it off rather than risk returning to the TNT. Yeah, the clip had close to three hundred dollars folded inside, but he was a rich man. If he had to eat the loss, he could afford it. He'd contented himself knowing the odds of anyone finding it among nearly four thousand acres of ponds, trees, and briars were thin.

Then Duncan and Donnie Bradley had mouthed off about seeing the Mothman and suddenly people were crawling all over the place again. If the clip turned up and the cops connected it to him, he could always say he'd been poking around looking for the creature, too. But there was always the chance questions might arise. Most people knew he hated the TNT and the wacky craziness it encouraged. Mothman, UFO's, ghosts. All bullshit in his opinion.

He'd probably lost the clip when he moved Amos's body, transporting the battered corpse from his car to the pond. He'd been careful to line the back seat of his Buick with plastic so no trace of blood or fibers were left behind, but what if he'd dragged Amos across the clip and smeared the bills with blood?

He wasn't dumb. He watched *Magnum, P.I.* and *Hill Street Blues.* A smartass cop like Ryan Flynn could trace those grisly stains back to Amos, then to him.

So for the last hour, he'd been scouring the TNT. First, in the area where he'd killed Amos, now near the pond where he'd dumped the body. Fortunately, he was alone, the area currently free of thrill-seekers and Mothman hunters. He didn't buy the Bradley brothers bullshit about the monster, but he'd slid a snub-nosed .38 into his trouser pocket to be on the safe side. Especially with the wacky phone calls he kept getting—screeches and shrieks—as though someone was messing with his head. He didn't want to draw attention to himself by calling the phone company, so he let the occurrences ride. If he ever found out who was playing games, it wouldn't go down well for the stupid sap on the other end. Just like it wouldn't go down well for any mutated bird like the Mothman that threatened him in the TNT.

Aside from Amos, he'd racked up two other murders over the years. With a past like that, he had no qualms about blowing away a flying freak.

Swearing under his breath, Reaper used a hand-held scythe to hack away at the plants clustered near the south end of the pond. Duckweed and algae caked the surface of the water, snuggling up to cattails and clumps of bulrushes at the edge. The muggy heat of the day amplified the reek of plant decay and sun-heated soil. Swatting a bug from his neck, he took another swing, parting the weeds with the old scythe he'd rummaged from his shed. He'd found it buried behind a bag of grass seed. An antiquated tool that had once belonged to his father, a man who'd eked out a hand-to-mouth living for his family on the coal barges of the Ohio River. Not him. He'd known early on he was destined for greater things, carefully planned and plotted to ensure that path as soon as he was old enough to take control of his destiny. Damn Rosie Parrish for throwing a kink into his life this late in the game.

Leaning forward, Reaper peered around the opening he'd cleared.

Nothing.

He hadn't been able to locate Rosie's negative, and he couldn't find the money clip. His wife would make an issue of the loss if she discovered the damn thing was missing. Especially since she'd given it to him as a gift on their last anniversary—only after making sure he knew it hadn't come cheap.

She was like that, always reminding him it was *her* money that put them where they were today. *Her* family who had given him his break, allowing him to rise to his current position. Sometimes he got so pissed with her snotty attitude, he had to make something suffer. Yesterday, it had been a crow with a broken wing. He'd come across it when he was looking for the scythe and had taken sadistic delight in using the instrument on the helpless bird. He hadn't killed it. That would have been too quick, negating the purpose. Knowing something suffered agony far greater than his helped him regain control of his volatile emotions.

As an afterthought, he'd driven to Rosie's old home and dumped the butchered bird on the side lawn, hoping it would be serve as a distasteful reminder of life in Point Pleasant for the girl, Eve. According to his source, she was thinking of remaining in town and had changed her mind about selling the hotel.

Not what he'd wanted to hear. He would have been more than willing to add the property to his portfolio if only to get her out of Point Pleasant. At least she hadn't found the negative yet. Maybe he was overreacting and there was nothing to worry about. Maybe Rosie had destroyed it, leaving his fate up to him as she'd suggested in her letter.

Stupid broad. As if he was going to confess to killing the girl.

The sound of muffled voices made him tense suddenly. Crouching, he concealed himself among the trees as footfalls joined the voices, alerting him of someone's approach. Peering through the branches, he spied a man and woman moving in his direction, the woman walking delicately as she picked her way through a maze of protruding roots and rocks.

"I told you to wear different shoes," the man complained, four steps ahead of her. "Those cork things aren't for hiking through woods."

"I didn't know it would be like this," the woman shot back, tiptoeing as if she was walking on hot coals. "How far do we have to go anyway, George?"

He swiveled to face her, walking backward. "Deeper. By that pond." He motioned in Reaper's direction. "Those people in town said a body was found out here. Maybe the Mothman got the guy. You bring the camera?"

"Yeah, I got it." She held up a 35 millimeter as proof. "But I don't want to end up on the menu."

"Don't worry, baby. We get a shot of that freaking bird-creature, we can buy our own restaurant and eat caviar."

What idiots. Worse, they were headed in his direction, making enough noise to raise the dead. Looking around, he tried to decide if he could slip away without being seen. As an alternative, he weighed the odds of walking out and saying hello—doing the local yokel thing and sending them off someplace deeper into the TNT—when he heard the man swear abruptly. Not in anger, but excitement. Reaper watched the guy stoop and pluck something from the ground.

"Holy shit, Glenda, you're not going to believe what I found!"

The woman pranced to his side. "What is it?"

Reaper couldn't see the object in George's hand, but the sick knot in his gut gave him a good idea what the man had discovered. Why the hell hadn't he seen it when he'd trudged through that area a few minutes ago?

"A money clip." George slipped the silver clamp from the bills and passed it to Glenda as if he couldn't wait to be rid of it. Hurriedly, he rifled through the cash, his expression growing more animated with each swipe of his fingers. "Oh, baby! There's close to three hundred dollars here."

"Someone must have dropped it." Glenda looked uneasy. "We should give it to the police."

George balked as if she'd lost her mind. "Are you nuts?"

"What if it's related to the man who was killed here? Maybe it was his, and it's the reason he was murdered. It could be drug money or something." She turned the clip over in her hand. "Look, George, there's a name."

Shit!

He was screwed. The woman was already thinking about giving the clip to the cops. Maybe he needed to play a bold card. Walk up and say he'd lost it. Problem was the guy would never believe him, and the woman would want proof. He had ID, but that opened a whole new can of worms. The two might head back to town and blab how they'd found the money clip near the pond. Ryan Flynn or Sheriff Weston would get wind and come sniffing around with questions. *Seems odd a man like you would be out in the TNT. You wouldn't happen to know anything about Amos Carter's death?*

No matter how he sliced it, he was screwed. Damn sloppy of him to lose that clip.

Reaching into his pocket, Reaper withdrew the .38. Things were getting messy. He couldn't afford two more bodies, but was running out of options.

He watched as George stuffed the wad of cash into his pocket.

"Just leave the damn thing here," he said. "I'm keeping the money."

That's it, George. Take the cash and get out of here. Make her leave the clip.

He could live with that scenario. He could even let *them* live with that scenario, as long as they kept their mouths shut. Odds were if George was keen on keeping the bills, he wouldn't mouth off in town about finding the clip. That would be equivalent to shooting himself in the foot.

The woman seemed indecisive, biting her bottom lip as if weighing the correct thing to do.

Screw this. He couldn't afford the risk.

Reaper tightened his hand on the revolver and moved from the trees. He'd only taken a single step when the woman looked up suddenly, blood draining from her face. He had the gun concealed behind his back, but she appeared terrified he was going to off her. Then he realized she wasn't looking at him at all, but something that loomed behind him. Something that blocked the sun and sent a massive shadow scrolling over the ground.

Reaper felt the hair on his neck stand on end. He had only a second to dive into the brush, chased by the woman's bone-chilling scream.

* * * *

Evening arrived and with it the planned excursion into the Witch Wood. Eve and Katie met Caden and Ryan at the Flynn house. While the men rooted for shovels in a storage shed, Eve and her friend said hello to Mrs. Flynn. They found Maggie's mother in the living room, contentedly knitting in her usual spot, the TV playing an old black-and-white rerun of *I Love Lucy.*

"You won't find the girl by the tree," she told them the moment they stepped into the room. The click-clack of her needles overrode any sputtered reply they may have offered at her bizarre greeting.

"I'm not sure what you mean, Mrs. Flynn," Eve said uncertainly. While Doreen Sue was "Doreen Sue," Mrs. Flynn was always "Mrs. Flynn," rarely ever "Elizabeth." There was something about this particular woman that made Eve feel like a child, uncertain of her place. Or maybe it was simply that Mrs. Flynn was Maggie's mother.

"Maggie said you have to go deeper, ten feet past the tree," Mrs. Flynn told them. "Look for the big rock you used to climb as kids. Dig there."

Standing inside the doorway, Eve exchanged a glance with Katie. Neither Caden nor Ryan would have mentioned the plan to their mother, feeding her eccentric behavior. If only Eve could speak to Maggie as Mrs. Flynn did so often and so easily.

"Mrs. Flynn," she prompted.

The woman looked up and smiled. "Oh, hello, you two. It's a pleasant day for a visit. Can I offer you some lemonade?"

Clearly befuddled, Katie stammered her thanks and declined.

Eve smiled pleasantly. The woman had been in one of her trances. "No thank you, Mrs. Flynn. We just wanted to say hello. Caden and Ryan are waiting for us outside. They're going to help Katie and me with a few things at the hotel."

"That's nice." Mrs. Flynn turned her attention back to her knitting, humming softly. Eve nodded to Katie, and the two left the room, heading for the front porch.

"That was creepy," Katie said as they'd stepped outside. "Does she do that a lot?"

"Frequently."

"How do you think she knew what we have planned? Do you believe she can talk to Maggie?"

"She was right about the igloo." Whatever force directed Mrs. Flynn— Maggie or something else—it wasn't to be discounted. "Let's tell the guys what she said."

Ryan scowled when they relayed the story, and Caden appeared uncomfortable. Eve guessed he didn't like the thought of his mother communicating with Maggie when he was denied the chance to tell his sister how sorry he was.

The drive to the Witch Wood wasn't long, but the hike between the trees took time. It had been years since Eve had played in the thicket, back in the days when Nana Flynn lived in the old home that bordered its northern edge. The house was still there, but it had new occupants now. Ones who cared little about its state of repair, judging by the peeling paint on the shutters and flowerbeds rife with weeds. A ratty wire fence had been erected at the edge of the yard to separate the overgrown lawn from the dense thicket behind it. As a result, they were forced to park elsewhere and enter the woods at a diagonal from a bordering lane.

It took Eve a while to locate the giant sycamore that resembled a woman reaching to the sky. "I can't believe it's still here." She traced her fingers lightly over the trunk, assaulted by a flood of memories. Maggie spinning in a circle, head thrown back and arms outstretched to the sky, her laughter giddy and bright like a flash of sunlight on water. Then months later, a different Maggie huddled beneath the blankets in her bedroom, whispering the Mothman wanted to kill her.

Eve sobered abruptly, appealing to Caden with a beseeching glance. "We're close." He had to feel his sister's spirit in these woods as much as she did. Maggie was here, held captive in the past. Whatever occurred that day fifteen years ago was the crux of everything that followed. Twining her fingers with Caden's, she tugged him past the tree. "Ten feet, your mother said. Near the big rock."

They found it exactly as Mrs. Flynn said they would. By then the sun had sunk lower on the horizon, bloodying the trees with bands of vermillion and copper-streaked brass. Twilight was still several hours away but the air had grown slightly cooler, ripe with the musky scent of ferns and soil.

"Let's get this over with." Ryan sank the tip of a spade into the earth.

Not content to stand around while the men dug, Eve and Katie pitched in as well. The ground was soft, but buried roots and hidden stones made the chore tedious. Thankfully, Caden had added a digging iron and pick to the shovels, allowing the men to hack through the roots more swiftly. Eve packed several thermoses with cold water and they took breaks as needed, sweaty from the laborious work.

Finally, after what seemed an inordinate amount of time, Ryan straightened with a huff of breath. Sweat glistened in his bangs, matting several strands to his forehead. His blue T-shirt was soaked at the collar, and his jeans bore streaks of dirt. "How deep do we plan on digging?" The pit they had created already reached a depth of approximately four feet. "Sooner or later we've got to face this is a waste of time."

Katie lobbed an irritated glare in his direction. "Quit if you want to, but I know Wendy didn't run away. I'm not giving up."

"Look, Katie, I know you're upset, but—"

"Hey, I think I found something." Caden tapped the point of his shovel carefully against the ground. "I think there's something buried here."

Ryan palmed sweat from his forehead. "Probably just another tree root or more rocks."

"This isn't rock." Kneeling, Caden held the shovel at his side, using his free hand to brush away bits of loose earth. Gradually, something took shape under his fingertips.

The edge of another stone? A surge of disappointment flooded Eve, only to be replaced by a sense of delayed horror seconds later. As Caden continued to work away the soil, the shape beneath his hand formed into the upper arc of an eye socket.

"Holy shit!" Swiftly, Ryan knelt to help his brother.

Moving to Katie's side, Eve wrapped her arm around the girl's shoulders, the two of them staring down at the ugly skull taking form in the earth. It wasn't long before the other eye socket and the dome of the cranium emerged.

Ryan grabbed his brother's wrist, preventing him from freeing more dirt. "We can't just dig this up."

"You're right." Sitting back on his haunches, Caden dragged a dirty hand through his hair. "Even if this isn't Wendy Lynch, the remains belong to someone. You need to let Pete Weston know so he can get a forensics team in here."

"It's Wendy." Katie's voice was flat, bordering on emotionless. The pain in her eyes spoke volumes. "Having Sheriff Weston exhume the remains won't make a difference. I know it's her."

"Katie, I'm so sorry," Eve whispered.

Caden stood. "If it is Wendy, she deserves to have her remains disinterred properly."

"There could be evidence here of how she died." Ryan seemed relieved to have his brother side with him but his words were plainly for Katie when he spoke. "We could damage the bones by continuing to dig and possibly compromise evidence that could brand this a crime scene." He stepped closer, taking Katie's hand in his. "If this is your sister, then she deserves whatever help we can give in finding her killer. Let me do this properly, Katie, through the proper channels."

She hesitated, clearly torn between proving the bones belonged to Wendy and wanting justice for her sister. At last she nodded. "Promise me if it is Wendy, you'll do all you can to find her killer."

Ryan nodded, his gaze for Katie alone. "I swear."

* * * *

Eve found it difficult concentrating on work the following day after everything that had happened. Fortunately, Katie had scheduled Sharon Tanner, their back-up employee for the front desk to work dayshift. With Roger Layton's birthday party taking place that night, Eve's business-savvy manager had left her and Eve free for any last minute party prep that needed to be addressed.

Walking into the lobby, Eve found Sharon behind the desk, her nose buried in a pop magazine with Steve Perry and Journey on the cover. Not up to arguing the merits of looking busy, especially when the hotel was quiet, she cleared her throat. "Have you seen Katie?"

The girl colored and lowered the magazine. "Oh, uh…hi, Eve. I think she's in the kitchen talking to the cook—um, chef."

Eve nodded, noting the correction. It was silly, but part of offering an alternative to the chain hotels across the river in Gallipolis had included hiring a head chef for catered events and the café. She had a lot riding on Roger's party. As a bank vice-president, he'd be hobnobbing with city officials and businessmen of note who might bring other business if they enjoyed the event.

"Oh." Sharon turned a page as Eve prepared to head for the kitchen. "By the way, Mr. Layton is in the ballroom. He came in earlier wanting to see the layout. Since you and Katie weren't around, and since it's his party, I didn't see any harm in letting him up there."

"Okay." Eve would have done the same, though she most certainly would have accompanied him in the event he had questions or comments. Then again, Sharon wasn't equipped to handle either and would have had to refer matters to her.

Finding Katie leaving the kitchen, she did a quick visual inspection of her friend, spying a telltale smudge of shadow beneath her eyes. Clearly, she hadn't slept well, not that Eve could blame her. It wasn't every day you came across bones that most likely belonged to your missing sister.

"Good morning." She tried to sound cheerful, sensing Katie's subdued mood. "How are things going with the party menu?"

"On schedule." Katie offered a weak smile in return. "Jack has everything under control. With his culinary skills, I'd be surprised if Roger Layton has anything negative to say about tonight."

Jack Devin, a Philadelphia transplant, was the hotel's recently hired head chef. Fortunately for Eve, he'd fallen in love with a local girl and had shown up a week ago sniffing for employment after moving to the area.

"How about you?" She hooked her arm through Katie's and steered her toward the lobby. "After everything that's happened, do you still feel up to helping with the party?"

"Of course. Besides…." Coming to a halt, Katie tugged at her ponytail. It was a trait Eve had come to recognize as a nervous habit. "There's nothing I can do for Wendy right now, and thinking about those bones in the Witch Wood will only drive me crazy."

"Ryan's working on it."

"I know he is."

"Did you say anything to your mom?"

Katie shook her head. "I won't. Not until I know it's Wendy for certain. I just hope the way rumors fly, it doesn't leak out and she hears about it from someone else. At least everyone is busy chattering about the Mothman photo right now."

"Mothman photo? Did I miss something?"

"You don't know?" In the lobby, Katie crossed to the sofa grouping below the front windows and grabbed a paper from the table. Whatever she planned to show Eve, it apparently wasn't newsworthy enough for Sharon to tear her eyes from her magazine. At the desk, the girl was still busy poring over Steve Perry.

"Here." Katie produced the local newspaper with a flourish. "Today's headline, courtesy of our hotel guests, George and Glenda Whitmore. They're overnight celebrities."

Eve's mouth dropped as she stared at the front page. The headline emblazoned across the top read *Mothman Captured in Photograph.* Below that was a large grainy image of…something.

Frowning, Eve turned the paper, hoping to spy a form among the wash of charcoal, white, and gray which resembled nothing so much as an elongated blob.

"You have to tilt your head." Katie demonstrated as she traced her finger over a corner. "This is a wing tip. See how it curves down? And this, part of the body." Another trace of her finger outlined a thin cylindrical shape. "It's a partial shot. According to Glenda, she was running and screaming her head off when she accidentally clicked the camera, certain she only had minutes to live."

Eve looked at her friend. "I don't really see…"

"I don't either, but apparently it's been picked up on a news wire and is being touted as the Holy Grail of Mothman evidence. While we were digging up bones last night, Glenda and George were at the police station sharing their story."

"Which is?" Eve still couldn't see anything in the picture. Maybe with a stretch of imagination, and if she tilted her head as Katie said…

"They were poking around the TNT out near the pond where Amos was killed when the Mothman made an appearance. According to Glenda, they barely made it back to their car. She said it chased them down Potters Creek Road, then veered off about a mile from town. They went straight to the sheriff—and then to the newspaper office. The lab developed the photo overnight."

"Did anyone else see it?"

Katie shook her head.

"Hmm." Undecided if she believed someone had managed to capture a photograph of the elusive creature, Eve couldn't find it within herself to dismiss the sighting as folly. Not after what Caden had told her.

Even as the thought surfaced, the phone rang, and Sharon answered with a chirpy "Good morning, Parrish Hotel."

"Sure, I can book those dates for you." Sharon set her magazine aside in favor of the reservation book. "Yes. We're only about five miles from the TNT."

Katie raised a brow as they listened to the conversation. "It's been on and off like that all morning. Mostly locals from neighboring towns, but I have a feeling it won't be long before we're flooded with people from all over hoping to catch a glimpse of the Mothman."

"The hotel could use the business." All the more reason for her to stay in Point Pleasant. The Parrish Hotel was beginning to feel like *her* legacy, not just her family's. It was a business she wanted to succeed.

"It looks like we're finalizing Roger's party just in time," she said to Katie. "Oh, and speaking of which…Sharon said he's poking around the ballroom, checking things out for later tonight. Want to say hello with me?"

"To that man?" Katie frowned, but nodded nonetheless. "Sure. Why not?"

Moments later, they entered the ballroom to find Roger Layton lingering inside—a tall man who stood in the center, hands clasped behind his back. Judging by his commanding posture, if there was something he disliked, Eve would certainly hear about it. The way he surveyed the room she would have thought he owned it. With a mental reminder he and his wife were paying a sizeable chunk of change for the party, she plastered a smile on her face and stepped forward.

"Mr. Layton." She extended her hand as he turned to face her. "I'm Eve Parrish. I don't know if you remember me. It's been many years."

"Eve." He smiled smoothly, revealing even, white teeth. "Look at you, all grown up." His gaze swept her in quick appraisal, the touch of his eyes strangely unsettling. She had nothing but vague memories of him, yet her father's written evaluation rang in her head: *I don't like him.*

"You have your mother's eyes," Roger said.

"Thank you."

His own were brown like his hair. Despite the relative heat of early June, he wore a crisply tailored business suit, the light cream color complementing his gold-striped tie.

"I believe you know my manager, Katie Lynch." Eve indicated her friend.

Roger nodded in Katie's direction but turned his attention back to Eve without as much as a verbal greeting for Katie. "You've done wonders with the setting."

Eve frowned. "Actually, Katie took care of that." She made a point of Katie's hard work, given that Roger's quick glance bordered on condescending. Her friend had an unjustified reputation in the town, and it grated on her nerves to see her dismissed so haughtily. As if accustomed to such snubs, Katie moved away to inspect the silverware on a nearby table.

"I trust everything meets with your satisfaction," Eve said to Roger.

Undaunted by the coolness of her tone, he made a show of letting his gaze roam the room. "Quite. I know Lillian likes all of this fuss.

Personally, I would have preferred a quiet birthday celebration at home. I was hoping she hadn't gotten carried away with decorations and whatnot. Thankfully, it seems acceptable."

Odd. According to Lillian, Roger was the one who expected a party and had felt the buffet wasn't fancy enough. His gaze strayed to Katie who fiddled with the floral arrangement on the nearest table. A flicker of something touched his eyes that made Eve uncomfortable. Just that quickly, he refocused.

"How rude of me not to immediately offer my condolences about your aunt."

Flustered by the swift change of topic, Eve fought to find her voice. "Thank you."

"You do remember she and I were engaged?"

"Yes. I was sad when she broke it off. I wanted her to be happy."

"I was crushed." He didn't sound anything of the sort.

Katie dropped silverware onto a plate, causing them both to glance sharply in her direction.

"Sorry." Lowering her gaze, she picked up the flatware and began placing it back on the table, taking care to arrange each dinner setting precisely. A marked tightness hovered about her mouth.

"It seems so long ago," Eve said to Roger. "I never understood why Aunt Rosie broke off the engagement so abruptly." The collapse of the Silver Bridge had altered everyone's life, but the tragedy shouldn't have stolen her aunt's chance for happiness. "I thought the two of you were happy together."

"We were. It's a mystery to me as well." Roger shrugged, then swiftly brushed the observation aside. "In any event, it's a pleasure to see you again." Extending his hand, he flashed another polished smile. "I'll look forward to enjoying the party tonight."

After he'd left, Eve turned to Katie. "You look perturbed."

"Does it show?" Setting aside a cloth napkin, Katie shook her head. "I seriously doubt he was crushed when Rosie broke off their engagement. He married Lillian six months later."

"Only six?" Eve had imagined him devastated and broken-hearted, reluctant to strike up another relationship, at least not so quickly. It must have been horrible for Aunt Rosie to see him remarried so soon. "I didn't realize it happened so quickly."

"Maybe that's why your aunt never married." Katie gave the napkin a final fluff. "Between losing her brother when the bridge collapsed and having Roger marry so soon, she had too much heartache in her life."

Eve pulled out a chair and sat down. "I'm sure it didn't help that my mother left, too, packing us off to Pennsylvania."

"I can understand why she didn't want to stay." Katie sat beside her. "I didn't lose anyone when the bridge went down, but it changed everything about Point Pleasant. Then Bruce Mechanical closed, and so many people were left without work. Overnight, Point Pleasant became a shadow of what it had been. There are ghosts in this town, Eve, and not all of them have to do with dying."

"Then why did you stay?"

Katie shrugged, lowering her eyes briefly. "I knew my mother wasn't going anywhere, and I really believed Wendy didn't run away. I'm not sure what I thought happened to her, but I knew if she tried to reach me, she'd look here. I couldn't leave without knowing what became of her."

Eve leaned forward, laying a hand over hers. "What if those really are her bones we dug up last night? Are you prepared for that?"

Katie nodded. "I already know it's her. I can feel it in my heart. I just want the bastard that killed her to be found. She didn't deserve to be tossed away like that. No one does."

Chapter 10

Roger Layton's party went smoothly. Eve made sure the meal was served and the tables cleared before she thought about taking a break in her office. Most of the work was over.

At the podium, Lillian offered a toast to her husband, then beckoned him forward to say a few words. His speech wasn't long, a thank you to her, a reference to his position as VP at the bank—drumming up more business, most likely—and a few anecdotes about getting older. When he was through, Katie dimmed the lights, setting the stage for a more relaxed environment. Violet Breeze, the local band Lillian had hired, launched into its first set, and a few dancers braved the spotlight on the highly waxed floor, Roger and Lillian among them.

Satisfied that all was going well, Eve headed for the door. A ten-minute break wouldn't hurt, and she could use the downtime after standing most of the evening in heels. She was almost to the threshold when she encountered Jeremy Layton returning from the hallway where he'd no doubt gone in search of the bathroom, his expression strangely mournful.

"Hi, Jeremy." She smiled as she approached. "Did you enjoy dinner?"

He shrugged without comment, his sullen look speaking volumes. The poor kid was probably bored out of his skull.

"Aren't there any other kids here?"

He shook his head glumly. "Dad didn't want that."

So it was Roger who'd called the shots with putting the party together. He wanted pomp and fanfare but didn't want to appear like the one orchestrating it.

"Don't you like to dance?" She felt badly for Jeremy. "That's always fun." Even as a kid, she'd danced with adults at some parties she'd attended. Both her dad and mom had always been accommodating when she couldn't coax one of her shyer friends onto the floor. And then there was Aunt Rosie, who'd often dragged *her* out for a fun and frivolous twirl.

He shook his head.

"Ok. Well, what do you like to do?"

"I like to read."

"Great. Did you bring a book?"

"Dad wouldn't let me." The kid looked miserable. "He said I need to be part of the party, make sure I'm seen."

Dad was a jerk. The more she learned about Roger, the more she disliked him. Between the orders he'd given Lillian about the party preparations and the rules he set for Jeremy's attendance, he was obviously an overbearing man. No wonder her father disliked him. What had ever attracted Aunt Rosie to a man like Roger?

Tapping a finger against her chin, she considered the pop magazine Sharon had stashed behind the reception counter. Would a twelve-year-old boy be interested in Journey?

"I might be able to find a magazine downstairs if you'd like."

"That's okay." A hesitant smile touched his lips, and she had the distinct impression he was pleased by the offer. "Thanks anyway. Mom stashed the book I'm reading in her purse. She said once Dad has a few drinks and is wrapped up in the party, she'll give it to me. He won't notice me reading then."

Lillian might be reserved, but she plainly had a soft spot for her son. "Your Mom is really thoughtful."

He nodded eagerly. "Yeah. We like a lot of the same things, too, like reading, funny TV shows, and gardening. Mom and I both love yellow carnations. Dad says flower gardening isn't masculine and reading isn't much better."

Dad was more than a jerk, he was a dyed-in-the-wool Neanderthal. Eying the tables, Eve was surprised he hadn't objected to the colorful centerpieces Lillian had delivered from the local florist. Apparently flower arrangements were acceptable for a banquet hall celebration. The summery blooms reminded her of the yellow carnations she'd found on Aunt Rosie's grave. Interesting that Lillian liked yellow carnations.

Curiosity made her pry. "Has your mom taken flowers to the cemetery lately?"

Jeremy looked at her in surprise, and she immediately regretted the question. What a strange thing to ask a young boy. He must think her crazy, at the very least, rude.

"How did you know?"

It was her turn to feel astonishment. "You mean she did?"

He nodded. "She put them on some woman's grave. I think she's a relative of yours."

"Rosalind Parrish?"

Another nod. "I went with her because she took me to McDonalds for lunch afterward. She said we shouldn't tell Dad about the flowers because he'd only get mad."

Eve's heartbeat quickened. Why would Lillian of all people feel compelled to put flowers on the grave of her husband's former fiancée? And why would that make Roger angry?

She was so absorbed in the thought she didn't realize when the Man of Honor came up beside her. "Is my son monopolizing your time?"

Eve tried to keep her growing distaste from showing as she turned to face him. "Roger. You surprised me. Jeremy and I were just chatting. Your son is charming."

He didn't spare the boy a glance. "Perhaps I can distract you for a moment? I'd like to talk to you about something."

"Oh?" Eve allowed herself to be steered away, thinking it had to do with the party. A backward glance over her shoulder showed Jeremy disappearing back into the hallway as if he hoped to vanish from his father's sight.

"I hope you won't mind doing me the honor of a dance as we talk." Roger pulled her onto the waxed floor before she could form an objection. Violet Breeze had morphed into the mellow notes of a song more appropriate for romantic dancing between couples. Eve stiffened to the feel of Roger's arm around her waist and the dwindling space between them. "Shouldn't you be dancing with your wife?"

"My wife and I have all night to dance, and she doesn't have a hotel to sell."

Eve almost came to a complete stop. "Pardon?"

His smile was smooth and effortless. "Eve, certainly you must have surmised by now that I'm Adam Barnett's client. Who else in town would have the wherewithal to make a solid offer on the Parrish Hotel?"

"You?" It made sense. Of course, it did. He was vice president of the local bank and, according to almost everyone in town, one of Point Pleasant's leading citizens. But why would a bank VP want to add an historic hotel to his portfolio of holdings? She bit her lip. Why not, especially if the tide turned and he could make it profitable again?

No, that was something *she* intended to do. Even without a resurgence of Mothman fever, she had planned on reinventing the hotel and establishing the type of traffic that had been common in her parents' day. She wasn't about to turn that legacy over to anyone else. If she'd been on the fence before about leaving Point Pleasant, she no longer had doubts she would stay. The Parrish Hotel would not fall into the hands of someone like Roger Layton.

Or anyone else for that matter. It belonged to her family. Always had and always would if she had anything to say about it.

"I'd like to discuss my offer with you." Roger moved closer as if attempting to use his height to intimidate her. His hand dropped lower onto her hip.

Rather than grow flustered, she became angry. "Mr. Barnett already discussed it with me. The answer is no. I'm staying in Point Pleasant. The hotel isn't for sale."

His lips thinned in a condescending smile. "What do you know about running a hotel?"

"It's in my blood." The man was such a conceited ass. "And I have Katie Lynch as my manager. She knows the operations of this hotel almost as well as my Aunt Rosie did."

"Katie Lynch—"

"Did I hear my name?" Like a godsend, her friend appeared at her shoulder, as poised as Eve had ever seen her. "Eve, I hate to interrupt, but I need to talk to you about the wine list."

Eve wanted to hug her. "Of course." Stepping away from Roger, she thanked him politely for the dance, then reiterated the hotel was not for sale. Katie gave her a strange look but led her across the room and into the hallway where they had more privacy.

"What about the wine list?" Eve moved a short distance away from the entrance. At the top of the stairs, a young couple chatted while taking in the view of the lobby and a few partygoers wandered past in search of the restrooms farther down the hall.

Katie shook her head. "Nothing actually. I just thought you needed rescuing from Roger. I saw him pawing you." She gave a theatrical shudder. "The man makes my skin crawl."

"Mine, too." Away from the ballroom and the party guests, Eve could admit the truth. "You're a lifesaver."

Katie smiled. "Glad to help. But what was that about selling the hotel?" The smile faded, replaced by an expression of worry. The hotel was Katie's livelihood, especially now with the promotion and raise she'd received. It would be bad enough for Eve to sell, but far worse if she turned the establishment over to a man like Roger.

"You don't have to worry. Roger Layton isn't getting his hands on my hotel."

"He actually wanted to buy it?"

"He did." She crossed to an ornate, padded bench positioned against the wall and sank to a seat. It was wonderful to get off her feet for a few minutes. A steady drone of music, voices, and laughter flowed from the open doors of the ballroom as Roger's party settled into full swing.

Looking worried, Kate joined her on the bench. "Are you thinking of selling to someone else?"

"Definitely not." Removing one shoe, Eve dropped it to the floor, then massaged her toes. She'd worn slacks, not a dress, but the heels had taken their toll on her feet. "I won't lie. For a time I did consider selling, but so much has happened, it's made me realize what the hotel means. I grew up here. Despite all the bad memories of the Silver Bridge, losing my father and Maggie, Point Pleasant is my home. I've decided to stay."

Katie's mouth dropped. "Permanently?"

Fully embracing the decision, Eve nodded. "As soon as I can finalize things in Harrisburg, I'm going to move here. I've already got Caden making repairs to the house so—"

She never got to finish. With a squeal of delight, Katie engulfed her in a hug. "I'm so glad you're going to stay! And not just because of the hotel. You've become such a good friend. I'd be lost if you went back to Harrisburg."

"Me, too." Laughing, Eve hugged her back. "I'll be counting on you to help me get things in order."

"I will. I promise. Rosie would be so happy."

The mention of her aunt shifted Eve's thoughts elsewhere. Drawing back, she looked at Katie intently. "Speaking of Aunt Rosie, you won't believe what I learned tonight."

"From Roger?"

"No. From his son, Jeremey. Apparently, Lillian put flowers on Aunt Rosie's grave when Jeremy was with her. She told him they had to keep it a secret from Roger because he'd be angry."

The smooth skin above Katie's eyebrows furrowed in a frown. "But Lillian and Rosie weren't friends. As far as I know, the only time they spoke was when Lillian booked the ballroom."

"That's what I thought. So why would Lillian go out of her way to put flowers on Aunt Rosie's grave, especially if she knew Roger wouldn't like it?" It didn't make sense.

"Uh-oh." Eve's friend stared past her down the hallway, a flicker of alarm passing through her eyes.

"What?"

"I hate to be the bearer of bad tidings, but Caden is headed this way, and he doesn't look happy."

Eve twisted around to see her boyfriend stalking toward her, his expression thunderous. Now what? With a sigh, she slipped on her shoe. "You'd better go. Whatever it is, I'm sure it's about me."

"Maybe I *will* check on the wine list." Katie patted her knee. "Be tough. That guy's putty in your hands." Breezing down the hall, she tossed a hello to Caden as they passed, but he barely acknowledged her, focused on Eve.

"You look upset," she said when he reached her. He'd obviously been working at her house, dressed in an old T-shirt and jeans that bore speckles of paint. Yesterday, he'd finished the repairs and painting to Aunt Rosie's old dark room and had intended to start on the upstairs hallway and bath today.

"Upset?" The word rolled from his tongue weighted with sarcasm. "When were you going to tell me?"

Puzzled, Eve stood. "Tell you what?"

He shook his head as if disbelieving she would act clueless.

"Caden." She grew exasperated. "It would help if I knew what you were talking about."

"I'll give you a hint. I needed turpentine to clean my paintbrushes but ran out, so I looked in your shed, hoping you might have some. Want to guess what I found?"

"Pff!" She blew air between her lips. The man was acting crazy. "No, I—" And then it hit her. The trash bag with the butchered crow. How could she have been so stupid to forget? Between the grave-digging excursion in the Witch Wood, the discovery of Wendy's remains, and the preparations for Roger's party, she hadn't buried the grisly thing. The bag had probably been swarming with flies. "Oh." She covered her mouth with her hand. "I forgot. I was going to tell you. Honestly."

His gaze was hard. "When?"

The intent had been there from the moment Katie lectured her, but somehow she'd forgotten. Especially after Caden had dropped his bombshell about coming in contact with the Mothman. With all the craziness taking place, she wasn't exactly thinking rationally.

"Eve." Grabbing her arm, Caden pulled her down onto the bench. "How am I supposed to protect you if you won't tell me what's going on?"

Fire stirred in her belly. "I don't need you to protect me, Caden."

"You do know I was a cop?"

"Yes, a sergeant. And I know why you quit. Doreen Sue told me what happened with Hank Jeffries and the Kline brothers."

His mouth twisted, a visible sign he hadn't expected her to dig up something so tragic. "She told you, huh? It's probably just as well."

"Would you have told me?"

"It's not something I like to talk about." Taking her hand, he softened his voice. "Look, Eve…what happened with Hank might have soured me on carrying a gun, but it hasn't made me any less aware of predators. You need to tell me about the crow and how it got there."

He'd avoided answering her question. Maybe it was cop instinct that kept him focused, or maybe he really wasn't sure. Either way, sitting in the hall with a party taking place a few feet away didn't seem the appropriate time to pick at his reasoning or the past.

"I found it the day you and Ryan came for dinner." Drawing a breath, she forced herself to retreat to that sunny afternoon, then relayed the whole story—how she'd found it outside, talked to Doreen Sue, then finally, how she and Katie had stowed it in the trash bag. "Katie wanted me to tell you that night, but I wanted you and Ryan focused on Wendy. Honestly, Caden—after that, I just forgot. I didn't even remember to bury the poor thing."

"I took care of that. It wasn't worth sending to the lab, but I'll check the area where you found it. Eve." He drew her hand into his lap, then lightly tracked his thumb over her knuckles. "Don't you see this is the next step? Whoever is trying to scare you away, for whatever reason, wasn't successful with the notes they left on your car. The guy is getting desperate, so he's upped the ante. Who knows what he'll do next."

"Well, I'm not leaving." She stiffened her back, sitting straighter. "I'm staying permanently. I made that decision tonight. I'm going to move into Aunt Rosie's house and run the Parrish Hotel just as she would have wanted. As my father would have wanted. I'm not going anywhere."

"Seriously?" The grim line of his mouth morphed into a slowly spreading smile. "You're going to stay—live—in Point Pleasant?"

She smiled right along with him. "Yes. It will take me a while to wrap up the loose ends with my job in Harrisburg, my apartment, and belongings, but I have no plans on reversing the decision. The hardest part will be breaking the news to my mother."

"Eve, that's great. Uh…not about your mother, but that you'll be staying." He cleared his throat and shifted awkwardly. "I probably haven't said it, but I care about you."

Her heartbeat quickened. The interlude with Roger aside, it was turning out to be a perfect night. "I care about you, too. Every time I thought about saying goodbye, I felt sick." Her fingers tightened around his hand. "Looks like you're going to be stuck with me."

"You won't get any complaints." Hooking his arm around her neck, Caden pulled her closer. His lips moved over hers in a soft kiss, sending a pleasant tingle down her spine. Before she could contemplate the delicious sensation, he drew back and stroked a finger over her cheek. "What time will you be done here?"

"Why?"

"Because I'll hang around, or I'll come back when you're through."

"Why?" she persisted.

"Eve, just about everyone in town knows Roger is having a party tonight. If someone wanted to catch you leaving the hotel, tonight's the perfect chance. I'd feel better if I was here when you left. I'll follow you home."

The man was being silly, but there was no use pointing out the obvious. His expression more than made it clear arguing would be a waste of time. Like it or not, she was stuck with her overly protective, ex-sheriff's-sergeant boyfriend. There were certainly worse ways to end a night.

"All right." She glanced at her watch. "Let me check with Katie. The dinner service is over, so there's not much left to do. If she's fine handling things on her own, I'll leave now. Give me ten minutes, and I'll meet you in my office."

"Done." He gave her a quick kiss and stood. A goofy grin spread over his face. "Damn, I'm glad you're staying."

A feeling of warmth washed over her. "Me, too."

There was no question she'd made the right decision.

* * * *

Roger tossed down another shot of Scotch and leaned against the bar, watching his friends, associates, and family members party on the dance floor. Somehow, Lillian had convinced Jeremy to join her, but the kid had two left feet. What an awkward bird. Not that his wife was much better, but at least she wasn't making a spectacle of herself. No, his perfect wife was too proper for that. She frequently reminded him they had an image to uphold. Her family came from old money—banking money—and had helped put Point Pleasant on the map. She might look like an eighteenth-century spinster, but underneath the woman was a shrewd cookie.

She'd supported him, recognizing the potential of a lucrative investment when he'd suggested they make an offer on the Parrish Hotel through Adam Barnett. Too bad the deal hadn't seen the light of day. Now he'd have to tell her it was a no-go. Not that he really wanted the old monstrosity, anyway.

Years ago, it had ranked high on his radar, but that was before he'd landed Lillian and her father's bank. It still wouldn't have hurt to tuck the hotel into his portfolio, but his main reason for making the offer had been to get rid of the girl. If Eve sold the place, she'd leave town without any need for him to resort to his "Reaper" persona.

Damn. He hated when things didn't go his way.

Motioning for the bartender, he nodded toward his empty glass.

"Sure thing, Mr. Layton." The man hopped to the task, splashing a finger of Scotch into the crystal.

Mr. Layton. He liked the respect the name implied, enjoying the recognition that came from being someone of note. Feeling generous, he dropped a few dollars on the bar as tip, then downed the shot.

Happy Birthday to me.

The liquid burned his throat, but the sting made him feel alive. He had a slight buzz going and would probably be drunk before the night was over if he kept the current pace. Hell, he deserved the luxury. Another year older and all that crap. Yesterday at the TNT, he'd been ready to shit himself, certain he wouldn't live to breathe another second.

The rational part of his mind insisted he hadn't seen the Mothman, but the part that functioned on survival instinct knew differently. He still remembered the red-haired woman's scream, a horrified shriek that had sent him diving for the ground. He'd burrowed among the bulrushes, trying to appear as small as possible, knowing something demonic loomed behind him. The woman and her husband hadn't spied him, but he'd feared "the thing" had.

Shit, he'd even whimpered. What a pathetic pansy-ass.

The monster's shadow had crossed over him as it flew past, dark and cold as a patch of black ice. A loud droning exploded in his head, somersaulting his gut into his throat. Terrified, he'd squeezed his eyes shut and pressed his hands to his ears, fearful of heaving his lunch.

He couldn't be sure how long he'd lain curled up like a spineless wimp. After a while, he became conscious of the sound of his breath, a harsh rasp that replaced the buzzing in his head. Other sounds followed...

insects nearby, the call of a bird, the rake of the breeze through the rushes. Drenched in sweat, he'd crawled unsteadily to his knees.

The Mothman, the nosey tourist couple, and even their car were gone.

Earlier today, he'd seen the photo the woman had snapped splashed across the front page of the local paper. Fortunately, the focus had been on the monster and how the couple had managed to escape. No mention of his missing money clip. According to the woman, *The thing chased us from the TNT, then veered off. George said it didn't want us there, but I got the feeling it was trying to protect us from something. It could have killed us if it wanted to.*

Stupid bimbo. What did some touristy broad know about a bird-creature? The only thing she and her dim-witted husband had needed protecting from was him.

Had the monster known he was there? That he'd intended to kill them? He shuddered.

It didn't matter. All he cared about was the money clip and the possibility of it being tied to him or, worse, Amos's murder.

He'd scoured the area thoroughly after recovering from his fright, but hadn't been able to find the damn thing. The woman must have pocketed the clip or dropped it. Hopefully, it was gone for good and the meddlers would leave soon, too. Even if the couple wanted to hang around, they probably had jobs waiting and wouldn't be able to linger indefinitely. If worst came to worst, he'd have to dream up an incentive to move them along.

Thinking about it, Roger cracked his knuckles.

"Hey, Roger." Stan Brogan, a colleague from the bank, joined him at the bar. "Some party. Why aren't you on the dance floor with Lillian?"

Roger motioned the bartender to pour another Scotch. "I'm enjoying the view from here."

"Yeah, great party." Brogan requested a bottle of Miller, then propped an elbow against the bar while he waited. "Of course, I wouldn't expect anything less from you and Lillian. You two always go for the brass ring." The bartender delivered his bottle, and he raised it in a toast. "Cheers, Roger."

"Cheers." Roger downed his Scotch. "So what do you think about this Mothman thing?" It wouldn't hurt to get another opinion on the sighting, maybe even learn a thing or two about the redhead and her money-grubbing husband. "What was the name of the couple who saw The Bird?"

Brogan grunted and scratched a chewed fingernail across his chin as if the question required excessive thought. No wonder. Habitual nail-biters overanalyzed everything. "Whitmore."

Lately, Lillian had picked up the nail-chewing habit, too. Strange that he hadn't realized the frequency until now. She couldn't have grown frazzled from planning a simple party, so why the sudden nervous tick? "They still around town?"

"Last I heard." Brogan took a pull on his Miller. "I think they're enjoying the attention, though I heard they were scared shitless by what happened. Can't say I blame them." He downed the rest of his Miller then shoved the bottle on the bar. Violet Breeze launched into the first punchy chords of "Eye of the Tiger" and he happily bobbed his head to the beat.

What a jerk.

"I don't think they'll be going back to the TNT anytime soon," Brogan continued, pitching his voice to carry over the guitar riffs. "I bet they'll hang around until everyone quits buying them free meals and beer. Tomorrow, something else will come along to snag everyone's attention, and they'll be yesterday's news. I already heard a rumor the cops dug up a set of bones in the woods near the old Flynn house."

"Huh?" Roger swiveled around as if he'd been slapped in the face. The loud crash of bass and drums was nothing compared to the roar of blood in his ears. "What's that?" His fingers cramped on his shot glass.

"Hey, can I get another Miller, here?" Brogan waved to the bartender, indicating his empty. Loosening his tie, he bobbed his head some more, clearly planning to cut loose.

"Stan."

"Yeah. What?" The beer arrived, and he dropped a dollar tip on the bar. "Hey, did you see that new blond teller anywhere?" Turning, he surveyed the dance floor, looking every bit the married man whose wife had gone out of town. "I thought this would be a good chance to say hello outside of work. You did invite her, right?"

"Stan, what about the bones?"

"Bones? Oh, that." A long pull on the Miller had Roger wanting to strangle the guy. How freaking long did it take to answer a simple question?

Brogan dragged a hand across his mouth, wiping up overspill from his beer. "I heard someone say Ryan Flynn found a grave in the woods near that old behemoth property at the end of town. You know—the one where his grandmother used to live. The cops are supposed to be exhuming the remains, but it could just be talk. Can't even remember who told me about it."

Roger clenched his jaw, the slight buzz he'd enjoyed earlier completely obliterated. The damn world was unraveling. It wasn't possible Flynn had found her bones. Not now. Not after all this time.

Part of him wanted to strangle the annoying little pipsqueak standing beside him, bopping his head to the music, drinking *his* damn beer. But the other part, used to playacting in public, put on a silky smile and clapped the bastard on the back. "Probably more hogwash like the Mothman. You enjoy yourself, Stan. I'm going to mingle with some of my other guests."

"Sure thing, Roger."

Yeah. Sure thing. What the idiot didn't realize—there wasn't a single person in the room Roger wouldn't willingly sacrifice to save his own ass.

Chapter 11

"Okay. I'm ready." Eve pulled her office door closed and stepped into the hotel lobby. She wasn't entirely sold on the necessity of Caden escorting her home but seeing him gazing out the front windows, hands in the pockets of his jeans, sent an unexpected jolt through her heart. With his back turned, she could almost imagine him the eighteen-year-old boy who'd caught her fancy when she was an impressionable preteen. "Katie said she'll stay until the party ends. Just in case there are any loose ends, or Roger or Lillian need something."

Caden turned to face her. "Yeah, she told me her mom is watching Sam tonight." He extended his hand. When she stepped nearer, closing her fingers around his, he tugged her close and kissed her.

When she could talk again, she smiled. "What was that for?"

"Because I know you think I'm being overprotective. Thanks for humoring me."

"Is that what I'm doing?"

"Are you forgetting I was a cop? I can read between the lines." The observation was accompanied by a measured glance. "And by the way, Roger left a while ago. He cut through here on the way to his car while you were in your office."

"Really?" He didn't seem the type to leave his own party when it was in full swing—too egotistical—but maybe he was miffed because she'd turned him down about the hotel.

"Pardon me." The sound of a woman's voice meshed with the pat-pat of approaching footfalls. "Eve, can I talk to you a minute?"

Somewhat reluctantly, she stepped from Caden's embrace, turning to find Glenda Whitmore behind her. Looking awkward for having interrupted a private moment, the woman tightened her fingers around the strap of a brown and yellow handbag hooked over her shoulder. "I'm sorry to bother you. I just wanted to say how much George and I enjoyed staying here."

"That's very nice of you." Eve guessed Glenda had come from the café. The crowd was probably smaller than usual, many of the regulars attending Roger's party, but there would be plenty of locals to ensure Glenda and George continued their reign as celebrity kingpins. Lately, everyone wanted to talk about the Mothman. If you were lucky enough to have spotted the creature, you automatically garnered superstar status. "I hope you're not leaving?"

"In the next day or two. We really like it here, but we have jobs waiting back home." Biting her lip, Glenda twisted her wedding band nervously. "George is still in the café, but I heard someone say you were here. Because of the party."

Eve nodded, not sure what the woman wanted. "We were just getting ready to leave." She indicated Caden, introducing him as her boyfriend.

Glenda offered a quick hello before glancing over her shoulder in the direction of the café.

"Is something wrong?" Caden asked.

"Wrong?" She swiveled her head back and parted with a nervous laugh. "No. Not at all. But I have something here." Lowering her gaze, she rummaged through her purse. "With me and George leaving, I thought I should give it to someone." She pressed a small silver object into Eve's hand, then quickly recoiled as if she wanted nothing to do with it. "We found it at the TNT area. By that pond where the man was killed."

Eve glanced down at the rectangular object. "A money clip."

"There was nothing in it," Glenda blurted. "Just the clip. That's all."

"Okay." Eve looked at her quizzically, puzzled by her nervousness.

"Well, don't you see? It might have something to do with that poor man being murdered. Here, look—there are initials on the back." Reaching forward, Glenda flipped the clip over in Eve's palm. She traced her finger along the neatly engraved letters. "See? R-A-L."

Eve nodded. "But someone might have just dropped this when they were hiking around."

"I know. But I wouldn't feel right if I didn't tell someone. Maybe you could give it to the police or something."

"Why haven't you?" Caden asked.

Glenda blinked owlishly. "Because I can't get involved. George and I have to get back to our jobs. We've already stayed longer than we should." Switching her attention to Eve, she hiked the strap of her purse onto her shoulder. "Do what you want with it, okay? I'm going back to the café to have another drink with George. For all I care, you can throw the thing away. Just don't tell anyone I gave it to you." Without waiting for an answer, she spun on the heel of her marmalade jelly-flat and strode from the lobby.

Eve looked from the silver clip lying in her palm to Caden. "Do you think this is worth giving to Ryan?"

"It can't hurt." He ran his thumb over the letters. "R-A-L. You know who this belongs to, don't you?"

She shook her head.

"Roger Layton. I've seen him pull it out at the café."

"He doesn't seem like the kind of guy to hike around the TNT, but I suppose it could have been stolen. Maybe Amos took it."

"Maybe." Caden gripped her arm above the elbow. "Come on. I'm going to take you home. We can decide what to do with it later."

* * * *

"This is silly." Eve shook her head and folded her arms across her chest. "Caden, be reasonable. I let you follow me home, but there's no reason for you to start acting like a bodyguard again. I'll be perfectly fine on my own."

It was like talking to a brick wall. The infuriatingly calm man she'd started to think of as her boyfriend checked the lock on the kitchen door to make sure it was secure, then turned to face her with a raised eyebrow. "I thought I'd visit for a while. Are you that anxious to get rid of me?"

He would throw *that* into her face. "Of course not, but—"

The jarring intrusion of the phone cut off her protest. Not that it would have done any good anyway. There were certain areas in which Caden wouldn't budge, and her safety had become one of them. Shaking her head, she turned to the wall phone and picked up the receiver.

"Hello." A whistling shriek erupted in her ear. Recoiling, she held the phone at arm's length and grimaced. "Not again." The screeching was louder than usual, magnified in the small space between her and Caden.

"What the hell?" He took the receiver from her. "What's wrong with your phone?"

"I don't know. I keep getting calls like that. Static and squeals."

"Did you report it to the phone company?"

"Yes, but they said they couldn't find anything wrong."

Her stomach tightened as a wave of fear buffeted her. The squawks and shrieks spilling from the receiver were far more jarring than in the past, mournful wails that seemed ripped from the throats of the dying.

"Someone's playing around." Caden lifted the phone to his ear. "Who is this?" he demanded.

Eve shivered and wrapped her arms close, wanting the gruesome orchestration to stop. Caden depressed the switch hook several times until the drone of a dial tone replaced the shrieks. Hanging up the phone, he kept his hand locked on the receiver as if he expected the caller to make a repeat performance. Frown lines tugged the corners of his mouth. "This has been going on for a while, and you haven't told me?"

She could see it in his eyes; they'd just gone through the same thing with the crow. How could he protect her if she continued to keep secrets? She hadn't considered the distressing calls something she'd deliberately kept private, but her omission made them seem that way now. "The first few times it happened, I thought it was static."

"Eve—"

"And then Doreen Sue tried to convince me it was Aunt Rosie."

"Rosie?" A look of incredulity spread over his face. She'd definitely caught his attention with that bombshell. "What are you talking about?"

"Not here." It had grown dark, night nestling close against the windows and the door to the screened porch. She felt exposed standing in the kitchen, knowing someone had once lurked outside. The kitchen wasn't a place to have a discussion about ghosts and communication with the dead. "Let's go into the living room."

Grabbing a can of beer from the refrigerator, she passed it to Caden, conscious of the scrutiny in his eyes when their fingers brushed. If he'd been worried about her before, a call from her creepy phone stalker hadn't helped. Claiming a Tab for herself, she tried to look at the situation positively. Having the call happen while he was here forced her to consider Doreen Sue's explanation. Even he couldn't deny the eerie screeching had sounded inhuman.

"You do know Doreen Sue buys into everything supernatural?" he asked as he followed her into the living room. "Anyone in town can tell you that. She was one of the people who claimed to see a UFO when all those sightings were happening in '66 and '67."

Odd that Katie hadn't mentioned her mom's attachment to the paranormal. Eve folded into a seat on the sofa, tucking one leg beneath her. She vaguely remembered the UFO sightings and the uproar they had caused in the town. "Interesting."

"Maybe." Caden paced across the room and took a swig from his beer. "Regardless, I can have Ryan put a trace on your phone."

"Won't he look foolish if it's a minor glitch somewhere on the line?"

His brows drew down as he turned to face her. "I thought you'd already ruled that out."

She sighed, suddenly tired. "I didn't press as hard as I could have. At the time, it didn't seem that important." Life had certainly been much simpler in Harrisburg. It would be wonderful to reside in Point Pleasant and not have so many issues hanging over her head. All she wanted to do was stay and run her family's hotel. Enjoy her time with Caden, but she'd attracted some nut who was set on driving her away.

Because they don't want me to find whatever's hidden in the house.

The being at the igloo had indicated as much, confirming her belief Aunt Rosie had hidden something in the house before she died. It had to be what Amos—or whoever had vandalized the property—had been looking for. Something of value. Money or jewelry, perhaps. Why else would someone focus on forcing her from town? And yet the creature at the TNT had hinted whatever was hidden had to do with Wendy Lynch.

Perhaps Aunt Rosie was trying to tell her where she'd stashed the item.

"What if Doreen Sue was right?" Eve wrapped her hands around the can of Tab as she tossed the idea to Caden. Surrounded by her aunt's possessions, most unchanged from the time she was a child, was like being enveloped in a shawl of her aunt's love. Now that the house was hers, she couldn't see herself replacing the heavy traditional furniture with something more contemporary. Even the colorful rugs that warmed the hardwood floor evoked memories of her beloved aunt. It was that sense of closeness that gave her the courage to plow ahead. "What if Aunt Rosie is trying to tell me something?"

Caden dismissed the idea with a backhanded wave. "Be serious." He started pacing again.

"I am being serious." Defensiveness stiffened her spine. "According to the being at the igloo, Aunt Rosie hid something in the house. What if she's trying to tell me where it is?"

He shook his head, dark hair spilling across his brow. "To believe that, I'd have to believe in the thing at the igloo." He turned to face her. "Which I don't."

"Even after it led us to Wendy's body?"

"We don't know if it's Wendy's body."

"And we don't know it isn't. Either way, it led us to a body." Leaning forward, Eve set her soda on the coffee table. "Caden, you know I'm not crazy. I certainly didn't imagine what happened out there. I don't doubt that you had an encounter—*two* encounters—with the Mothman. All I'm asking is that you extend me the same measure of belief."

She'd struck a chord with that one. A frown flitted around his mouth, and his gaze dropped to the gashes on his arm. He nodded. "Okay, you're right. Say I do believe you. What exactly did Doreen Sue tell you?"

Elated by a surge of victory, she bit away a smile. "That spirits often try to communicate through electricity or phone lines. She'd told me about a woman whose dead husband contacted her by using clicks and static delivered over the phone. Kind of like what I've been experiencing. Given all the other strange things we've encountered, it's not outside the realm of possibility."

"I can't argue that." The admission came reluctantly, but he joined her on the couch. Setting his beer on the coffee table, he leaned back with a loud exhale and scrubbed a hand over his face. "It would be a lot easier if we knew what Rosie was trying to tell you."

"Isn't it obvious?" Eve twisted to face him, her knee butting against his thigh. The fact he was onboard with the idea—at least the *possibility* of the idea—brought a renewed rush of excitement. "Aunt Rosie hid something in the house. It's what the vandal was looking for. I think she's trying to tell me where to find it."

"Why now?"

She tilted her head, puzzled. "What do you mean?"

"If it's something important, something she wanted you to have, wouldn't she have told Adam Barnett about it?"

"Not necessarily." Thinking it over, she tapped a finger against her lips. "She might have had a change of heart. Something that didn't seem important while she was alive, or maybe wasn't critical to her until those last moments." She snapped her fingers. "The gray vines."

Caden looked at her askance. "The thing she told Katie about?"

"Yes. Don't you see? That has to be it." Caught up in the idea, Eve bolted to her feet and began to pace. "It wasn't important to her until those final moments of life. She tried to tell Katie, but she was already slipping away." *Gray vines. Gray vines.*

It made no sense. Her aunt didn't even like gray. Everything about her had been vibrant, full of life. She'd favored bright clothing, stylish hats, and chunky jewelry. Even the furnishings in her house reflected her personality. From the vibrant gold swirls in the rug under Eve's feet, to the vivid green grape vines embroidered in the living room drapes, Aunt Rosie's zest for life was evident. True, that vivaciousness had dimmed when the Silver Bridge collapsed, but—

Something clicked in Eve's mind. "That's it!"

Caden raised a brow. "What is?"

"Gray vines!" Eve darted to the bow window, her heart hammering wildly as pieces of the puzzle fell into place. Giddy, she fingered a drapery panel. "At the end, when Aunt Rosie was with Katie, she was doped up on morphine. She wasn't speaking clearly. Katie even told me she slurred her words."

Caden spread his hands. "So?"

Eve's gaze tracked over the twining vines embroidered on the drapes. "What if she hadn't been saying 'gray vines'? What if it only sounded like that, but what she meant to say was '*grape* vines'?"

Caden followed her glance to the drapes. "You think that—"

"Yes, I do!" Excited, Eve flipped the edge of the panel so the backing was exposed. Running her finger along the white fabric, she noted where the panel and backing were stitched together. "This has to be it, Caden. Whatever Aunt Rosie was hiding…whatever her secret was, it has to do with these drapes. I think she must have hid something inside the panel and sewn it back together."

He frowned, joining her to examine the heavy curtains. "Didn't your aunt make these by hand? I remember Maggie talking about that years ago."

"She did. Aunt Rosie loved these drapes."

"And you want to rip them apart?"

Her stomach fell. He was right. If she tore them to pieces only to find nothing inside, she would have destroyed one of her aunt's prized possessions. After the horrid vandalism to Aunt Rosie's house, it seemed heinous to even consider tampering with the drapes. And yet inborn conviction told her she had to be right. "I can have them repaired if I'm wrong. We'll be careful with the stitching so we don't tear the fabric. Help me get them down."

"You're decided on this?"

She nodded. "I can't explain why, but I feel certain I'm right."

Exhaling, he dragged a hand through his hair. "Okay. Let me grab a chair from the dining room so I can unhook them without tearing them."

It took longer than Eve thought. Probably because of the inordinate care she placed in examining each panel. First, she rolled the fabric between her fingers, hoping to feel an obstruction if something was hidden inside. Unfortunately, the fabric was too thick to yield anything by touch. Eventually, she resorted to snipping the seams with scissors, going stitch by stitch, until she could separate the backing from the fabric.

By the time she reached the third panel without discovering anything, doubt had crept up her spine. Her aunt's beloved curtains lay folded over the opposite end of the couch, ruined until she could have them repaired. She wanted to sob. She'd been so certain. How could she have been so utterly wrong?

Shifting, she stretched her legs under the coffee table, adjusting the panel on her lap. She was about to embrace regret when her movement dislodged a white triangle, pushing it through the half-open seam. For the span of a heartbeat, she didn't breathe. "Caden!"

He stood on a chair by the window taking down the fourth and last panel.

"Caden, come quick. I found something."

Without waiting, she snipped away the rest of the seam, exposing the edge of an envelope.

"I don't believe it." Caden peered over her shoulder, then quickly took a seat next to her.

Eve eased the envelope from the panel, suddenly terrified of what she would find inside. Plain white, without any markings, the envelope was the size someone might use to send an invitation or thank-you card. Her heart quickened as she clutched it in her hands. Is this why her house had been vandalized? This single innocuous-looking item? It certainly wasn't money or jewelry. Perhaps it contained a message revealing the location to something of value. Or maybe it was connected to Wendy Lynch.

"Careful with it," Caden said.

"Do you think we should give it to Ryan? If it's related to the vandalism..."

"We don't know that."

"Then you open it. I'm too nervous." The idea Aunt Rosie harbored secrets sent dread tunneling through her stomach.

Caden held the envelope up to the light, squinting to decipher what was inside. "Can I have the scissors?"

She passed them without speaking, consciously gnawing her bottom lip. The air in the room felt abruptly oppressive, ballooning in her lungs, pushing against the back of her throat. Placing the envelope on the coffee table, Caden opened the scissors on a butterfly. Carefully, while holding the white square in place, he slipped one end under the flap and slit the seal from edge to edge.

Eve held her breath.

Gingerly, Caden withdrew the contents of the envelope—a note-sized piece of paper folded in half. Like the cover that had contained it, the sheet was plain and without markings.

"What is it?" Her voice was strained in the weighted silence.

"Something's tucked inside." Even as he spoke, a small piece of transparent film dropped from the open edge into Caden's hand.

Eve stared at the object incomprehensibly. "A negative?" Her aunt had been an amateur photographer and occasionally had even taken shots for the local paper, but they'd been simple slice-of-life and human interest type photographs. "Why would someone vandalize the place for a negative?"

Caden withdrew a small black and white picture from the envelope, his face draining of all color.

Eve's gaze fell to the image she surmised had been lifted from the negative. Expecting to see a candid shot of Wendy Lynch or something that would tie Katie's sister to her aunt, she recoiled at the ghastly sight in horror.

"Oh my God, Caden. Roger Layton killed Maggie!"

Chapter 12

Caden bolted for the door intent on one thought only—*find Roger Layton*. He didn't know why, but the bastard had killed his sister. He'd held the photographic evidence in his hands—an image of Maggie struggling to thrash free of the river. Roger Layton had loomed above her, knee-deep in the water, hands throttling her neck. All this time, Caden had thought the bridge collapse killed Maggie, but she'd survived the tragedy. If not for Layton, she would have been one of the lucky few pulled from the water.

"Caden, no," Eve yelled behind him.

He barely heard, remembering those first raw moments of rescue—the sting of headlights in his eyes, screams and sobs reverberating through the night, the icy bite of wind cutting beneath his sopping clothes. He should have seen Maggie in the confusion. He should have saved her. A bonfire of anger and grief crashed over him. Ripping open the door, he imagined doing the same to Layton's gullet.

"Caden, think!" Eve caught up to him and clutched his arm. "This isn't the way."

"Layton has to pay." He didn't recognize his voice, thick with hatred. The need for vengeance bubbled hot in his gut.

"I know that. I do." Eve refused to release him, staring up into his eyes. Her gaze, troubled and beseeching, mirrored the pleading tone in her voice. "But if you go after Layton in a rage—if you hurt him—you'll only make things worse, and it won't help Maggie. Roger needs to be brought to justice for his crime. Call Ryan and let him handle this legally."

Legally? He grunted at the bothersome thought. The justice system hadn't been worth a damn when Layton wrapped his hands around Maggie's neck and choked the life from her. "Eve—"

"Listen to me." Anger mingled with the desperation in her voice. "Do you want Roger to go free because you acted impulsively and did something stupid?"

"He *killed* her." For fifteen long years he'd held himself accountable for his sister's death. Even saying the words sent a stab of pain through his gut. "Killed her. An innocent child who'd done nothing wrong." Wrenching his arm free, he stalked onto the porch.

"You know I'm right," Eve yelled, trailing behind him. Her voice was choked, as if she fought tears. "You were a cop, Caden. Think like one!"

Her admonition was a slap to the face. He drew up short at the bottom of the porch steps, the first nagging tentacles of doubt dampening his inferno of anger. Vigilante justice wasn't the answer, but the system was slow. The system would take time. It would be so much easier to settle the score with Layton personally. But committing such a crime would only hurt his mother and brother, who'd already suffered the tragedy of loss. And it would do nothing for his sister.

Raising his hands to his face, he dug his fingers into his skull. Eve was right. Of course she was. But—*oh, God, Maggie!*

Sucking down a lungful of air, he bent double, hands braced on his knees. Every time he closed his eyes, all he could see was his sister's trusting face. He shook his head. "This is shit."

Hovering behind him, Eve slid a hand onto his bowed back. "Think of what Maggie would want."

That was the problem. His sister wouldn't want him to toss his life away in a violent hell-bent act of retribution, but he needed to avenge her. The conflict made him want to kick something. To punch. To drive his fist into the hardboard siding and feel pain explode the length of his arm.

Instead, he pulled Eve close. His voice of reason. His sanity. She folded willingly into his arms, burying her face against his neck.

"I'm sorry." He stroked a hand over her hair, conscious of her tears on his skin. Beating Roger to a pulp might selfishly satisfy his need for vengeance, but it wouldn't help Maggie, and it wouldn't put the banker behind bars where he belonged. The man deserved to rot in prison. For the first time since he'd made the decision, Caden regretted turning in his badge.

Slipping a finger beneath Eve's chin, he tilted her face up toward his. Her gaze held a mixture of love and concern, as starkly visible as the tears on her face. A sense of calm washed over him. From the start, she'd been a healing tonic for his soul, soothing the anger and grief that had kept him bound in darkness for fifteen years. She believed in him, and that belief made him take a harder look at himself.

"I'll call Ryan. We'll go through the proper channels and do this legally." He thumbed the tears from her face. "I'm sorry I lost my head."

"You had a right."

Cupping her face in his hands, he kissed her. What might have he done if she hadn't been there to stop him? Now that he could think rationally, a new troubling thought wormed into his brain—Layton had killed Maggie, but why hadn't Rosalind Parrish reported him for his crime?

* * * *

Eve waited in the living room for Ryan to arrive. She'd chosen not to eavesdrop on Caden's call when he'd retreated to the kitchen to phone his brother. It was hard enough managing the tumbleweed of emotion in her stomach. The ghastly photo she and Caden had discovered lay face-down on the coffee table in front of her. She couldn't bear to look at it, but the grisly image remained seared into her mind.

Tears burned Eve's eyes.

What had motivated Roger to kill Maggie? And why was he still free if her aunt had witnessed, even photographed, the crime? The sick feeling rooted in her stomach mushroomed into a wave of nausea. Shocked, angry, and scared, she wanted to demand answers, but Aunt Rosie was gone, taking the ugly secret to her grave.

Why, Aunt Rosie? How could you have let Roger get away with something so monstrous?

And he *was* a monster. Suddenly, it all made sense.

Maggie had never seen the Mothman in the Witch Wood. She'd come face to face with a human monster. A man who'd already committed murder and was digging a grave to conceal the body of his victim. In her terror, Maggie had turned him into a creature that couldn't be real, and thus, couldn't hurt her.

But Roger had seen her. Chased her. When she'd told everyone she'd seen the Mothman, making no mention of him or a body, he must have felt momentarily safe. Like so many others, he'd probably wandered to the river the night the Silver Bridge fell to help with the rescue efforts. When he'd come upon Maggie struggling from the water, he used the opportunity to make certain she could never betray him.

Did that mean Roger had killed Wendy Lynch, too? If he'd been the "monster" in the Witch Wood and the remains proved to be Wendy's...

Overcome with grief, Eve bit her lip to hold back tears. When Caden returned from the kitchen five minutes later, his face was grim but calm. Thank God, the worst of his anger had passed.

"Ryan's on his way." He sat beside her and wrapped his arm around her shoulder, drawing her against him.

She needed his strength every bit as much as he needed hers. Maybe it would have been better for both of them if they'd never learned the truth. As soon as the thought surfaced, she banished it. Caden needed the truth to be free of guilt, and Roger Layton had to be made accountable for his crimes.

A steely sense of determination washed over her. The resolve was still there fifteen minutes later when Ryan arrived, breathless and flushed.

Caden took him aside, speaking swiftly and urgently as he showed his brother the gruesome photograph. Ryan's initial reaction—anger and a personal need for justice—was much like Caden's had been, but his brother eventually managed to calm him down.

"We're going to get this bastard, Ryan," Caden said. "But we're going to do it legally. I want you to arrest the S.O.B., and I want to be there when you read him his rights."

Standing in the middle of the living room, the picture clutched in his hand, Ryan shook his head. His face relayed his shock. "I don't understand. Why would he do this?"

"I think I have an idea." Eve had been quiet since Ryan's arrival, allowing Caden to explain how they'd discovered the photo and negative. As brothers, they'd needed those moments without her, a brief time to absorb the horror, anger, and grief. She wasn't a police officer, but she'd been a little girl once and could easily understand how Maggie had twisted witnessing a horrific act into something that wasn't real. Drawing a deep breath, she steeled herself for their reaction. "It goes back to what Maggie saw that day in the Witch Wood." Quickly, she shared her thoughts about the Mothman, Maggie, Roger, and why he'd killed her.

Silence reigned when she was through.

Finally, Caden exchanged a glance with his brother. "She might be onto something."

"So why didn't Rosie go to the police with this evidence?" Ryan lifted the photograph between two fingers.

"I wish I knew." The omission left a raw wound in Eve's heart. Moving from the sofa, she joined them in the center of the room. A short while ago, the surroundings had comforted her with memories of her beloved aunt, but now they brought bitterness. Maggie had been Eve's closest friend.

How could her aunt have protected the man who'd taken her life? "I can only guess she couldn't bring herself to turn Roger in, even knowing what a monster he was. She loved him too much. Now I understand why she broke off her engagement."

"Well, I don't care how much she loved him," Caden snapped. "The man killed my sister."

She understood his venom, the dread in her gut slithering into something thorny. "It's why Aunt Rosie didn't seek treatment for her cancer." Suddenly her aunt's willingness to let the disease claim her made sense. "She viewed it as payment for her sins. According to Katie, she prayed God would forgive her at the end."

"God might, but I won't." Caden's expression was hard, his mouth compressed in a rigid line. She couldn't fault his bitterness. At the moment, she wasn't even sure *she* could forgive her aunt, regardless of how conflicted Rosie might have felt.

"A deathbed confession more or less," Ryan said quietly. He shook his head, looking down at the photo. "She must have planned to take the secret to her grave, but had a change of heart at the last moment."

"Maybe." Caden raked fingers through his hair. Hands on hips, he paced off a small circle. "So if it was Amos who trashed the place, why did he want the negative?" He paused only briefly. "To blackmail Roger?"

"Not a smart move considering how he ended up," Ryan observed.

"Which could explain the money clip," Eve said.

Ryan shot her a glance. "What money clip?"

Withdrawing it from her pocket, she explained how Glenda Whitmore and her husband had found it near the pond where Amos's body was discovered. "See?" She passed it to Ryan. "Roger's initials are on it— R-A-L."

"A judge would say that's circumstantial." Examining the clip, Ryan turned it over in his hand. "It could belong to someone else."

"I've seen him with it before," Caden said. "All we'd have to do is ask to see his clip. If he can't produce it, we know this belongs to him. The lab might be able to lift his prints, too."

Ryan frowned. "That still doesn't prove he killed Amos."

"But we know he killed our sister." Caden tapped the photo in Ryan's hand.

"Yeah." Ryan paced a few feet away. "Don't be surprised if some slick defense attorney doesn't try to twist this."

Eve was appalled. "How?"

"Lack of a body at the time it happened. No witnesses. Roger could say he was trying to help her, and she was swept away in the current."

"No sane person will buy that." Caden stalked to his brother's side. "Did you *look* at that flipping picture? The man is strangling her, trying to shove her under the water. Look at his face for God's sake. That is not the face of a man trying to rescue someone."

Exhaling, Ryan nodded. "You know how the system works, Caden. I'm just trying to cover all bases so he doesn't walk."

"Right now I'm more worried he'll rabbit. If Amos was trying to blackmail him—"

"But how could he?" Eve interrupted. "He didn't have the negative."

"Maybe Roger is the one who trashed the house," Ryan said.

Caden shook his head. "He wouldn't risk getting caught. Not with a high profile career at the bank." He looked from Ryan to Eve and back again. "But he might have hired someone. Someone who botched the job and didn't deliver the goods."

Eve caught on immediately. "Amos."

"So how did Roger know about the negative in the first place?" Ryan asked.

Clenching his fists, Caden smiled tightly. "I vote we ask him."

* * * *

He didn't find Roger and perhaps that was for the best at the moment—Caden's emotions still seesawed between anger and restraint—but Lillian served almost as well.

"Where is he?" he demanded, his gaze narrowed on the thin woman standing inside Eve's office at the Parrish Hotel. Having quickly realized Roger wasn't in the ballroom, nor was he anywhere else in the building, they'd found Lillian among her party guests. Taking charge of the moment, Eve had asked Lillian if she would accompany her, Ryan, and Caden to her office where they wished to discuss something with her in private. Caden had to admire the way Eve handled the request, asking him and his brother to remain outside the ballroom so as not to cause a scene.

He'd fidgeted, every bit as agitated as Ryan who'd stood scowling beside him, but bided his time until he saw Lillian nod and head in their direction. Once they'd reached Eve's office, Caden wasted no time in demanding to know where Roger had gone.

"I told you already." Lillian's mouth was a thin, white line as she faced the two brothers within the confines of the small office. "I didn't even realize he'd left until a short while ago."

"Kind of unusual for a guy to skip out on his own party, isn't it?" Ryan had taken a position in front of Eve's desk, arms crossed over his chest in a hardline stance. His gaze was as coolly unforgiving as the edge in his voice. Only Eve kept up a slim measure of cordialness, inviting Lillian to sit in one of the chairs.

The older woman shook her head, then turned her attention back to Ryan. "Roger does what he wants, when he wants." She paused briefly, her mouth compressing further. Her gaze tracked back to Ryan, then shifted to Caden. "This is about the photograph Rosalind took the night the Silver Bridge collapsed, isn't it? You must have found the negative."

Cadent felt like the floor had buckled beneath him. "You know about it?"

She gave a clipped nod. "I only found out after Rosalind died. She mailed me a copy of the photo with a letter."

Shifting, Caden fisted and unfisted his hands in an effort to leash his anger. How many freaking people had known about his sister's murder and done nothing? If Roger had been standing in front of him, he would have smashed the guy in the face, but Lillian required different handling. "Why didn't you go to the police?"

"Why should I?" Lillian's gaze snapped with the same sudden fire as her voice. "Rosalind kept what happened that night a secret for fifteen years. Then to ease her own conscience, she shifted the burden to me. I pitied her at first. I even put flowers on her grave a few times thinking how horrible the knowledge must have been. But then I realized she wanted me to destroy the man she'd been too cowardly to betray. Not only him, but my family as well. All over a girl who died fifteen years ago."

"That girl was my sister." Ryan took a threatening step forward. "You're lucky Caden and I don't take Roger apart, rather than hauling his ass to jail."

Lillian lifted her chin like a stern-faced schoolteacher staring down an unruly student. "I don't care what happens to Roger, but you're not going to drag my family down in the process—or the business my grandfather and father built. That's Jeremy's inheritance. He's the only one I care about."

"Maybe we should back up a bit." Playing peacemaker, Eve moved between Ryan and Lillian, gingerly touching the woman on the forearm. "Please, Lillian. This is difficult for all of us. Won't you have a seat?" She motioned to one of the chairs in front of her desk.

Lillian's gaze remained icy, but she complied. Swearing under his breath, Caden paced a short distance away and braced a hand against the wall. Where the hell would Roger go? He almost believed Lillian. She was a doting mother, but her marriage to Roger had always seemed an unlikely match. Turning, he rested his shoulders against the wall, tamping down the urge to act like a cop in an interrogation room. "Start at the beginning, Lillian. You said Rosalind sent you a letter."

"Yes. It was mailed without a return address and arrived a few days after her death. I'm assuming she had someone send it for her."

"Probably Adam Barnett." Eve slid into the chair opposite Lillian, speaking neutrally as if to ease the tension in the room. "He took care of settling her estate."

"That may well be. When the letter arrived, I thought it was odd." Lillian paused for a moment, looking down at her hands. "When I read it…" For the first time, she faltered, the hesitation in her voice a clear sign of her inner struggle. "No one wants to believe something so heinous of the man they married. Roger and I have never had an ideal union, but I didn't think him capable of murder." Clearing her throat, she sat straighter and faced them.

"I still have the letter somewhere, tucked away. I should have destroyed it, but I hid it instead, the same way Rosalind hid the negative to the photo. She called herself a coward for not being able to report Roger to the police. She said she loved him too much to betray him." Lillian made a soft scoffing sound. "I don't know how he inspired such devotion from her, but maybe he was different in those days. Not as ruthless."

"He was a killer," Caden reminded her flatly.

Lillian cast him a glance, then continued without commenting. "In her letter, Rosalind said she'd been walking along the river that night with her camera, just as she often did. She got caught up in the chaos when the bridge fell and tried to help. When others took over, she snapped several photos. Some made it into the *Point Pleasant Herald* but there was one shot she didn't realize she'd captured."

"Roger and Maggie," Eve said softly.

Lillian nodded. "She refused to believe it when she developed the shot. She even enlarged that part of the image, examining the details under a magnifying glass, but couldn't deny what she saw. Afterward, she broke off her engagement with Roger, but kept telling herself Roger was innocent. That maybe he'd been trying to *help* Maggie."

"What kind of shit-logic is that?" Caden pushed away from the wall with a snarl. Clenching his jaw, he stalked across the room and loomed over her chair. "My sister was on the Silver Bridge that night because of *me*." He jabbed a thumb against his chest, overcome by a crushing wave of guilt. "I couldn't save her. The least Rosie could have done—the least you can do now—is bring her killer to justice."

Lillian blinked up at him. "Caden Flynn, you're talking about my husband."

"Somehow I don't think you love him."

"Who are you to judge?"

"You just said the only one you care about is Jeremy."

"Yes!" She surged to her feet, a tiny combatant when measured against his height. "Rosalind blocked the incident from her mind. That's what she said in her letter. That she put the photo and negative away and made herself believe they didn't exist. It was only when she was diagnosed with cancer and started going through old papers to get her estate in order that she found them. Even then she didn't have the courage to do anything about it. She sent a copy of the photo to me and a copy to Roger, urging us do the right thing—what she couldn't."

Caden felt the blood drain from his face. He exchanged a sharp glance with Ryan before looking back to Lillian. "She sent Roger a copy?"

"Yes." Lillian sagged into her chair. "He doesn't know I have a letter, too. Rosalind hoped Roger would turn himself in, but if he didn't, she wanted me to follow through and do what she couldn't."

"So all this time he's known the negative is hidden somewhere in Rosie's house?" Caden ground his teeth. "He must be the one who left notes on Eve's car, trying to scare her away."

"No, that was me." Drawing a deep breath, Lillian shifted her attention to Eve. "I couldn't risk you might find the negative. I thought if I could frighten you enough to make you leave Point Pleasant, life would go back to normal. Roger wouldn't have to worry about the past hanging over his head, and I could forget about Rosalind's letter."

Eve's lips parted as if in shock. "Did you kill the crow in my yard, too?"

"Crow? What—no." Lillian shook her head. "I don't know anything about a crow. You have to understand what a scandal like this would do to my family. Roger is vice president at my father's bank. The town would never trust us again, and Jeremy's inheritance would be forfeit in disgrace. I've known all along Roger was only after money and position when he married me, but I will not allow him to rob my son of a future because of some sordid atrocity in his past."

"At least you acknowledge the atrocity," Ryan said bitterly. "Unfortunately for you, Caden and I are going to take this as far as we can and see that your husband spends the rest of his life in jail. If you don't want to end up as an accomplice, I suggest you tell us where he went before I think about booking you as well."

"But I told you!" Lillian looked truly frightened now. Desperate, she glanced between Ryan and Caden. "I don't know. He was talking to Stan Brogan at the bar and then just took off. That was a few hours ago."

"Who's Stan Brogan?" Caden asked.

"Someone from the bank."

"What were they talking about?"

"The usual stuff, I guess." Lillian looked flustered. "Work, the bank… rumors around town. Stan said the last thing he mentioned was scuttlebutt about bones being found in some woods at the end of town. After that, Roger excused himself and left."

Caden cast Ryan a glance. "Eve's idea about Maggie seeing Roger in the woods is starting to sound more plausible."

Lillian's brows knitted into a crease. "What are you talking about?"

"Nothing that concerns you," Caden replied.

"Well, if it doesn't concern me, I'd like to return to my party and my guests."

"Fine." Ryan made the decision for all of them. Stepping forward, he adopted his sternest "lawman look," eyes narrowed and direct, mouth flattened into a stiff line. "But I caution you to keep this discussion to yourself. Do not share any of it with Roger or anyone else. And should your husband return, call the sheriff's department immediately. I'm going to have a warrant issued for his arrest."

"Arrest?" Lillian blanched. "Because of a photo?"

"Yes. And because of Rosie's letter."

Lillian stiffened like a rope. "That's hearsay without my confirmation. A wife can't be made to testify against her husband."

"But I can get a search warrant for your house. Don't make this difficult, Lillian." Ryan's gaze remained resolute. "If you care about Jeremy the way you say you do and want to save what's left of his legacy, do the right thing. The town could well see you as a victimized wife who had no idea what her husband was really like. You can still walk out of this with your head held high and garner sympathy for yourself and Jeremy if you play your cards right. "

The corner of her mouth curled slightly, the hint of a sneer. "Why should I?"

"Because." Caden spoke firmly with a controlled effort to keep anger from his voice. If there was any way to reach Lillian, it was through what mattered most to her—her son. "Someday it could be Jeremy who dies at the hands of a murderer. Wouldn't you want his killer brought to justice?"

Her demeanor changed instantly, her body seeming to cave in on itself as the reality of the situation struck her. Her husband had killed a *child*. If that didn't strike a nerve with her, Caden didn't know what would.

Nodding, Lillian sank back into her chair. "You've made your point. I'll give you Rosalind's letter, and I won't say anything to Roger."

* * * *

His wife had betrayed him!

Roger drove, heading away from town. He needed time to think. After talking to Stan Brogan he'd made a hasty trip to the woods where he'd buried the body fifteen years ago. As Brogan had hinted, the earth was disturbed and roped off with police tape. He'd been close to panicking then, but knew it would take weeks, possibly months, before officials had a positive ID. They had no idea who was buried in the grave, so he was safe temporarily.

He'd decided to return to the party and put on a game face until he formulated a plan. The sight of a police cruiser parked outside the Parrish Hotel acted like a double punch to his gut. But there was no way anyone could have put two-and-two together. He'd convinced himself the cruiser had nothing to do with him and boldly walked into the lobby.

That's when he heard his wife's voice coming from the office behind the reception desk, followed by the deeper voice of Ryan Flynn. Luck favored him for a brief while—someone had left the door ajar, and no one was in the lobby—but the streak died quickly as he registered the gist of the conversation. Lillian admitted to having a copy of the photograph and a letter from Rosie. Worse, she planned to give both to the cops.

Backpedaling, Roger hurried from the lobby and into his car. He'd slammed the thing in gear but was careful not to squeal the tires when he left, hoping to make a low-key exit without drawing attention to himself.

He drove aimlessly for a time, drumming his thumbs against the steering wheel as the flash of streetlights came and went. Fortunately for him, most everyone he knew was still at the party—*his* party. The irony didn't escape him that he fled like a scared rabbit while everyone was toasting another year to his health.

With effort, he tried to fit the pieces together: Lillian had a letter from Rosie detailing what had happened that night and a copy of the photo. But what had prompted her to confess in the first place? Had she decided she'd finally had enough of him, or had Rosie's witch-of-a-niece said something that prompted her to spill her guts?

He'd always been discreet with his affairs. Even though he guessed Lillian knew about most, he'd considered himself safe. Their marriage had never really been about love so much as appearance, and what each was able to do for the other. She'd wanted a kid and someone who could fill her father's shoes. He'd wanted money, a career that took him off the docks, and gave him position.

It didn't make sense she'd turn on him now.

He'd heard no mention of the negative, but hadn't heard the whole conversation. Maybe Ryan didn't have it? Maybe it was still hidden somewhere in Rosie's house. Without the negative, there was no case against him. He'd already destroyed the letter and the copy of the photo Rosie sent him and was confident if he could get Lillian alone, he'd be able to convince her to do the same. If nothing else, he'd play the Jeremy card—*Think what this would do to our son.*

The kid was far from what he'd hoped for in his bloodline, but Jeremy had value when it came to Lillian, and value was how Roger saw everything. Rosie Parrish had equaled the potential of owning the Parrish Hotel. When that scheme had gone belly up, he'd zeroed in on Lillian and her father's bank. If he had to use Jeremy to save his hide, he would.

As he turned a corner, he remembered Eve was at the hotel along with Lillian, Ryan, and Caden. What better chance to toss Rosie's house for the negative? Amos had botched the job, an imbecilic fool who couldn't find his butt in a chair. It was Roger's own stupid fault for hiring the jerk, but he was desperate now. He probably had a few hours before the party wrapped and Eve returned home.

Yeah. That was it. He'd toss the house, find the negative, destroy the damn thing, and then convince Lillian to trash her evidence. Ryan and Caden Flynn would be left with their mouths hanging open, and he'd walk away without a blemish of misconduct.

Grinning, Roger turned another corner and steered the car toward Rosie's house. A lot could be accomplished under the cover of darkness.

Chapter 13

"I'll be fine here." Placing her hands on Caden's chest, Eve leaned into his embrace and raised her head to brush a kiss against his lips. The office had cleared, Lillian putting on an impassive face to return to the party, Ryan loitering in the lobby while he waited for Caden.

"The party is still going on upstairs," she said. "Under the circumstances, I don't feel right leaving Katie to manage alone. Besides, if Roger does return, I can alert you he's back."

He frowned, much as she'd expected. "I don't like it."

"I didn't think you would, but you won't have to worry about me being alone if I stay here. When you're through at the sheriff's office, you can come back and take me home."

Although he was no longer a cop, Caden had made it clear he had every intention of accompanying Ryan while his brother relayed matters to Sheriff Weston and ensured a warrant was issued for Roger's arrest. At some point, they would also have to break the news to their mother regarding the true nature of Maggie's death. Neither brother was looking forward to that moment, but it couldn't be avoided.

"Ryan's impatient," she told Caden with a nod to the half-opened door of her office. Beyond the gap, the younger Flynn brother shifted from foot to foot, his face set in a perpetual scowl. She wanted both brothers to leave before Katie inadvertently wandered into the lobby and someone mentioned Wendy. Although there was no concrete evidence the remains in the Witch Wood belonged to Katie's sister, circumstance pointed that way.

"Go." She kissed him again, then urged him toward the door with a gentle push. "I'm going upstairs to see how Katie's doing with the party. Give me a call when you're through at the sheriff's office. By then, I'll be ready to head home."

The discoveries of the night had left her mind reeling, her stomach in an unsettled knot. She needed time alone to think about what Aunt Rosie had done—or more precisely, what she *hadn't* done. Her aunt's silence was nearly as devastating as Maggie's murder.

At last Caden relented. He looked every bit as edgy as Ryan to start the wheels turning that would lead to Roger's arrest. Pulling her tightly against him, he gave her a final kiss, then left in a rush.

"Let's go," he called to Ryan as he breezed into the lobby.

Eve waited until she heard the front door shut before collapsing into her desk chair. What a night! At least she had solved the mystery of why Aunt Rosie had broken off her engagement with Roger. Thank God, her aunt hadn't married the man only to discover what a monster he was later.

Exhausted, she rubbed her eyes and replayed the night through her head. The jumble of thoughts made her briefly consider calling her mother just to hear a soothing voice. But her mom would no doubt ask when she planned to return to Harrisburg, and Eve wasn't ready to share her decision to remain in Point Pleasant. That was a conversation for a night when she was more alert, able to defend her choice.

The jarring ring of the phone coaxed a sigh from her lips. Now what? She picked up the receiver. "Hello?"

A high-pitched whine danced across the line. Gooseflesh rippled down her arms as the unnerving sound spawned a burst of static. Shrill clicks and a hollow jangling exploded in her ear.

"No!" Her strange caller had never contacted her anywhere but at the house. Her gut reaction was to slam the phone down as she usually did, but she hesitated with the receiver halfway to its cradle. What if it *really* was Aunt Rosie on the other end?

She'd discovered the negative of Roger and Maggie as a result of the last spine-tingling call. Maybe her aunt was still speaking to her, communicating the only way she could.

Swallowing hard, Eve raised the receiver to her ear. "Aunt Rosie?"

A horrible shrieking wail.

"Aunt Rosie is that you? Are you trying to tell me something?"

The screeching continued, punctuated every few seconds with a grating symphony of rapid taps and clangs. If it wasn't her aunt, someone had a sick sense of humor. Propelled to her feet by fear, she clutched the phone to her ear.

"Listen to me, whoever you are. If you don't leave me alone, I'm going to report you to the police. Do you hear me?"

A scream. Like someone being murdered.

Her hands shook, and a cold knot of fear spread roots in her stomach. A single word pierced the static. "House."

Eve held her breath. Had she heard correctly? The voice sounded inhuman, a keening wail that might have resonated normally in some chaos-spawned, primal world. An icy sensation bloomed in her gut, and in that instant, she knew she communicated with her dead aunt.

"Aunt Rosie?" Her mouth was dry.

Three seconds of silence.

Click. Click. Click.

The word came again, joined with another, both distorted and muffled as if shrilled underwater. "House...now."

The line went dead.

Limply, Eve folded into the chair, her heart rattling out a frantic rhythm. With shaking fingers, she returned the receiver to its cradle, half afraid the phone might ring again. She'd been given a directive—*house now.*

Was her aunt instructing her to return home? Had she and Caden missed something in their search for the negative? Perhaps the reason Roger had killed Maggie was hidden in the house as well.

Should she go with her instinct and do as the phone call instructed? There'd been urgency in the message, an instruction to go "now." Caden would be angry if she took off without him, but she'd look foolish if she begged him to go with her and they came up empty-handed, especially when he had more important matters to address at the sheriff's office.

Biting her lip, she considered calling him. Or maybe she could leave a message with someone so he'd know where she was. She could borrow Katie's car, perhaps even be back before Caden returned to the hotel. If Mrs. Flynn could speak to Maggie in her dreams, then it was equally possible Eve's aunt could communicate with her over the phone lines.

Crazy or not, she intended to put the idea to the test.

* * * *

Caden paced in Sheriff Pete Weston's office while Ryan relayed the details involving Roger, Rosie, and Maggie. He offered the photo and negative Caden and Eve had discovered as proof. There was no question Weston was stunned. A big man with a burly frame and a normally ruddy complexion, the sheriff's face turned the color of boiled cabbage when Ryan showed him the incriminating photo.

Weston sank into his desk chair, the old wood squeaking loudly. "Shit, boys, this one isn't going to go down easy. Roger Layton carries a lot of clout. You might as well be arresting the governor of West Virginia."

"Boys" because Weston had watched them grow up, a close friend of their father's when Donal Flynn had been alive. Caden stopped pacing long enough to lob Weston a glare. "Lillian's family is the one with the clout, and I don't give a damn who it is. If the governor were involved, I'd slap him in cuffs, too."

The sheriff raised bushy gray eyebrows, a match for his salt-and-pepper hair. "You're not a sergeant any longer, Caden. You're here as a courtesy for past service and because of your brother."

Caden muttered an oath. Weston might be informal when it came to running his office, but there were specific things he couldn't do, and that included extending certain privileges to civilians. Caden had made his choice when he'd trashed his career over the debacle he'd made with Hank Jeffries and the Kline brothers. He'd walked away from a job he'd worked hard to achieve, convinced he'd never want to carry a badge or gun again.

But Roger Layton had changed that.

Unfortunately, the knowledge did little good. Turning away, he scraped a hand through his hair. "Thanks for the timely reminder."

"Don't be so huffy."

A desk drawer scraped open. Caden glanced back in time to see Weston toss a badge onto his desk. A badge he recognized. Raising his gaze from the shiny gold object, he met Weston's eyes with a silent query.

"I've kept it handy, hoping I'd have a chance to offer it again someday." Weston nodded toward the badge. "It's yours if you want it. We can do the paperwork later."

The offer was every bit as unexpected as the helter-skelter events of the night. Caden shot his brother a questioning glance and read the message in Ryan's eyes: *Take it, you jerk.*

Could he? Could he go back to law-enforcement, knowing there might be another Hank Jeffries or Parker Kline in his future? He'd trained to "serve and protect." There was no guarantee he wouldn't have to use his gun, perhaps even take a life to save another.

Decision made, he stepped nearer the desk and closed his hand over the badge.

Weston grinned. "Good deal. Ryan said you were a shitty contractor, anyway."

"Ryan doesn't know squat." Caden slipped the badge into his pocket. "Now, are you ready to issue that APB?"

* * * *

Aunt Rosie's house was only a few miles from the hotel, a drive Eve made with her hands clasped tightly to the steering wheel of Katie's powder blue Ford Pinto. Her friend had known immediately something was wrong but agreed to lend her car, even after Eve had convinced her a full explanation would have to wait until she returned.

Now, as Eve pulled to a stop in front of the house, she realized she had no idea what she was looking for. Maybe Aunt Rosie had hidden something in the final curtain panel she and Caden hadn't dissected, or perhaps she'd stashed something elsewhere in the house. It would have been so much easier if her aunt had only shared her secrets before she died. What would ever possess her to protect a man like Roger?

Eve turned off the ignition.

Love. Denial. A willingness to forget the truth.

They were plainly the motives that had driven her aunt and sustained her ignorance through the years. She hadn't told the authorities the truth because she'd *chosen* to forget. Death likely brought a new perspective. In the world beyond the veil, she'd recognized her error and was doing all she could to correct it.

Slipping from the car, Eve was thankful for the passing traffic on the road, headlights and taillights that illuminated the night and made her feel less alone. The air was warm, scented with summer grass and the fragrant perfume of Mrs. Flynn's flowers next door. Yet despite those comforting touches, a chill settled into her bones. She locked the car and started for the house, wishing she'd left a light on to welcome her back. Foolishly, she hadn't wanted the house looking so exposed without draperies at the front windows. At the very least, she should have flipped on the porch light.

Fishing her keys from her purse, she located the correct one by feel, then inserted it into the lock and stepped inside. A soft glow brought the room into focus when she switched on a table lamp. Instantly, alarm pricked her nerves. Her aunt's draperies lie scattered haphazardly over the furniture and floor.

She was fairly certain she hadn't left them in that condition, but the night had been nothing short of chaotic. She'd probably just forgotten her own sloppiness amid the confusion. Testing the door, she made sure it was secure, then moved about switching on more lights. The lack of curtains at the windows made her feel exposed, but the brightness was comforting. A gradual sense of relief settled over her as she walked to the kitchen. She'd double check the back door, make sure it was locked, then examine the final drapery panel, the one she and Caden had left untouched. It was possible the phone would ring and Aunt Rosie would relay another mysterious word or two. If she discovered nothing within fifteen minutes to a half hour, she'd head back to the hotel and wait for Caden. The plan made her feel safe and secure.

Until she stepped into the kitchen.

The sight of the broken back door greeted Eve like a kick to the stomach. Someone had worked hard to bust through the deadbolt, hacking away at the wood until the door had splintered under the assault. The intruder had punched a hole, then simply reached through and released the lock from the inside.

Fear crashed over her in an icy wave. There was no longer a question of whether she was alone in the house. Was the intruder upstairs, waiting for her to retrace her footsteps, or did he lurk on the screened porch? For three terrifying heartbeats, panic held her immobile as she debated whether she should chance calling the sheriff's office. In the end, fright spurred her to action. Breathing rapidly, she wrenched open the door and scrambled onto the porch.

"There you are," a man's voice said from the dark. She slammed up against something solid, a wall of flesh that blocked her escape. A massive hand clamped over her mouth, muffling her scream. She clawed at the fingers, but the man spun her around, pinning her back to his chest. The smell of mossy aftershave and Scotch engulfed her. She screamed into his hand and squirmed, digging her elbow into his ribs.

The futile efforts had no effect.

"Stupid woman, I've been waiting for you."

He released her long enough for her to gulp air. Before she could make a dash for the door, he struck her on the side of the head, dropping her to her knees. The hard boards of the porch bit into her hands, and a sound like water bouncing off tin, rang in her ears. Swaying, she managed a feeble gasp before folding completely. The last thing she saw before surrendering to the crowding darkness was the axe he'd confiscated from her garden shed.

* * * *

Caden itched to be out looking for Roger, but there were i's to dot and t's to cross—precise procedures that had to be met so the scumbag wouldn't be able to cry a technicality when apprehended. As Caden waited for Ryan to put the finishing touches on the order for Roger's arrest, he paced to the coffeepot. Not that he wanted any of the overly strong liquid, but it gave him something to do rather than rehash Maggie's death.

Again.

Since learning the truth, he'd replayed the bridge collapse a dozen times in his head, and a dozen times he'd been left with the same glaring reality—he couldn't have saved her. Maybe it was time to let go of the guilt and give them both the peace Roger had stolen.

"Hey, Caden." Wayne Rosling helped himself to a cup of coffee, filling his Cleveland Browns mug to the brim. Once white, the inside of the stoneware had turned the color of toasted caramel from years of accumulated stains. It had been a standing joke in the department that the best way to work Rosling into a huff was to hide his Browns mug. He refused to drink from any other cup, insisting the accumulated stains added flavor. "Rumor has it you're going to be joining us again."

"Rumor spreads fast." Rosling, like most everyone else under Weston's command, was a good cop. Officers pulled their weight or shipped out. As informal as he was, Pete Weston didn't tolerate slacking.

"In this case, it's a good one." Rosling offered his hand. "Welcome back."

"Thanks." Caden shook, then glanced around the room. "Quiet in here tonight." Evening shifts were generally low-key, but tonight, more so than most. A good chunk of local residents were no doubt at Roger's party. As a result, the phones were quiet, Mothman sightings likely cut to a minimum. The few officers on duty attended to paperwork and fielded the occasional call. Caden wondered how those same officers would react when the APB on Roger was announced. Weston planned on sharing it once Ryan supplied him with the official forms.

Anytime now.

Impatiently, he glanced at his watch.

Rosling took a swig of his coffee. "With any luck it'll stay quiet. I'm not looking forward to citing drunks from Roger Layton's party."

Caden was about to tell him the night was going to explode for an entirely different reason when Rosling tugged a slip of paper from his breast pocket. "By the way, I took this message for you when you were in with Pete." Unfolding the scrap one-handedly, he passed it to Caden, who frowned down at the phone number for the Parrish Hotel. Rosling had scrawled a name beside it.

"Katie. That's odd. Did she say what it was about?"

"Sorry." Rosling shook his head and downed another gulp of coffee. "Anyway, good to have you back." He clapped Caden on the shoulder, then headed for his desk.

Caden glanced about for a phone, noted Ryan using his own, and promptly took over the nearest empty desk. The hotel was within walking distance, just a few blocks away, but he didn't want to miss Weston's announcement. Eve must have asked Katie to call him about something, but if the women were in the ballroom, they'd never hear the phone ring.

He dialed the number regardless, surprised when Katie answered after a single ring. "Caden, thank God you called."

The breathless rush of her words sent a spike of fear lancing through him. "What's wrong? Where's Eve?"

"That's why I'm calling. She borrowed my car half an hour ago."

"What?" He shot to his feet, the phone clutched to his ear.

"She said she had to check something at the house and that she'd only be a few minutes. But I know something happened tonight, and I'm worried. I tried to call her, but she isn't answering the phone. She told me you were at the sheriff's office with Ryan, so I thought—"

"I'm on it." He couldn't say the words fast enough. He was about to cut the phone call short when he remembered to ask if Lillian was still there or if Roger had shown up.

"Lillian's here, but Roger's been missing most of the night. What kind of host ditches his own party?" He could picture the bafflement on Katie's face. "Roger's guests are starting to talk. Caden, what's going on?"

"Not now. Thanks for the tip, Katie. I'm going to drive to Eve's place and make sure she's okay."

"But—"

He clicked off the call, hating to be rude, but propelled by urgency. "Ryan," he called, striding for his brother's desk. "I need the keys to your cruiser."

His brother glanced up. "What for?"

"Eve borrowed Katie's car to head home a half hour ago. Katie's worried because she isn't answering the phone and hasn't come back."

Ryan swore. "You don't think Roger—"

"That's exactly what I think."

"Then I'm going with you." Ryan shoved from his chair, paperwork clutched in hand. As the two bolted for the door, he tossed the forms on Wayne Rosling's desk. "Weston's waiting on that. Make sure he gets it."

The older officer glanced down at the APB order. The last thing Caden heard as he ran outside was Rosling's stunned voice.

"Holy shit! Is this for real?"

* * * *

It seemed mere moments until the world swam back into focus. Eve moaned as she regained consciousness, a knot of pain rolling from her temple to her jaw. She thought she heard a phone ringing in the background, but before she could focus on the noise, it stopped.

It took several seconds to remember what happened, the resulting panic propelling her clumsily to her knees.

"It doesn't have to be like this." Roger's voice sliced through the pounding in her ears.

She wobbled to her feet, then tottered behind a chair, clutching the frame to steady herself. The barrier placed an obstacle between her and Roger, but also effectively cut off her escape. She hadn't imagined the ringing or the phone call that had brought her here. But she'd obviously misinterpreted what her aunt wanted her to do, for Aunt Rosie would never place her in a dangerous situation. Frantically, she tried to think of what she'd overlooked.

Unconcerned by her mounting dread, her tormentor bent and picked up the axe he'd used to hack through her back door. "I saw what you did to the drapes and realized I was too late." He spoke indifferently, almost cordially. A predator who viewed his prey as a pitiful threat. "Is that where Rosie hid it?"

Eve licked her lips, her mouth dry. Her gaze darted about as she sought an avenue of escape, but he'd backed her into a corner like a wolf herding sheep. The chair was flimsy protection at best. The only buffer she had, she clung to it, trying to anticipate his next move.

"I don't know what you're talking about," she said, attempting to play dumb.

He snorted softly. "Eve, a word of warning—if you continue to annoy me, I can almost guarantee you'll end up like Amos Carter."

A cold finger of sweat trickled down her neck. "You killed him?"

"The oaf didn't deserve to live. He trashed Rosie's house and couldn't come up with the negative." Roger took a casual step closer, forcing her to shift the chair like a shield in front of her. "So you see there's a lot of blood already wrapped up in that negative. A little more isn't going to make a difference." He tossed the axe lightly from hand to hand, an unspoken threat.

Her stomach rose to her throat, her pulse fluttering like a hummingbird's wings. "I don't have it. I gave it to Ryan Flynn. Lillian knows about everything, Roger. She's going to cooperate with the police."

"So I heard." Even in the dark, she could tell his face hardened. "I came back to the hotel and was outside your office when the spineless witch spilled her guts."

"Then you know I don't have the negative," she blurted.

He frowned, momentarily uncertain. Clearly, he hadn't heard everything, or he would have known Ryan had the incriminating film. By the same token, had she just surrendered her security? He'd killed Amos without qualm, and he'd killed Maggie.

"Why did you do it?" If she could keep him talking, maybe she could figure a way past him. At the very least it would buy her more time, and she needed to know the truth. "Why did you kill Maggie? She was innocent. A child!"

He grimaced. "She saw me in the woods."

"Burying a body?"

He nodded. "You're a smart girl. More's the shame you stuck your nose where it doesn't belong."

"The body…" She grew cold realizing the extent of his crimes. "Was it Wendy Lynch?"

A look of surprise crossed his face. After a second, he chuckled coldly. "So, you figured that out, too? Yeah, it was her." He tugged his bottom lip thoughtfully. "Sixteen years old and pregnant. Stupid girl thought I'd be elated and marry her. When I said I wanted nothing to do with her, she threatened to tell Rosie what we'd done."

Poor Wendy! It all came together in Eve's head. "And you couldn't risk that because Aunt Rosie would break off her engagement. It was bad enough you'd been unfaithful to her, but statutory rape of a sixteen-year-old…" She felt nauseous. The man was a reprehensible killer. "You never loved my aunt, did you? You were after the hotel the whole time."

Roger straightened his shoulders. "I was after anything that would get me off those damn docks. I wasn't going to be a river rat for the rest of my life, like my father and grandfather. When Rosie bailed, I went after the next best thing."

"Lillian."

He flashed a feral smile. "Like I said, you're a bright girl. You should have sold me the hotel and walked. All of this unpleasantness" —he waved the axe in the air— "could have been avoided."

Eve tensed, prepared to run. "You're a monster."

"I'm an opportunist." He narrowed his eyes, signaling a growing impatience with the conversation. "I took what I wanted. Wendy Lynch was nobody. A slut who'd been used up and spit out by the time she got her claws into me. I should have dumped her body in the TNT, but it was overrun with all those lunatics looking for the Mothman and UFOs back then. I thought that thicket at the end of town was the next best thing. I wasn't going to ditch my shot at a future for a piece of teenage trash."

If he'd been closer, she would have spit in his face. "My aunt was right to dump you." He needed to be locked up, banished to a prison where he couldn't hurt anyone ever again. "I'm only sorry she didn't report you to the sheriff years ago. If you've got any sense, you'll turn yourself in." She thought quickly, grasping for anything that might make him run. "You heard the phone ringing."

"So?"

Roger wouldn't believe it may have been her Aunt Rosie, and certainly wouldn't care, but he'd reconsider if he thought his neck was on the line. "That was Caden checking in with me. Since I didn't answer, he'll be coming to the house. Soon, there'll be nowhere for you to hide."

Silence greeted her. His expression grew grim as he digested the truth. "Maybe. But I won't leave you behind as a witness."

He lunged to grab her, one meaty hand closing the distance between them. Recoiling, Eve shoved the chair, using it like a battering ram. Roger howled, solid proof it connected painfully with his knees. Sensing freedom, she stumbled for the door, knocking over a small table lamp. Her balance off-kilter in her high-heeled shoes, she'd only managed three steps when Roger grabbed a fistful of her shirt and wrenched backward.

Eve yelped, yanked off her feet. She sprawled against his chest, pinned in place when he wrapped an arm around her waist. The cold blade of the axe pressed against her cheek.

"If you as much as flinch, I'll cut you. Do you understand?"

Terrified, Eve choked out a "yes."

"Good. You and I are going for a drive." He grinned, his breath hot against her ear. "It's time I showed you where Amos breathed his last."

Chapter 14

Caden thrust the door of the cruiser open before Ryan brought the car to a complete stop. The sight of Katie's Pinto parked in front of the house sent a flood of relief crashing over him, but the knot in his gut wouldn't unravel completely until he talked to Eve and assured she was fine.

As he sprinted for the front porch, Ryan bolted around the side, heading to the rear yard. Caden rang the bell, impatiently shifting from foot to foot. He rolled his hand into a fist and pounded it against the door.

Come on. Come on.

She should have stayed put like she'd promised.

Inwardly seething, he dug the house key she'd given him from his pocket. Before he could insert it in the lock, the door swung open, revealing Ryan on the threshold. His brother's taut expression alerted him something was wrong.

"What is it?" Caden demanded.

"You better take a look." Stepping clear, Ryan motioned him inside. "Someone hacked through the kitchen door. Eve isn't here."

A torrent of alarm rocketed through Caden. He dashed for the rear of the house, acid bubbling in his gut. The sight of the busted door drew him up short, his sense of dread mushrooming into raw-boned fear. On the porch, he found evidence of a struggle—an overturned chair, a table knocked to the side, a broken lamp. Switching on a light, he stood blinking against the glare.

No blood, thank God.

"Eve?" Even as he yelled her name, he knew it was useless. She wasn't there.

Returning to the living room, he found Ryan on his handheld radio, talking to the dispatch operator at the sheriff's office. Caden's brother had switched on several lights, revealing Eve's keys and purse on an end table to the left of the door. She must have placed them there when she'd stepped inside, not realizing anything was wrong.

The intruder had probably been waiting for her in the kitchen. He paced off an agitated circle, thoughts firing helter-skelter through his mind. Where had she been taken? Was she hurt? And damn it all to hell, why hadn't he insisted she stay with him at the sheriff's office where he could have assured she was safe?

Switching off his radio, Ryan turned to face him. "I've requested a crime scene unit and put out an alert she's missing."

"It's Roger." Caden spat the name like something vulgar. "He has her. I know it's him."

Ryan nodded. "He's the only one that makes sense, but where would he take her?"

Trying to think rationally, Caden scrubbed a hand over his face. "To the TNT. To the place where he killed Amos."

"You're guessing."

"Damn right, but it's all I've got." Brushing past Ryan, he raced for the door. "I'm taking the car."

Ryan hurried after him. "Where?"

"Where else?" Caden sprinted across the lawn. "To find Eve."

He prayed to God when he did, he would find her alive.

* * * *

Roger was a cruel man.

If Eve had any doubt of how cruel, she learned firsthand when he dragged her from the house, through the backyard, and down the creek bed. Despite his threat of harm, she'd known her life depended on breaking free. Once across the water—a trek that had her wobbling in her heels, her feet soaked—he'd pulled her into a gully that ended two streets away where he'd stashed his car. When she spied the sedan, she'd known her only chance for safety was flight. There was no one around to help, no one to hear her scream on the deserted, darkened street. When he'd dragged her toward the car, she'd twisted frantically, fighting his grip despite the lethal threat of the ax at his side.

Her gamble ended when he struck her. Not a slight clip like the one he'd given her on the porch, but a brutal crack of his fist that sent the world plummeting into darkness.

When she awoke, it was to the feel of cool leather pressed to her battered cheek, her body cushioned against the rear seat of his car. He'd dumped her unceremoniously on her side, her feet near the back passenger door, head inches from the rear door on the driver's side. Shadows, black as nighttime soot, scrolled across the roof spanning above her. Only a glimmer of light pierced the windows. They must have already made the turn onto Potters Creek Road. The deeper Roger drove into the TNT, the less chance she had of ever being found.

She was petrified he would bludgeon her with the axe or pummel her with his fists like he'd done with Amos. Dear God, what had she been thinking going back to the house? Why would Aunt Rosie send her there?

Her brows creased as she digested the horror of her situation. Perhaps the phone call had been a way to alert her where Roger could be found. Yes, that had to be it. She'd been meant to notify Caden and Ryan, not stupidly venture there herself. She'd made a horrible, reactionary mistake and was paying for it now.

Eyes narrowed to slits, she forced her breathing to remain even so as not to warn her captor she was awake. Roger was apparently unconcerned she'd regain consciousness because he hadn't restrained her in any way. In the darkness, he appeared as a hulking silhouette, his form outlined by a faint glimmer of light from the dash's instrument panel. The man had killed three people without a flicker of remorse. He'd never spare her after confessing the extent of his crimes. But even if she managed to escape, where would she run? The TNT was an endless hodgepodge of dense woods and scattered ponds, dotted sporadically by igloos and the stark shells of abandoned buildings. With luck on her side, she might be able to hide until daylight. There was a distance chance she'd be able to stumble across a campsite or a hiker roaming the grounds in the morning.

The decision was taken from her when the car rolled to a stop. Not as if Roger had braked or slowed, but as if everything mechanical—headlights, taillights, motor, instrument panel—abruptly died.

"What the—" Roger hunched forward, shoulders bunched as he cranked the key in the ignition. The gas pedal made a hollow sound when he pumped it up and down, but the motor refused to turn over.

Potters Creek Road. Cars inexplicably die here.

The thought pinged through her, exhilarating and equally chilling. If there was any hope of escape, she had to seek it now while he was occupied trying to restart the car. Ducking low behind the seat, she scrunched closer to the passenger side of the vehicle. The pin in the door was pushed to the locked position, a simple metal peg standing between her and freedom. She envisioned wrenching it upright, popping the door handle, and fleeing into the night.

One motion flowing fluidly into the next, a surreal but critical ballet.

Roger cursed and pumped the gas pedal again. When he turned the key in the ignition, there was only a click, not even the feeble attempts of a battery sluggishly trying to chug to life. Eve tried to quell the fluttering of her heart and rummage a shred of courage. For Maggie and Wendy. Even for Amos and her misguided aunt, who through her silence, had let this monster go free.

Praying her legs would support her, she lunged for the door, yanked the lock-pin upward, then swiftly engaged the handle. The barrier gave before her, spilling her unsteadily into the night. Her palms struck the ground and she sprawled to one knee, dizziness crashing over her in a spike of vertigo. Behind her, Roger grunted in surprise.

Panicked, she propelled herself forward, the sound of an opening car door igniting a fresh blaze of terror. She ran clumsily. Into the dark and the trees. Choking on tears, her breath ripped from her lungs in forceful gasps. Her vision swam, the cuff she'd taken when Roger knocked her unconscious leaving her weak-kneed and disoriented.

The cluster of the surrounding trees engulfed her, pulling her deeper into the TNT where darkness blanketed her in a sheltering cloak. Roger shouted threats of retribution and prolonged death behind her, but his footfalls faded, lost in the tangle of intertwined sycamores, oak, and ash. She tripped more than once, her heels catching on clumps of ferns and protruding roots. The air was sticky and clung to her skin with a clammy film. Or maybe it was only fear, pumped through her veins in a toxic cocktail of adrenaline and grief that made it feel that way.

"When I get my hands on you, you'll wish I'd killed you earlier," Roger bellowed from the darkness. His voice sounded far away as if she'd increased the distance between them.

Coming to a halt, she bent over, hands on knees, and drank hungry gulps of the night air. She thought about kicking off her shoes, but there were too many roots and rocks on the ground to slice up her feet. She had no idea where she was and no idea of where the car had stopped. Trying to get some sense of bearing, she struck off in what she hoped was a parallel path to the road, heading back toward the entrance to the TNT. If only she had some idea of how long she'd lain unconscious, she might be able to better judge how far he'd driven into the remote area before losing power. She could only hope that enough time had passed for Katie to grow concerned over her absence.

* * * *

Caden didn't know if he was relieved or panicked by the sight of Roger's abandoned car on Potters Creek Road. Rolling Ryan's cruiser to a stop behind the vehicle, he snatched the mic from the dashboard and depressed the call button in one swift motion.

"This is Caden Flynn. I've located Roger Layton's car approximately five miles in on Potters Creek Road. Black Buick Regal, tag number three-Charlie-Victor-nine-four-one. Vehicle looks abandoned, but there's reason to suspect Layton has abducted Eve Parrish."

A woman's voice crackled over the airways with a burst of static. "Say again, Caden."

Damn reception. Swiftly, he repeated the basics, added a request for back-up, then dropped the mic onto the seat, not bothering to wait for acknowledgment. He didn't have a sidearm, but the 12-gauge shotgun, standard issue for every police car, would serve. Pocketing several shells, he pulled the gun from its cradle, checked the load, then eased from the car.

He approached Roger's sedan from the rear, advancing on the driver's side, the butt of the scatter-gun snug against his shoulder. Both the driver's door and the rear passenger door hung open as if the occupants had fled in a hurry. He didn't know if he should be grateful or alarmed Eve wasn't in the car. It seemed odd Roger would stop here, only five miles into the sprawling wilderness. Caden could only hope Eve had escaped and was hunkered down somewhere in the darkness.

Darting from the road, he wound his way into the knot of trees and leafy undergrowth. He should have grabbed a flashlight from the car, but it was too late for regrets. He wove through the darkness as best he could, zigzagging beneath branches and hoping to spy some telltale signs of passage. Crushed vegetation, broken twigs, a piece of fabric snared by thistles. Anything to indicate Eve had passed this way.

Something rustled behind him, and he immediately turned toward the sound, hoping it was Eve. He didn't know if Roger was armed and feared forcing a confrontation if she was a hostage. On the flip side, a careless man made careless mistakes.

He was about to shout to Roger—a threat to warn him the police were on their way when the rustling came again. Closer this time, off to his left. He half-turned as someone thrust from the trees in a quick blur of motion. Instinctively, he raised his arm, blocking the blow of an axe as it angled for his chest.

The impact of the hard wooden handle against his forearm nearly shattered the bone, and the force dropped him to his knees. Roger swung again. Driven to the defensive, Caden reeled backward. The deadly blade grazed his cheek, releasing a thin trickle of blood.

Layton grinned manically as though inflamed by the sight. "You're finished, Flynn."

"The hell with that." When Layton swung again, Caden rolled to the side, snapping the gun into firing position. Barrel and axe cracked together and the shotgun spun from Caden's pain-numbed fingers.

Too late, he kicked out, trying to hook Layton by the ankle. The banker scrambled clear as Caden got his hands under him. The sound he feared most echoed in his ears—Roger Layton engaging the pump on the riot gun.

"Don't move," Layton said behind him, "unless you want a shotgun blast to the back."

* * * *

Eve bit her lip, halting a second to listen. Roger had stopped shouting threats, but a new game had begun—the hunt between predator and prey. She strained her ears for any betraying sound, trying to decipher if he was near. Noise seemed to be sucked up in the TNT like a vacuum that drank in any microscopic disturbance. She heard nothing, not even the hiss of the breeze through the grass.

Cautiously, she started walking again, wincing when a twig cracked beneath her shoe. She needed to move silently, but it was hard to see, and everywhere she turned something obstructed her journey—trees, thistles, clumps of vegetation she couldn't even name. There was no path, just a snarl of weeds and vines that grasped at her ankles and tangled around her legs with every step she took. Raising her arm, she pushed a low-hanging branch out of the way, its jagged leaves scraping across her cheek. Something wet and filmy brushed against her face, and she fought a knee-jerk urge to scream. Spiders, ticks, and God-only-knew-what had probably dropped into her hair. Frantically, she whisked her fingers over the top of her head in a frenzied attempt to dislodge any creepy-crawlies. She wanted to cry for help, but the only person within hearing distance was the man who intended to kill her. A sob caught in her throat.

Is this how Wendy and Maggie had felt at the end? A soul-sucking hopelessness that whispered death was inevitable?

No, she wouldn't die like a cornered animal. Maybe she didn't have a weapon, but she'd fight Roger until the end. Stooping, she felt along the ground for something to use to defend herself—a rock, a stout branch—anything she could wield against him. Her fingers blundered through the wet undergrowth, even as the raspy sound of her breath drowned out any other noise. Focused intently on the task, she reacted with a violent start when Roger's voice cut unexpectedly across the distance:

"It looks like you have a rescuer, Eve. If you don't want me to blow Caden Flynn's head off, you'll come out where I can see you. Now."

Eve squeezed her hands into fists, still as a statue in the darkness.

"Do you hear me?" Roger's voice made her heart pound faster. "If you don't want me to kill your boyfriend, you'll come out here now."

Was it possible? Had Caden tracked her to the TNT?

Her stomach rolled over in a queasy somersault.

"I'll give you ten seconds to make up your mind," Roger yelled.

"Eve, don't listen to him."

Oh, dear God, it really was Caden. His voice sounded weaker than usual, as though he was hurt. Panicked, she ran toward the voices, unconcerned by the roots that attempted to trip her and the grasping branches that scraped her clothing. It was her fault Caden was in danger. If she'd done as he'd asked and waited at the hotel, none of this would be happening.

"I'm coming," she shouted, fearful she was already too late.

"Eve. Damn it. Stay away." There was no question Caden was angry, his voice fueled by fervent emotion. She broke into a small clearing in time to see him stagger upright. Roger hovered five feet away, a shotgun leveled in Caden's direction. The axe Roger had threatened her with was stuck through his belt. Where had he gotten the gun?

"Over there." Roger motioned her toward Caden.

She was only too eager to comply, ducking under his shoulder to hold him steady. He held his free arm awkwardly, and a dark streak of blood slanted across his cheek. This was all her fault. "I should have listened to you. I got a phone call, and—"

"Don't." He silenced the breathless rush of her words with a single glance of his eyes. Raising his hand, he touched her bruised cheek gently. Dried blood stretched her skin taut, but it was fear and regret that brought tears to her eyes.

"I shouldn't have left you."

She shook her head and buried her face against his chest. It was unfair of life to end here when they hadn't yet been given the chance to explore a future together.

"How sweet." Roger's voice dripped honey. "I'd hang around and prolong the show but circumstance dictates I kill you both quickly."

"Like you killed Maggie?" The challenge in Caden's voice was equal parts heat and ice.

Tension rippled through his body, transferred to her where she gripped his arm. Two blasts from the shotgun, and it would be over. Roger would kill Caden first, eliminating the greater threat, then her. Sickness churned in her stomach.

Roger shrugged. "Your sister saw something she shouldn't have. She didn't leave me any choice."

"I'll kill you." No boast or bellowed threat, just a man's cold promise.

Roger chuckled. "That might prove difficult since I have the shotgun."

A low-level hum made Eve turn her head slightly to the side. Neither Roger nor Caden appeared to have heard the noise, intent on the power-play stretching between them.

"I called for backup." Caden smirked, a twist of the lips that made Eve wonder if he was playing a game. "Pull the trigger, Layton, and you won't make it out of the TNT alive."

The humming grew louder. Caden flinched, indicating he'd heard, but Roger was too engrossed in defying the boast.

"Don't count on it." He raised the shotgun. "You've already provided me with transportation. I'll be gone before your pitiful cavalry gets here, and you two won't be able to say a word about what happened." Grinning, he snugged the butt of the shotgun against his shoulder, raising the site to his eye. "Since you'll be dead."

A sudden screech erupted from the trees, a shriek so shrill and inhuman, Eve screamed in response. Startled, Roger looked toward the sky.

Caden used the distraction to tackle him around the waist and throw him to the ground. A single blow of his fist spun Roger's head to the side. Quickly, he wrestled the shotgun from the banker, then backed away, raising the weapon to his shoulder. "Don't move."

Something large and winged hurtled into the clearing, blocking Roger from view. The powerful beat of enormous wings washed over Eve. A roar like a cyclone exploded in her ears and the wind sucked her breath away.

Roger screamed.

Horrified, Eve choked out a cry. All around her, the humming spun into a jarring drone, worming into her skull. Steady and low, it thrummed like current through a fat wire. The sound filled her head, throbbing and growing until it rattled deeper into her chest. Her field of vision was consumed by two almond-shaped eyes, dark red like aged wine. Lethal, clawed hands and massive wings, thinly-veined in white, loomed before her.

No face. The thing has no face.

That was the most terrifying element of all.

Roger tried to run, but the Mothman blocked him like a cat cornering a mouse. Beating its wings to stay aloft, the creature reached forward and gripped the banker by both arms.

Bones cracked.

"No!" Roger howled in pain and terror.

She didn't realize she was screaming until Caden grabbed her arm and tugged her close to his chest. He bowed his head against hers, locking her in place. The droning intensified, then was joined with an inhuman screech and the punishing boom of the creature's wings.

Roger screamed a final time. A wet, gurgling cry that signaled death. At last, the wings retreated. A deafening roar of thunder that was sucked into the night-blackened sky.

The rapid hitch of Eve's breath was the only sound to break the silence that followed.

Chapter 15

Eve sat in the back of the police cruiser, sore and too numb to move. The light bar mounted on the roof sent a red and blue stain leaping through the darkness. Earlier, Caden had rummaged a blanket from the trunk, wrapped it around her, then helped her to a seat where she wouldn't be subject to prying eyes. A number of cars were parked along the road, Ryan and several deputies engaged in scouring the surrounding terrain.

Sheriff Weston had already questioned them about what happened. By mutual consent they'd agreed not to mention the Mothman—who would believe them?—or that the creature had killed Roger, carrying his broken body into the sky. Caden suggested the banker had grown disoriented in the darkness and was lost somewhere in the woods.

Even as Eve replayed the scene in her head, she wondered if the encounter was a figment of her imagination. She couldn't understand why the Mothman, a terrifying creature of myth, would save them from certain death. Had it protected them, or was it merely responding to the threat Roger presented? A threat to the wild, rambling habitat it considered home.

She shuddered, recalling the intelligence she'd seen in the monster's eyes. It was a perceptive being. One that calculated, planned, and hunted. The creature had left no visible tracks, and those belonging to Roger were muddied beneath her and Caden's, revealing only that he'd crossed the same area. If his body was ever discovered, it would likely be miles away, dumped in a pond or left to rot in the empty shell of a derelict building.

Gathering the blanket, she huddled more deeply beneath the folds. A vision of the Mothman's burning red eyes flashed into her mental vision. *No face.*

She'd seen the creature up close but couldn't recall a single facial feature other than those horrible blood-red eyes. Caden had said he'd felt a flood of emotion from the Mothman when he'd come across it in the

TNT on that Halloween night so long ago, but she experienced nothing of the sort. In her fear, she'd probably been too focused on Roger's blood-curdling screams, a memory that made her stomach clench even now. Thankfully, movement outside drew her attention to the window. In the next instant, Caden opened the door and bent down.

"Hey." His voice was soft, accompanied by an equally gentle smile. "How are you holding up?"

"Fine." She managed a weak turn of her lips. "Just tired. How's your arm?"

"Better." He moved it somewhat experimentally to show her. "I'll probably have a hell of a bruise."

Far better than the alternative, a frightening reality she didn't want to contemplate. "Can we go soon?"

He nodded. The blood on his cheek had dried, the cut superficial. "The search is going to continue through the night, but we're clear to leave. Ryan got in touch with Katie at the hotel and brought her up to date on everything that's happened. She's anxious to see you and said you can spend the night with her if you'd like."

Katie.

The thought of her friend sent a new ribbon of grief unfurling in Eve's stomach. Traumatized by the arrival of the Mothman and the manner of Roger's death, she'd forgotten why the banker had dragged her to the TNT in the first place.

"Caden, I completely forgot about what Roger told me earlier. Maggie wasn't his only victim. Wendy Lynch was pregnant with his child and threatened to tell Aunt Rosie. Roger killed her to keep her quiet, and Maggie caught him in the act of burying her body. It's why he had to kill Maggie."

All trace of softness left his face, his features settling into a grim mask. "It seems to me the true monster here tonight wasn't the Mothman."

Mention of the towering birdlike creature made her flinch. With a cautious glance for the deputies milling beyond the car, she lowered her voice. "Do they know he was here?"

Caden shook his head. "But I'll make sure they know about Roger's crimes. All of them." The rigid control in his voice was painful to hear. "His confession to you will make identifying the bones we found in the woods that much easier. Right now, I want to get you out of here."

She nodded tiredly. "Right now, there's nothing I'd like better."

* * * *

Katie swept Eve into her embrace the moment she stepped through the door of the hotel.

"I was so worried," her friend said. "I can't believe that creep abducted you."

Eve cast a glance over her shoulder to Caden. She needed time alone with Katie to tell her about Wendy and hoped he'd understand.

"I'll go up to the banquet room," he said as if reading her mind.

"No one is up there." Katie stepped back, looking between them. "You don't seriously think I was going to let a party continue with everything that happened tonight? Someone got wind of the APB for Roger, and the whole thing turned into a mess."

"What about Lillian?" Caden asked.

"She hustled Jeremy home the minute things started to go sour."

He nodded. Eve suspected he'd want to talk to Roger's wife again and suggested he leave to handle the situation. "I'll be fine here with Katie." He appeared ready to object, reluctant to leave her, but she deflected the protest before he could voice it. "I'll stay put this time, I promise. When I'm done talking to Katie, I'll go upstairs and crash in one of the guest suites."

"I don't know," he hedged. "You've been through a lot tonight. Maybe I should hang around."

"Caden." When she sent him a stern glance, he finally pulled her close and kissed her. "I'll be back in a little while to check on you. Call if you need me."

"I will."

After he left, Eve collapsed onto the sofa in the lobby. "I can't believe how tired I am." Kicking off her shoes, she stretched her legs. The hem of her dressy slacks were ruined, ripped and shredded where briars had snarled them. She'd probably end up tossing the shoes, too.

Katie sat beside her and leaned forward to grip her hand. "Tell me what happened. Do you have any idea how frantic I've been?"

Eve lowered her gaze, chagrined to have put Katie through so much worry. "Roger was waiting for me when I got to Aunt Rosie's house."

"Why did you go there in the first place?"

Eve recalled the phone call that had triggered her ordeal. It was quiet in the lobby, the stillness of the hotel like a clinging shroud. The heavy silence made her think of ghosts and hauntings. "I thought Aunt Rosie wanted me to go." She shook her head, too tired to explain the eerie call. "It doesn't matter. I think I was supposed to send Caden and Ryan to the house, not go myself. When I got there, Roger—" She swallowed hard, shaken by the memory of how Roger had taunted her. "He told me he'd overheard our discussion with Lillian. He'd been in the lobby."

Katie blanched. "The whole time?"

"Most of it. He thought I had the negative, and when he realized I didn't…" Closing her eyes, she pinched the bridge of her nose. The memory of Roger's ugly confession made her stomach roil. "Katie, there's something I have to tell you. Something that won't be easy to hear."

Her friend drew back as if steeling herself. She regarded Eve warily. "It's about Wendy, isn't it?"

"Yes." She wished there were an easier way to break the news. "Roger said she was pregnant."

Katie's face contorted. "Not by him. Please, not by him."

"I'm sorry."

With a strangled cry, Katie lurched to her feet. "Why would she do something so stupid?"

The anguished sound of her voice made Eve tear up in sympathy. "Wendy was only sixteen, Katie. Roger was a predator, in his thirties. He seduced her. You can't blame her."

"I don't." Bowing her face into her hands, she wept softly. "I just wish I could have done something to stop her. He killed her, didn't he?"

"Yes." Eve pulled the sobbing girl down beside her, wrapping her arms around her friend. She pressed her cheek to the crown of Katie's head, and let the grisly memory of Roger's death wash over her. "If it's any consolation," she whispered. "I promise he'll never hurt anyone again."

* * * *

Three days later a sheriff's deputy found Roger's body while scouring the TNT. The decomposing remains surfaced in a pond, the public cause of death listed as drowning after blunt force trauma. Secretly, Eve suspected the coroner had uncovered much more. According to Caden, most of the bones in Roger's body had shattered. Deep gashes consistent with knife wounds were found on his arms and head, an ugly detail that made Eve recall the Mothman's sickle-like claws.

By the end of the week, Wendy Lynch's remains were buried in the local cemetery. Eve attended the service along with Caden, Ryan, Mrs. Flynn, and most of the staff from the hotel. As she stood at the graveside, offering silent support to Katie and Doreen Sue, she couldn't help thinking of what Maggie had witnessed that day in the woods. When she crawled into bed that night and closed her eyes, she dreamed of her friend.

Eve sat on a grassy slope that slanted down to the creek behind Aunt Rosie's house. The property belonged to her now. She'd made her decision to stay. Perhaps that was why she appeared as an adult in this dream, and

Maggie was still a child. Her friend had never been given the chance to grow up.

Tilting her face to the sky, Eve drank in the fragrant scent of the honeysuckle and sweet clover that grew wild along the bank. The sun warmed her skin and danced upon the water in a flickering shower of gold. In that moment, the carefree innocence of summer felt like it might never end.

"You shouldn't feel sorry for me," Maggie said. She wore jean shorts and a pink T-shirt with a picture of Scooby Doo on the front. Her ginger-colored hair was caught up in a ponytail but several strands had wormed free, contouring the curve of her face. She tucked a loose curl behind her ear. "I'm glad the truth came out. About Wendy and why I was so scared."

Eve understood. "You couldn't talk about it then."

Maggie shook her head, rifling her fingers through the grass. She found a pebble and tossed it into the creek where it landed with a plop. "It was easier to pretend I saw the Mothman." A ring of ripples fanned outward, kissing the reeds huddled at the bank's edge.

"But the night the bridge collapsed..." Eve swallowed hard, unable to continue. Dear God, how her friend must have suffered.

Maggie glanced at her hands. "If I'd told someone the truth, maybe I'd still be alive."

"You can't blame yourself. You did nothing wrong." Tears burned Eve's eyes. "I don't understand why my Aunt Rosie didn't go to the police when she realized what happened."

"I think she blocked it from her head. Like someone who goes into shock after seeing something awful. I can sense her on this side, and she's sad she kept silent. She tried to tell you about the negative."

"The phone calls?" Eve sat straighter. "They were from her, weren't they?"

Maggie nodded. "She tried to communicate with Mr. Layton, too, hoping he'd confess."

"He was a wretched man, caring only for himself." She swallowed hard. "Can you talk to Aunt Rosie? Can you tell her it will take time, but that I'll try to forgive her?"

"That will make her happy."

Smiling a little, Eve gripped her friend's arm. Maggie felt frail and insubstantial, a wraith who might be whisked away in the wind. Was she truly a ghost?

"I don't have much substance in this world," Maggie said as if reading her thoughts. "I've stayed here too long. It's why I told my mom I can't

talk to her anymore. I have to let go, and so does she. Now that the truth has come out, it's time for me to move on. Even if others can't."

Eve didn't understand. She wiped her cheeks with the back of her hand, then shifted to face Maggie. Still seated, she clutched her friend's thin fingers. "What others? Who are you talking about?"

For a time, Maggie said nothing, her gaze steady. Finally, she wet her lips. "They've lived here for a thousand yesteryears. There's only one left now, the last of his kind."

"The Mothman." Despite the warmth of the sun, Eve was wracked by a sudden chill. She wasn't sure she wanted to hear more.

"His species thrived when the world was new. Long before the dinosaurs roamed the Earth or land masses were formed. The world was old then." Maggie's voice had taken on a formal cadence, her words like the stilted speech of an antiquarian. "He and Caden are connected." She slipped her hands from Eve's and turned away.

"Wait!" Eve scrambled to her feet, "What do you mean connected?"

"You've seen the marks on his arm. A life for a life. It's a bond between them."

"I don't understand."

Maggie's form dwindled, swallowed in a waning shower of sunlight. In another moment, she was gone.

Fresh tears spilled from Eve's eyes. A thousand yesteryears.

Caden.

The Mothman.

Sinking to her knees on the sun-warmed grass, she prayed for an answer to the riddle.

Epilogue

August, 1982
Point Pleasant, West Virginia

Eve took a deep breath and surveyed the freshly decorated living room. At first she'd felt guilty about removing Aunt Rosie's things, but the furnishing, particularly the embroidered drapes, reminded her too much of the past. All that had been dark and ugly when she'd first arrived in Point Pleasant.

She'd replaced the paisley rugs with fawn-colored carpet, the heavy furnishings with sleeker contemporary pieces in shades of parsley and mint. Caden had painted the walls for her, agreeing the soft cream she'd chosen complemented the maple-stained trim, and the potted plants she'd transported from Harrisburg. Well…he'd transported them, renting a U-Haul for the trip. He'd helped her pack her belongings and made time to reintroduce himself to her mother.

Her mom still wasn't happy with Eve's decision to relocate, but at least she'd stopped calling the move "a heartbreaking, crazy idea." Perhaps in time, she'd even visit. Eve would love to have her opinion on the changes she'd made to the house.

The living room was the first of several she intended to redecorate. Caden had already finished most of the repairs to the other rooms. The few remaining, he'd subcontracted to a friend. As a full-time sergeant with the sheriff's office, he preferred to spend his free hours with Eve, not hanging drywall or refitting plumbing. She'd even convinced him to take up the guitar again. He'd been reluctant at first, but within a short while, his new six-string became a cherished friend. His friends, Glen and Wyatt, were trying to talk him in to performing with them, but so far he'd been reluctant.

Perhaps with time.

Even Mrs. Flynn was doing better, seemingly having put her connection to Maggie behind her. She was no longer obsessed with her daughter and hadn't been surprised to learn how Maggie had died. According to Caden, Maggie had told her mother in a dream shortly before Eve arrived in town. That dream had been the catalyst to propel Mrs. Flynn into a renewed bond with Maggie's ghost. A link that had gradually intensified, ending only when the truth about Maggie's death was brought to light.

Exposing Roger Layton's guilt had allowed Mrs. Flynn and Caden to start over, both free of guilt.

Smiling, Eve adjusted a small speckled plant on the windowsill for better light. This one hadn't come from Harrisburg, but was newly purchased two days ago in Point Pleasant. She hadn't been able to resist the yellow freckles peppered like sunlight on the dark green leaves. It would grow here, in her new home, joining the collection transported from Pennsylvania. Perhaps she'd even take a few to her office at the hotel, now that she was fully settled and business continued to grow.

She had the Mothman to thank for that. Although the creature had not been seen since the night it carted Roger's body into the sky, curiosity-seekers continued to flock to Point Pleasant where her hotel was the establishment of choice—the only lodging within town limits. She'd framed the front page of the *Point Pleasant Herald* with Glenda Whitmore's photo of the Mothman. Glenda and George had autographed it for her, and she proudly displayed the newspaper in the lobby. As soon as someone stepped through the front doors, they immediately knew they stood in the famed hotel where the Mothman photographer had stayed. With the boom in business, Eve told Glenda she and George were welcome back any time—free of charge.

Even Katie agreed. Her friend was quieter these days, but tended to smile whenever Ryan was near. Maybe one day soon, Caden's brother would work up the nerve and ask her out.

If it weren't for the troubling memory that still awakened her during the night, Eve would label life close to perfect. But in the back of her mind, she couldn't forget the disturbing dream about Maggie, or her friend's words concerning the Mothman.

He and Caden are connected.

She wondered if it had become a protector to the man who'd once saved it when everyone else was intent on killing it.

"Hey." Her boyfriend suddenly appeared behind her, balancing a pizza take-out box on his palm, a six pack of Miller in his free hand. "I see there's a new addition to the jungle." He nodded to the speckled plant on the windowsill. "What is it?"

Engrossed in her thoughts, she'd forgotten he'd left to pick up dinner and hadn't heard him come through the front door. "I don't know. It had a tag on it, but I didn't pay attention. I just liked the looks of it." She took the Miller from him and gave him a kiss on the cheek. "It's cute, isn't it?"

"Eve, you say all of these things are cute." He swept his hand to encompass the collection of ferns, vines, and potted greenery ensconced in the living room. "I can't imagine the amount of time it must take to water them."

"It's not that bad." She nudged him toward the kitchen, the odors wafting from the pizza box making her mouth water as she followed behind. Hot melted cheese, marinara sauce, and… "You got sausage, didn't you? I can smell it."

"What's wrong with sausage?"

"I wanted pepperoni."

He set the box on the kitchen table, then turned to take the beer from her, popping a can from the white plastic ring. "I got half each. I call that compromise."

"Do you?"

His satisfied grin coaxed a smile from her. As he stashed the remaining beer in the refrigerator, she rounded up plates and napkins. He poured her a glass of Pinot, and she located a bottle of hot sauce, knowing he liked the added flavor.

"I ran into Doreen Sue at the pizza parlor," Caden said as he pulled out a chair and sat down. He flipped open the cardboard box, then drew the nearest slice topped with crumbled sausage onto his plate. "She was with Martin Ward."

"From the Amoco station?" Eve joined him, pausing to sip her wine. "That relationship seems to be going well." She slid a slice of pepperoni onto her plate. "Katie likes him."

"Yeah." Folding his pizza lengthwise, Caden bit off the end. "It's about time Doreen Sue hooked up with a guy who isn't an ass—jerk." He offered a half-hearted shrug at the quick correction. "You haven't lived here long enough to see some of the winners she's had."

Eve couldn't argue. Given what Katie told her about her mom's taste in men, Doreen Sue had a bad habit of scraping the bottom of the barrel. Finally, she'd met someone who treated her with respect. In Eve's opinion, Doreen Sue and Katie would probably continue to suffer ups and downs in their relationship, but at least the discovery of Wendy's remains and the truth about why she'd been killed had brought them closer. Add Martin Ward—a man Katie clearly approved of—and the road to healing spanned invitingly between them.

"I saw Doreen Sue at the bank yesterday." Eve nipped a small piece of Mozzarella with her fingers and popped it into her mouth. Eyes averted, she focused on the pizza slice as she experimented folding the tip. "She told me she's felt a greater sense of peace these last few months since burying Wendy. We talked for a while, and then somehow ended up chatting about the TNT. It got me thinking about the Mothman again and that igloo." Eve raised her gaze to find Caden frowning at her across the table. "There's still so much we don't know."

"And I have no problem leaving it that way."

His answer didn't surprise her. Maybe it was because she'd only returned to Point Pleasant two months ago that she could see what he didn't. He'd spent his entire life in the old river town, constant exposure to the oddities of the TNT and Point Pleasant's dust-shrouded history making him numb to the possibilities. Undaunted, she plowed ahead.

"You can't deny you have some kind of unusual connection to the Mothman, Caden. Doreen Sue believes the thing"—she didn't know what else to call it—"in the igloo is different. Another creature or being." Maybe just as old. Perhaps infinite. "It told us where to find Wendy. Maybe it can tell us about the Mothman."

She thought he'd grow angry that she continued to press. Instead, he shook his head and slumped in his chair. "Did it ever occur to you I don't *want* to know?"

"But…" The word faltered on her tongue.

"It's been fifteen years, Eve. Fifteen years since I first connected with that creature and felt it inside of my head. I can't explain to you what that was like. The emotion and despondency from it. It saved me twice, and for that I'm grateful, but if I never see it again, I'll be elated."

She opened her mouth to speak, but no sound came. She should have recognized his feelings. He accepted the Mothman and the strange bond sealed between them. He even carried proof of that connection branded on his arm, but he had no desire to continue the link.

"Caden, I'm sorry." She reached across the table to take his hand. "I thought—"

"I know what you thought." His fingers curled around hers. He smiled. "That's why I care about you the way I do."

Suddenly, the potential of shadowy creatures lurking in alternative realms was no longer important. At least not at the moment. Later, when she was alone, she'd go back to pondering Caden's strange connection to the Mothman. Whether he wanted to acknowledge it or not, his life was bound up with the archaic mysteries of the TNT and Point Pleasant's resident creature. He couldn't escape that.

Not now. Not in a thousand yesteryears.

Meet the Author

Mae Clair opened a Pandora's Box of characters when she was a child and never looked back. Her father, an artist who tinkered with writing, encouraged her to create make-believe worlds by spinning tales of far-off places on summer nights beneath the stars.

Mae loves creating character-driven fiction in settings that vary from contemporary to mythical. Wherever her pen takes her, she flavors her stories with mystery, suspense, and romance. Married to her high school sweetheart, she lives in Pennsylvania and is passionate about cryptozoology, old photographs, a good Maine lobster tail, and cats.

Sign up for Mae's newsletter to learn about her new releases, book specials, and author promotions as they happen!
http://maeclair.net/newsletter-sign-up/

If you enjoyed A Thousand Yesteryears, you will love
Myth and Magic by Mae Clair.

Available now!

Myth and Magic

AS CHILDREN THEY PLAYED GAMES OF MYTH AND MAGIC...

Veronica Kent fell in love with Caith Breckwood when they were
children. As a teenager, she was certain he was the man she was destined
to marry. But a traumatic event from Caith's past led him to fear a future
together. He left Veronica, hoping to save her from a terrible fate. Twelve
years later, Caith, now a P.I., is hired to investigate bizarre incidents at
the secluded retreat Veronica manages. Returning to his hometown, Caith
is forced to face his nightmares—and his feelings for the woman he's
always loved.

THEN ONE DAY THE MONSTERS BECAME REAL.

After the callous way Caith broke her heart, Veronica isn't thrilled to
see him again. But strange occurrences have taken a dangerous toll on
business at Stone Willow Lodge. Forced to work together, Veronica
discovers it isn't ghostly apparitions that frighten her, but her passion
for a man she has never forgotten. Or forgiven. Can two people with a
tarnished past unearth a magical future?

Chapter 1

"Stone Willow Hounded by Dead Dog"

Veronica Kent frowned at the newspaper headline. She'd hoped for a diversion from monthly budget projections, not another tabloid report to fan her irritation, but should have known better. Stone Willow Lodge and Breckwood Industries made it into Kelly Rice's *Coldcreek Herald* so frequently she'd been forced to become a regular reader in order to counter fallout. Managing the lodge for BI made it a necessity.

Standing, she pressed her hands to the small of her back and stretched. The clock on her desk read 9:14, an hour supported by the creaks and groans of the old house as the lodge settled around her. Her office was comfortable, a stroll down the hall from the main reception area, tucked around the corner from her suite. She should call it a night and curl up with a book on her couch. The budget reports weren't due until the end of the week and quitting time had been hours ago. If she had any sense at all, she would have met Merlin at the Jade Club.

Her gaze returned to the newspaper and its revolting headline. Curiosity got the better of her and she sank into her desk chair, focusing on the article.

"Stone Willow Hounded by Dead Dog"

Unexplained circumstances continue to escalate at Stone Willow Lodge where everything from random thefts to rumors of supernatural occurrences plague the struggling corporate retreat. Yesterday, the mutilated carcass of a dog was discovered in a guest suite. Avoiding specific details, Sheriff Duke Cameron would state only that the grisly remains, likely those of a stray, were found by a guest Tuesday evening. Not your typical turndown service.

Damn, the witch! Veronica bit her lip, silently fuming as she continued to read.

Site manager, Veronica Kent, was unavailable for comment, but Breckwood Industries chief operations officer, Aren Breckwood, insists the corporation has the situation under control. According to Mr. Breckwood: "Our primary concern is for the safety and continued enjoyment of our guests."

Stone Willow Lodge remains an established landmark in Coldcreek. The retreat incorporates part of the original Warren Barrister House, the site where Barrister brutally murdered his wife and children on a winter night in 1873. Coincidentally, an employee of the lodge claims to have seen Barrister's ghost, while several guests have reported the apparition of a sobbing woman roaming the hallways at night.

Fantasy or hoax? Either way, Breckwood Industries has managed to ensure their dying retreat is in the limelight once again.

Veronica flung the paper on her desk. Kelly Rice had been a thorn in her side since high school when they'd butted heads over everything from boys to clothes to grades. Kelly was determined to share Stone Willow's misfortunes with the rest of Coldcreek, writing up every mishap and problem as headline news.

Incidents had begun several weeks ago when one of the guests had spotted a "glowing apparition" by the lake. *A woman in a long white veil,* the guest, Kay Porter, had said. When she'd tried to speak to the mysterious woman, she'd retreated into the surrounding woods and vanished.

Other incidents followed: disembodied lights weaving through the trees, a room that stayed frigid despite attempts to heat it, locked doors yawning open, creaks and groans that had nothing to do with the settling of the lodge, even spoiled food and missing items.

Let me get my magic wand, Merlin Breckwood had joked. *I'll send the demons packing.*

Her sometimes-boyfriend rarely took anything seriously. Probably why their on-again off-again relationship never lasted more than a few weeks at a time. Like his three brothers, Merlin had been named for a character from myth, something that had played an important part in their childhood. If only myth still held the same magic.

The phone rang a shrill intrusion, and she snatched up the handset in an attempt to quell her irritation. "Hello?"

"Veronica, it's Melanie." The hesitation in the other woman's voice gave Veronica a sense of what was coming. "I thought you should know I ran into Merlin at the Jade Club."

"Who was he with? A blonde or a brunette?" Surprisingly, she didn't care. Twenty-nine and single. Her love life was going nowhere. "It's no big deal, Melanie. Merlin and I are in the friend stage again."

"Hmm…" Melanie didn't sound convinced. A good friend, she was the wife of Aren Breckwood, Merlin's older brother.

"I know exactly what Merlin's like," Veronica said. For all his outward sparkle, Merlin Breckwood was self-centered and thoughtless. A sad turn of events for a boy who'd been charismatic and fun-loving in childhood. "Merlin and I are…convenient. I don't think we were ever in love. He's free to see other people."

"What about you?"

Her throat closed up as she thought of Merlin's younger brother, Caithelden. "There isn't anyone for me. Pretty pathetic, huh?"

She'd been eleven when her parents had moved to Coldcreek and she'd met Caith. He'd been the boy with the funny name until Derrick Trask taught her how to pronounce it—*Caith-el-den*—pausing on each syllable until she got it right.

Her eyes shifted to a small framed photo on her desk, a cherished keepsake of better days. Eager young faces smiled back at her: Merlin, and his dark-haired brother Caith, Trask in a battered green ball cap, and her, all freckles and straight blond hair, as gangly-limbed as a newborn colt. It was the last photo of the four of them together.

"I don't want Merlin to hurt you," Melanie said.

"Don't worry. I told you we're just friends. One of these days I'm going to find someone as wonderful as your Aren and have a storybook romance."

"Well, you're probably right about Merlin. As much as I love the little brat, he's clueless about relationships. I say dump the cover boy and move on."

Veronica laughed. "I'll consider it. Right now I owe Aren budget reports."

"Mr. Taskmaster." There was a smile in Melanie's voice.

"He's adorable, and you know it."

"True, but it would be nice to see him blow a gasket now and then. Just to know he's human like the rest of us. I'll let you go. I know you're busy."

"Okay. Talk to you later." Veronica's thoughts returned to Caith as she hung up the phone. He'd been sandwiched between Merlin and Aren in personality, not as extroverted as Merlin, not as willing to bend as

Aren. His stubbornness was the reason he'd left Coldcreek and his family twelve years ago after a horrible falling-out with his father.

Merlin was a pale imitation and a convenient replacement. Was it any wonder he flirted with other women? He had to know her heart had always belonged to his brother. She was a pathetic mess, in love with a memory.

Her eyes dropped to her desk calendar. The anniversary of Trask's death was fast approaching. Halloween. What might have been different if he'd lived? If they'd all grown up together, unscathed by tragedy? Caith might never have made the choices that drove them apart.

The phone rang a second time.

Thinking it was Melanie, Veronica snatched up the handset. "Hey, I thought you were going to let me get back to my budget reports?"

"Go to the lobby," a man's voice said.

"Excuse me?"

"Go to the lobby," the unfamiliar voice repeated. "I left something in the fireplace."

Click. The line went dead.

Suddenly uneasy, Veronica suppressed a chill. The familiar creaks and groans of the old lodge had stopped, replaced by unnatural stillness. She felt trapped, confined behind her desk, a target for a faceless assailant lurking outside. The hair prickled on the nape of her neck, sending a string of goose bumps racing down her arms. Crossing to the door, she held her breath then paused on the threshold, listening for telltale signs of intrusion. She'd always enjoyed the lodge's remote location, tucked in the woods of northwestern Pennsylvania, but at the moment wished it weren't so isolated. She couldn't hear anything over the frightened thumping of her heart.

Some creep's playing a game. He probably saw Kelly's article and thought it would be fun to scare me.

It was working.

Before the incident with the dog, Alma Kreider, Stone Willow's cook, had sworn she'd seen the ghost of Warren Barrister standing on the basement stairs. Veronica had heard eerie sobbing during a routine check of the vacant third floor two days earlier. Whether the occurrences were supernatural or contrived, they were mounting and unquestionably spooky.

Forcing herself to stay calm, she crept down the hallway, her tread light by nature. As a child, Merlin had compared her to a fairy queen, saying she looked the part with honey-kissed hair and green eyes. They'd been enraptured by myth and magic in those days, unaware there were real monsters in the world. Monsters like the men who'd murdered Trask and destroyed Caith's life.

Shaking the memories aside, she stepped into the lobby. All looked as it should be. The back of the check-in desk was visible, webbed in patches of velvety shadow. Towering glass windows hugged a cathedral ceiling, crisscrossed by thick wooden beams. Scattered rugs in earthy shades of russet, cinnamon, and pebble gray added warmth to the wide-plank pine floors. A fire crackled in the massive mountain stone hearth. Lew Walden, the lodge's caretaker, must have kindled it earlier. By habit, he'd return later to ensure it was out before retiring to his cottage at the southwest corner of the property.

I left something in the fireplace, the caller had said.

Veronica hugged close the collar of her bulky green sweater and padded across the waxed floor in stocking feet. She was still several feet away when her mind processed the sight.

A charred, cracked lump, broken by knobby protrusions of white, burned on top of the stacked logs. Something popped with the sound of cooking meat.

Choking on terror, she stumbled backward with a scream.

A severed human hand was swaddled within the dancing flames.